Swagbelly

Swagbelly:

A Pornographer's Tale

D. J. LEVIEN

First published in Great Britain in 2002 by
Allison & Busby Limited
Suite 111, Bon Marche Centre
241-251 Ferndale Road
Brixton, London SW9 8BJ
http://www.allisonandbusby.ltd.uk

A catalogue record for this book is available from the British Library

ISBN 0 7490 0498 3

Printed and bound in Spain by
Liberdúplex, s. l. Barcelona

Swagbelly is DJ Levien's second novel, following the highly acclaimed *Wormwood*. A novelist, film director and scriptwriter, Levien's first feature, *Rounders*, starring Matt Damon, was released to great acclaim in 1998. His most recent film is *Knockaround Guys*, which stars Vin Diesel and John Malkovich.

Afternoon Tryst

Two-bedroom luxury condominium. Upper East Side, New York. Yvonne and Antonio are married—only not to each other. Every day Yvonne stops by at their secret, pre-arranged time. Tommy, the doorman, discreetly tips his cap to her as she moves wordlessly by him to the elevator. Yvonne's cascading hair is so blonde it is almost white, but her eye make-up is dark in striking contrast. Her full lips are glistening pink, a ring of slightly mocha-colored lip liner around the outer edge sets off her natural pout. Her sheath dress is translucent and shiny. It fits her like a mermaid's tail. Her only piece of jewelry is a pearl and diamond choker.

Yvonne uses her key. She knows Antonio's wife is gone for the day and that he is waiting for her. She steps into the beige modern-decorated living room and there he is, by the window. Antonio turns to her. He wears a vest over his slim, hard torso, faded jeans below. A lock of his tousled brown hair hangs coyly over one eye. Not a word is spoken. They do not smile. There is a breathless quality in the air.

–Yvonne presses herself close to Antonio and tilts her head up at him. He grasps her snugly with a chiseled arm. Her lips part hungrily and her tongue extends forward. He brings his mouth to hers, his hair sifting down over their faces.

–She steps out of her white high heels and her bare feet, toes polished pink, sink into the plush carpet. She

9

is much shorter than Antonio now, and lays her cheek against his masculine chest. He cradles the back of her head with his powerful, veined hand.

–Antonio pushes the straps of Yvonne's dress off her shoulders as she similarly peels his vest off his arms. He cups her full breasts, nipples already stiffening. Both open their lips and tongues explore.

–Free of her dress, Yvonne is pushed roughly, but not too roughly, onto the couch by Antonio. He moves behind her, burying his face in her neck and pressing her breasts together. Her mouth opens in a gasp. Both have their eyes closed, such is their ecstasy, so forbidden is their passion.

–Yvonne leans back against him, his muscular thighs wrapped around her.

–Her blonde hair spread about, Yvonne has dropped to the floor on her back. Antonio's jeans have vanished and he is on top of her. All eyes are still blissfully closed.

–He is inside her from behind now. The lovers move together, backs arched, fitting together like bananas in a bunch.

–Skin, smooth, pink skin, so close that it overwhelms the eye. Nothing more can be seen.

–Antonio grips a bundle of her hair violently, yet with tenderness, in finish, and for the first time she opens her eyes fully. Wistfully. Gratefully.

Wordlessly, Yvonne gets up off the floor and walks to the bathroom. I hear the water running in there as she wets a washcloth and wipes my semen from her body. My eyes are still closed and I am breathing hard. I'm wondering where is that improved cardiovascular recovery time that my personal fitness trainer Brett is always talking about when I'm on the treadmill. I feel my heart. It feels fine. I figure when I go it will be a heart attack. Myocardial infarction. I had my first baby heart attack when I was twenty-nine. I figure it will be during sex. I half hope I'm right, I half hope I'm wrong.

I am not Antonio. I am Elliot. Elliot Grubman. Mine is a pornographer's tale. One year ago I was rich. I had everything in the world. I lived with my wife and young son in a five-story New York townhouse with six in help, and a seventh, a fucking major-domo, to run them. Now I've got my divorce. My boy won't talk to me and I live in this two-bedroom rental condo. All I have now is the money. I still have money. I'm a *gontser macher*. I'm worth a hundred mill. Even that much though, it can be lost.

The carpet is really itching my ass at this point, so I get up off the floor and scratch a little. I am not trim and muscular. I'm a bit flabby at age 54. I'm working on it. I have to now. My hair is not soft, and sharply coifed. It does not hang sensually or flip playfully when I move my head. The texture of my hair is closer to that of steel wool—fine gauge. Jew turf, as I've heard it referred to. I had an idea that Jews' hair is so wiry because it helps keep a slippery yarmulke on in temple. My hair turned white-gray in color, similar to 000-gauge steel wool. I dyed it recently. 'Sable' is what the stylist called the color. It is also known as brown. The dark stuff only took on the top though, the roots are more of a manila hue. I don't kid myself, it resembles a piece of tiramisu on my head. It does not particularly flatter along with my skin color, which has lately become orangey. I missed a few tanning appointments and tried some tan-in-a-can products. They do not work in the long term.

I look around the apartment. It is a new place. Two-bedroom, two-bath. Not bad. Nice building off Third. There's nowhere like the Upper East Side. Nowhere. Specifically Lexington, Park, and Madison in the 60's. Sometimes it is hard to tell if the women are fifty years old or twenty. It is a sea of rhinoplasty. This bothers some people, but I'm no purist. The television is switched on in the bedroom and I hear Bugs Bunny call somebody a "maroon." Cartoons. Yvonne likes to watch them. Why not, she's only twenty. Yvonne. I am not Antonio—not even Antonio-like—but Yvonne is really Yvonne. She is a model. I *date* models. Not the limp-postured, walking down the runway, high fashion models who are tall and thin and perfect, but look like shit without their make-up. Not the kind that never stop whining, have boyish chests, heroin routines, and puke up their Caesar salads, yet can take your breath away with a single twirl anytime they want. Not those kind of models. I'm talking about full-figured models, with large, luscious tits, real or fake, and firm round asses. Big-haired girls with dye jobs better or worse than mine, who can sock away filet mignon and lobster and work it off later. Girls with perfectly groomed pussies, so kept because they model those luxury liners. Porno-mag models who look good all the time, are not afraid to look like women, and if anything appear a bit overdone on a casual occasion. Like Yvonne. She is from the Czech Republic, with a laugh like a bottle of *slivovitz* frozen in a block of ice. The only part that isn't perfect are her teeth. A little dingy and crooked like most foreigners have. Except she smiles with her lips closed and then she's perfect. I get to date her, and those like her, because I own the magazine. *Swagbelly,* the magazine for today's gentleman.

Once in the bathroom I notice the toilet paper roll is empty. I'll have to make a note of that. I can hear the television louder in the next room. Yvonne, I think, with a smile in my chest. Then I look down past my slack stomach to my prick and wonder. I will always wonder at what draws a woman to me now. I stare at myself in the mirror for an unpleasant moment. I hate the way I look. Always have. The hair. Lips like a puckered anus. My mouth never looked more like that than when I was smoking a cigar. That's why I quit. I smoked most of five Punch Double Coronas every day. Straight from Cuba via James J. Fox and Robert Lewis on St. James's Street in London at £300 per box. I fucking loved those things. The texture. The aroma off a perfectly lacquered Elie Bleu humidor full of them. The fragrant smoke. The tingle on the tongue, and calm head they provide. Mouth cancer meant nothing to me. Only vanity overcomes nicotine addiction. I am not a man who understands women's *needs*, who seems to have grown up reading women's magazines such is his comprehension of the female mind, or one who, when all else fails, can fall back on being *adorable*. No, I *had* to become rich, and even then, when I caught a glimpse of myself with the cigar, like a turd in my lips, out they went.

I walk into the bedroom and there is Yvonne, laying on her stomach on the bed. Her face is three feet from the television, her feet kicking in the air behind her. Her ass is a double handful of joy mountain. I think I might actually be able to give her another bullet right now. I walk up behind her and crawl onto the bed. I slap my hand into her crotch. Hot and damp.

"Ellie," she says in her accent.

"Yeah?"

"It's *Fabulous Four*." I get between her legs, shuffling on my knees, and lay myself against the cleft of her ass.

"Uhh," I say. She rolls over and starts paying attention to me. We kiss and I get some stirring down there. Then she starts her muttering.

"Fucking, cock me, pantyline, pussy, diaper bag..." Her broken English. That does it. I don't know what the hell she's talking about. It doesn't matter. I put myself in her,

13

missionary style. The freeze-frame, multi-position stylistics of an adult film star are fine—for magazine pictorials and porno movies. In the real world simply getting the hardness into the wetness is artistry enough. It just feels so good.

I look down on Yvonne, her eyes shut, head thrown back. Something close to real feeling wells up deep in me. Even as my orgasm begins—I see her eyelids flicker and she reaches down and starts working herself furiously—I know she wants more. For a frightening, hollow moment I feel regret. Regret that I'm not satisfying her and touching her deeply in even a physical way. But that regret is of a size that is dwarfed by the wave of my own sexual pleasure. It is reduced to a mere twinge that serves only to threaten the other force's momentum. To interfere with it. So I sweep it aside. I ride the thrashing, surging wave of my own orgasm to the sounds of animated laser guns on the television. No sense in us both having an unsatisfying experience.

Later we get ready to go to dinner. Yvonne showers and I sit on the closed-lid toilet and watch her through the glass shower door. She washes her hair and I can hardly make out the difference between the stark white of the lather and her locks. She soaps herself, running the bar over her slippery breasts, getting clean. She is clean. She is my thirty-fifth lover of this, the year of my divorce. My thirty-sixth in fifteen years, counting Lauren, my now ex-wife. I was faithful to her for fifteen years—a few remorseful mistakes related to work notwithstanding. They should not stand and not be considered, for I don't know anyone with a better record. Still, re-entering the dating pool at my age and position I have to reckon with disease. AIDS. Why do these girls who pose for my magazine think they need to present written proof of a negative AIDS test when they sign their pictorial releases? I even send them to my own special man, Dr. Bobby Gold. Do they imagine it is to protect the male models whom they suck for the photos, and who lay a money shot all over their faces? Would I be devastated if some hard-body, swinging-dick got AIDS? The tests are for *me*. For my protection. Legal and physical, and not in that order. My centerfolds, my feature models, my *employees*, had been my dating pool. Until Yvonne. Four months ago she stopped the procession.

"Anytime you finish singing that minor-key dirge, you can get out of the shower."

"Oh Ellie, to sing in the shower is so happy. We never have so much hot water like this, and so hot in my country," Yvonne says. It is always what they didn't have back in her country. And that means I'm providing it for her, which makes me feel like a capitalist king. It may be a scheme she's running on me, one that I'm playing into, but it works nonetheless.

She steps out of the shower and reaches for the towel, which is not where it should be on the rack. I open the cabinet under the sink and flip one to her. She leaves the bathroom and I take my own shower. Afterwards I put my robe back on and start leaving notes. If there is one thing I detest, it is instructing maids in person. I keep a pad of yellow sticky notes and a pen in my robe pocket instead. Sticky notes are the most useful invention since the cellular phone. The guy who invented them should get a Nobel Prize.

TOILET PAPER! I write, and stick it to the empty spindle. TOWELS HERE ALWAYS, I affix to the towel rack. Back in the bedroom I assess things. The socks in my drawer are wrong. I throw several washed and folded pairs into the garbage, leaving only the new ones. I like a new pair of socks every day, with a crinkly piece of tissue paper between them and label wrapped around. When I was a kid I promised myself not only fresh, but new socks every day when I had the money. NEW SOCKS ONLY, I write, and sticky note it. I peel the wrapper off a new pair and put them on. I put on underwear too. Starchy boxer shorts from Brooks Brothers. I will wear my underwear more than once.

Clad in underwear and socks I go to the closet. A disaster, but first things first. Dinner tonight. I'll go suit, I think. I always go suit. I have between one and two hundred of them. Mostly blue, black, and charcoal. Pinstriped in those colors. I hate Armani. I hate Yves Saint Laurent. I hate Ralph Lauren. I hate Canali. I could go on. I wear custom suits by an Italian, a private tailor named Furio Fulvanti. They go back to him for cleaning and pressing. Regular cleaners will not even accept his suits because of the price. They start at $7,500 per. You'd think he would give a price break on bulk, but he does not. So meticulous is his fitting, he even checks to which side a customer's manhood customarily hangs, and leaves extra fabric in the trousers for it. I have him cut my suits conservative as can be. Double breasted mostly, the lapels crossing high on the chest. Close to Saville Row, although, it may be guessed, I'm not a fan of Saville Row. Dapper as hell with a few Double Coronas tucked behind the handkerchief—now only the hanky. Still sharp with just the hanky. Serious. That's the trick. That's *one* of the tricks—act serious. Dead-serious dour. When a smile or a light moment comes, then it's like a holiday, or a cloud passing from the sun. It is such a *relief* to people that they are then grateful to me. The suits though, are not hung properly in the closet. The hangers are pushed together here, and spread apart there. Wrong. TWO INCHES, I write on a note paper and

stick it to the closet rod between the first two suits.
TWO INCHES, I write on a second, and stick it in the
next space. I continue until I'm out of the papers, perhaps thirty-five sheets. I like to make a point. Then I get
dressed.

The shirts, fortunately, are as they should be. All seemingly new. Ascot Chang. I do not have them sent out to
be laundered. They go back to the maker where they are
washed, and re-packaged with pins and everything. It
costs five bucks a shirt, but is worth it. Unlike the socks,
this is a merely a little illusion I like to cast for myself. A
new shirt, a new day. I knot my tie and slip on the jacket. As I button up, Yvonne comes into the closet behind
me.

"What is this, Ellie?" she says of the sticky notes. "You
ah so fahnny."

Give it ten or fifteen years, I think to myself. Lauren
never thought it was so funny, my notes. That's the amazing thing—that the marriage could go down, essentially
spared infidelity, based on things like sticky notes.

"Where are we going for dinner?" Yvonne asks. I notice
her dress for the first time.

"Tre Fiori," I say. I usually eat there. "Gorgeous dear, but
can you turn it down about three notches. I'll wait in the
den." I have to say it, it leaps up into my throat and I cannot keep it in. "I want it to look like I'm with a model, not
a hooker." She doesn't bother appearing hurt or upset,
she just goes to change.

Tre Fiori is a little step-down restaurant serving regional
Italian food. They have ten specials each night listed on
a piece of paper inside the menu and ten more that the
waiter recites. Sponge painted walls, paintings of flowers, ornate bottles of grappa on shelves, and demure

lighting. The cozy cove effect. For rich people. Stuffy Park, Mad, and Fifth Avenue types. The guys there—the waiters, and Rez, the maitre d' hotel and part owner—love me. They admire what I walk in with, from Lauren right on down to flavor of the week. I drink Sassicaia or Gaja Brunello, the good years, at $175 a bottle. "Only the best-a for-a Mr. Grubman," Rez says, as he trots out the next bottle he sticks me with. Yeah, they stick me, but not too badly. Kind guys in there. When I am sick they give me hot tea with homemade honey from their village near Trieste. They treat me like family, and this is unusual in Manhattan.

I remember the first time I went to Tre Fiori. Summer, a year and a half ago. Lauren and I are taking a walk around on a Saturday night. Bored with our each other, and as such, looking for a new restaurant. Nothing like going to old Elio's or Elaine's, or Parma, even Campagnola, to deepen the usual conversational sloughs. We stroll by, hardly looking, and see Tre Fiori in the foot of a brownstone. We walk in the door and the place is packed, yet still hushed quiet. All eighteen tables are full, and there are six couples on the door. I step up to the podium and speak to Rez, who is behind it in a decent Pal Zileri three-button three-season.

"We have no reservation, but can you take two for dinner?" I ask.

Rez looks at me with narrowed eyes. I hear him thinking, *this man is serious. The suit, the handkerchief. He likes good Barolo. A good customer to catch.* I watch as his eyes make the twin Punchs. "Ten minutes please, and we will have a nice table for you," he says.

Nine minutes and fifty seconds later we're seated. A good table next to the window. Before three of the other couples waiting, I notice. Lauren and I drink two bottles of red. We eat risotto with white truffles and grilled langostine over linguini. Rez offers us coffee and cognac on the house, which we turn down. I leave a fifty percent tip, shake hands with Rez, and we're all happy, though Lauren and I have had the same conversation as always. Now I hear when she has been in, and I've managed to miss her there on my many dates over the past year.

Yvonne and I enter the foyer at Tre Fiori. It is crowded, but there is no question. My table next to the window awaits us. A few gentleman diners I know vaguely nod my way. None of the women in the place have great fondness for me. Maybe they've heard of my profession, or my divorce for which they naturally blame me. They hardly need reason to hate me more than the fact that the women I show up with make them look dried up, lumpy, almost misshapen, with everything strapped down and painted over. To their husbands these wives represent stable family, fidelity to some extent, the love of a good woman, a partner to a certain degree, or perhaps the best they could do, while my women seem like an adolescent fantasy, a rollicking dream rampage. The husbands don't look too long when I walk in, it is too painful. The wives whisper I should grow up. These men probably don't imagine the broken English, cartoon watching, the endless prinking, and AIDS tests. To them I represent the *other choice*. I know this because nearly thirty years ago I almost made the same choice they made. Her name was Barbara Schafer and she was from Brooklyn, where I grew up. But I didn't go that way, and it was a long time ago.

"*Buona sera*, Mr. Grubman," Rez says, shaking my hand. "*Buona sera, Signorina* Yvonne." He had only met her once when he started addressing her by name. If he is good it is safer for him to merely call all my women *Signorina*, but he is the best. Rez has never missed or mixed up a single name during my parade of dates. The wine is opened, decanted, and poured. We start in on anchovies, baked clams, and fried calamari. "Plate of fishies," Yvonne calls it.

There is a long, quiet lull before the entrees, prompting Yvonne to wonder "Is it kitchen or service that is slow? I always think it is waiter's fault."

"Wrong," I say. "Always the fault of the kitchen, but when they get backed up they're backed up. Blame them."

"How do you know?" she inquires. Because I worked at Lundy's in Sheepshead Bay for years, I want to say, slinging crab, jockeying plates for tips, and we were a damn hustling crew taking shit off the customers because the kitchen forgot to put the steak or lobster on the grill.

"I've owned restaurants," I shrug.

"You have?" She is amazed. They don't have capitalism up and running quite like this in Eastern Europe yet.

"I own a lot of things," I add. Then a veal chop bigger than Primo Carnera's fist arrives, along with a steak the size of the glove that covered it.

"We never have so much food like this in my country," Yvonne says, starting on her dinner.

"I know baby, they had one can of peas for the whole village back home," I say.

"Don't be fahnny, Ellie, you know I am from Prague, not village." I signal for another bottle of Gaja Brunello. It has a penetrating nose, velvet fruit, and a finish that rings off about the mouth in stages that go on for several moments. I begin to figure how many bottles I could buy with my entire net worth and come up with a number close to 571,148, and start to break that down into a bottles per day time frame, before I realize that as a Jew, that kind of drinking really isn't in my blood.

"Damn, Yvonne, you're a meat-eater. You've got appetite," I say without much expectation of an answer. Then I look up at the door and feel my breath solidify in my chest. Standing there is my wealthy, recently ex-wife Lauren. Fifteen year marriage and a fifteen million dollar settlement, pre-nuptial right out the window. The only thing iron-clad about it was the fee I paid my lawyer to prepare it. Fifteen million is a pretty good wage for a former secretary no matter how you slice it. Rez looks over at my impassive face, then has no choice but to greet her graciously. Stepping inside behind her is a tall, rangy fellow wearing a bright polar fleece pull-over and a droopy mustache. I recognize him as Ricky, the private mountain climbing instructor from the gym in Aspen. I can picture the name tag on his lycra tank top. A fucking yokel, and she's parading him right through upper Manhattan.

Lauren nods her tanned face at me. She looks good, well-fucked and well-rested from taking a little break with this backwoodsman before getting into training for some billionaire next-husband. Ricky looks over and I can see him want to smile and greet me. That's how he was raised back in Missouri or Michigan. He thinks better of it though, and not knowing what to do, stands there until Lauren leads him by the hand to their table on the other side of the restaurant. Yvonne has her face tilted down at her plate and probably wouldn't know my wife anyway, having only seen a photo or two of her. I'm relieved I had her change clothes. Yvonne wears a low cut black dress with spaghetti straps—what she had on before was indescribable—and still looks trashy next to Lauren, who has taste to burn. Twenty years of youth on Yvonne's side balances the equation. I wonder what Ricky thinks of Yvonne, which one of them he wants more.

"Don't be destroyed because your wife is here, baby," Yvonne says. I look at her, surprised.

"Distraught?"

"Yes. Have dessert. The nice man here is waiting." Yvonne reaches out and takes the hairy hand of the towering baritone waiter who stands bent over his dessert tray. He ticks off our choices while he looks at Yvonne's tits. There is pear pie, apple tart, raspberry tart, crème brulee, flourless chocolate cake, Italian cheesecake of fresh ricotta, and tiramisu. "They all look so good, Ellie."

"Make us a combination. A large plate with a small piece of everything. Except the tiramisu." It clashes with my hair.

"Oh sweetie, that is so good an idea. You know we hardly ever had such dessert back home in my—"

"I know, except for the big blini festival, there was hardly anything to eat at all," I smile understandingly. "Don't flirt with waiters unless you want to pay the check, my dove."

Dessert passes, while Lauren and her beau eat salads and pizzas, which I did not know Tre Fiori made, but suppose Rez did specially for them. I conclude that simple, hearty people eat salads and thin-crust individual gourmet pizzas at fine restaurants, and that Lauren is now one of them. I suppose the psychotherapy, personal shopper at Bendels, chauffeur-driven, Xanax ingesting Lauren who starts on her bottle of Gavi La Scolca by 2:00 in the afternoon is on hiatus. They skip dessert. Rez comes to my table and mentions that the Mrs. has showed up without a reservation, and offers cognac, on him, as consolation, which we accept, being as I am now in a Mexican stand-off with Lauren over who will leave first.

22

The restaurant empties out and only the bartender stands in the back, going over receipts and glaring at us for keeping him so late. The checks arrive and I figure on Lauren paying, and her leaving thirty percent. I get a prickly feeling when I realize I am, in effect, buying this Ricky dinner, but the tip I leave answers any question as to who is the preferred customer. I will leave fifty percent generally. Tonight eighty. Lauren would consider such a move gaudy and classless, and it is in a certain light. I see now though that I need Rez to protect me on these coincidences in the future, and that I can buy this protection. This is when Ricky lifts up his polar fleece top, and draws a cigar from his shirt pocket.

I can tell by the size and shape that it is a Punch Double Corona. It amuses me that obviously Lauren has instructed him in the kind of cigar a discerning man smokes. He wields the cutter clumsily, and from the way it lights, the cigar is obviously dry. I think how mountain air must be no aid in keeping cigars moist, before I realize the truth—it is an old one of mine from the townhouse. It has to be two years old, found in some neglected humidor, but the schnook looks plenty satisfied with it just the same. He sits there trying to look thoughtful with the Havana. He waves it around never letting it rest though, and he doesn't ash it either. The ash grows and grows as I watch him, and he just lets it build. He is an architect with that ash. Ricky Jones, climbing instructor, is clearly the I.M. Pei of cigar ash. I nuzzle close with Yvonne, though I haven't any sweet nothings to whisper in her ear, and understand in a moment, perhaps not a brilliant one, that I will buy Tre Fiori so that this scene, nor any like it, is ever repeated.

Yvonne excuses herself to the ladies room, and I am alone. I sit for a long minute without cover until I can't take it anymore. I stand up, pushing my chair across the dining room floor behind me with a loud scraping sound. Ricky starts at this. His edifice of ash falls and leaves a white slash across his denim covered knee. I walk toward their table, and try to smooth and modulate my steps. I suppose I will wait for my wife's lawyer to extract a large sum of alimony through my own lawyer. I will wait in a rental condo until I have decided on my next living arrangement. I will wait until my weekend visitation to see my son, and I will wait for barely post-teenage nude sex queens to change their clothes. But I will not wait for a guy, a guy whom I have previously paid to teach my wife a foolish skill and who now instructs her in some others, a guy for whom I have bought dinner, to finish smoking one of my cigars.

By the time I stand over them, and Lauren has made a play of how engrossed they are before noticing me, I am breathing a little hard. Even so, she takes it a bit far.

"Oh, Elliot," she says, faux-startled, "I didn't see you standing there....Elliot, you might remember Richard." Richard.

"Paying a visit to the big town, Rick?"

"Sure, I thought I'd—"

"I want to talk about May, Lauren," I move on. *Richard* sits there and chugs on the Punch, consternation written across his wind-chapped face.

"May?" Lauren trills, innocent as a fawn.

"May 22nd. We need to have those final meetings with Rabbi Weiss."

"Oh, you're talking about the *bar mitzvah*." *Bar mitzvah*. She says it as if it is something she has heard of, a rare and difficult condition, like beriberi or the bends.

"Yes, Andrew's bar mitzvah. It's an important occasion in a young man's life, especially with all that's been going on, and I want the family organized. It's going to take plenty of string pulling to get someplace decent,

Windows On The World, or Cipriani, on a Saturday night. The kid's been in Hebrew school for five years, so the big show may as well come off properly."

"You know I'd forgotten about that with all the changes I've been undergoing *spiritually*," Lauren says with passion. Has she been seeing God when the climbing instructor is laying her? I wonder what other spirituality she could possibly be talking about.

"What changes?"

"You know I've gone back to the Church," Lauren says. Perfect. My little *shiksa* wife. Ex-wife. Hadn't been to church in five years when I met her, and now she's going back to Catholicism. "I find it so much more forgiving. To try and follow the example of Jesus, to forgive the wrongs of others. It's so *inspiring* to not stand in judgment of people," she says, seemingly for Ricky's benefit.

"Yeah? I prefer the justice of the Old Testament," I tell him. "Has Andrew been learning his *haftorah*?" I ask Lauren, finding myself worried for the first time in years.

"Six months ago, when you finally moved out, he started losing interest in Hebrew school, so I told him he didn't have to keep going," she says, picking up her cappuccino and taking a sip.

"You what?" I hear my pitch rise. I sound overly involved, my shock too evident.

"If you ever spoke to him you would know—" she begins.

"*Me* talk to *him*? I try. I call and call, but the kid won't talk to me. Whether he's at home or school, I can't reach him. Twelve years old and he has an answering machine. He could be a great Hollywood agent he's so unreachable." Suddenly I feel a tremendous vise-like pressure across my chest. My heart is squeezed by it. The feeling

25

could be mistaken for a heart attack if I hadn't already experienced one. I realize it is emotion. Intense emotion.

"He decided he wasn't getting much out of Hebrew school anymore, and it just didn't seem right to force him to go, so..."

"He's a kid. He doesn't *decide*. We're his parents. We *tell* him."

"You think you can control everything, Elliot, but you're wrong. My parents forced me to go to church, and I've just now found a true sense of—"

"He's a boy. He's a Jew. Jews get bar mitzvahed when they're thirteen."

"Well, I don't know about that." She is smug. Her boyfriend looks like a gargoyle—deaf, dumb, and carved out of stone. He's perched there looking. A ruddy, handsome, cigar smoking gargoyle.

"Have Jews stopped bar mitzvahing thirteen year olds? Am I not aware of something?" Good, a little sarcasm. A little condescension. Some of the tools to direct a conversation. The fist gripping my chest relaxes a bit.

"I don't know if he *is* Jewish. He's feeling his Catholic roots. He's my son too, you know?"

"You? You converted to Judaism before you married me."

"I switched back. I took my first communion last month. I confessed my sins. It was *wonderful*. You should try it."

"We have Yom Kippur."

"One day a year? It doesn't seem like enough for some people." This one lands on me like a scud missile on the West Bank.

"You're putting these ideas in his head, confusing him."

"He just didn't seem to care about anything religious," she says. Good. Thank God. My God, the God of

26

Abraham. "He didn't seem to care about anything at all for a while there, other than karate and Playstation..." This gets a little snicker from Ricky, that Lauren shares intimately with a squeeze of his hand. They're so comfy together. It makes my heart beat black ink. I want to crucify them with pitons. "...Until he tried the Church."

"You get bar mitzvahed. You understand the importance of it later," I fairly bark.

"Your turning purplish, Elliot, and I don't know why, you haven't dated a Jewish girl since you were eighteen," I feel more blood rush to my face at this. "Anyway, Andrew has been considering taking the host and joining the Church—"

"That will not happen..." It is all I can manage to stutter out, as my world has suddenly stopped revolving. The idea of losing my son to that religion and I can feel the tremble and white fear of an onrushing subway train upon me.

"Who's your little friend, Elliot?" Yvonne stands next to me holding our light trench coats.

"No one," I say, snatching my coat. "Next week is Father's Day up at the Academy and I'm going to talk some sense into Andrew when I'm there. You can just forget about this church nonsense."

"I—"

"It's not happening." With that, I storm out of the restaurant. I hear Rez's sing-song "Good evening, *Buona notte*. Thank you," ring over my shoulder and the clip-clop of Yvonne's high heels chasing after me.

I sit on the bed in my Sulka pajamas, starched crisp, and find my fists are clenched. I open my right hand and pick up the liter of mineral water that sits next to me on the night table. I drink four liters per day, and today I am way behind, as I've had only two so far. I drain half the bottle and look up at Yvonne's livid face. She is still wearing her clothes and her coat.

"'Confessing your sins once a year isn't enough for *some* people,' she says. How's that for judgmental? In the same breath as 'forgiving like Jesus.'"

"Why are you so worried about what she says?" Yvonne asks.

"Did you see her, sitting there like that? As if she were so happy." I practically spit the last word.

"Yes, and so what? You called me 'no one.' Is that what I am, 'no one?'"

"It's a figure of speech." I really don't have the patience for any sort of argument with Yvonne. "So loaded with judgment. Almost intimating that my money is dirty. It's clean enough to buy her and her boyfriend a nice little romantic evening. Why are you standing there in your coat?"

"I don't want to stay here with you tonight if you think so little of me." She looks right into my face when she says it. She is bluffing. She is representing that she will leave, but she wants to stay. She just wants me to apologize. I'm too familiar with the ploy. I played plenty of poker while I was in the army. I even flirted with becoming a professional gambler. I was taking fifty, a hundred, bucks a day at the poker tables in the enlisted men's clubs, skinning under-educated kids from the South. I no longer gamble with cards, but one thing I learned at those tables, one of the many things I learned in the army, was that people looked into my face when they were bluffing, so I'd think they weren't. Yvonne and I have already gone twice in the afternoon, and it is a long shot that I'll be able to go again. Especially with the current situation—Andrew's defection. Pot odds don't warrant working things out.

28

"So go," I say.

It's time for her to show. "Stay here with her ghost then," she says. A decent line, loaded with emotion, in that foreign accent. I hear the door bang shut as Yvonne leaves. With her go my hopes and chances for sleep. Truth be known, the reason she halted my serial dating had nothing to do with her beauty or sexual technique. No, she whispers to me late at night in bed, tales of home, the sound of the forests of Eastern Europe in her voice, and I fall asleep to it. Sound sleep for the first time since the beginning of my marriage. I consider calling down to Tommy, the doorman, to stop her, but it would be a shame to spoil such a parting line, and I couldn't bring myself to apologize anyway.

Instead I sit up late into the night drinking mineral water. I concentrate on how it slides down my throat, and soak in memories. Four liters a day to cleanse the system. I let it filter through the organs and tissues and wash me of impurities. My style of confession. Let it settle into my cells and replenish those precious fluids. I am in the bathroom pissing, my last liter of the day tilted to my lips with my left hand, my prick in my right. It brings me back to a moment in my life. My brilliant moment, if you will, upon which all the rest hangs like trimming. I had decided I was going make a success of myself, and in my brilliant moment hit upon exactly how. I was sitting in a shitty apartment on 89th Street near Ralph Avenue, just back from the army. If there is one thing that every guy in the army has in common, it is a hard dick. Hard-ons are as prevalent as olive drab around there. Guys can stay away from the army, and they can leave the army when their time in is finished, but guys can't quit or escape their erections. I figured, and I might have even had mine in my hand at the time, that there had to be a way for a man to make a fortune off the ubiquitous horny cock.

It was a crooked path after that, but I eventually became a publisher, with *Swagbelly* as my vehicle. I'm no seer. No force reached down from the heavens and told me I could print pictures of tits and crackle, and shoot to the top of the business world. It was no stroke of genius for me to launch a magazine displaying naked women devoted to arousing the male member when there was a such slim niche in the first place. See, the shelves of newsstands were plenty full of these periodicals already, as they still are. Just a glance and there is *Playboy,* so decorous and refined, literary even, with the most beautiful women. Then *Penthouse,* nicely packaged as well, yet *the* gateway to the pink. After those two come what I refer to as the first tier—*Hustler, Club, Chic, Cheri, High Society,* and I am proud to include, *Swagbelly.* Beneath the first tier the competition gets thick and furious. This is where defining characteristics become few and quality is not of essence. There is *Hawk, Gallery, Velvet, Showgirls, Live Dolls, Teaser, Wild Ecstasy, Hot Bodies, Fox, Gent, Erotic Film, Playpen, Player, Portfolio, Mustang, Swing, Swank, Score* and *Genesis.* Check further down for the fetishes, specialties, and more exotic fare—*Sable, Sugah, Black Tail, Asian Beauties, Barefoot, Shaved Oriental, Over 50, Plumpers, D Cup, 40 Plus, Juggs, Dairy Queens, Milk Maids, Leg Action, Thrust, Naughty Neighbors, Just 18, Beaver, Close Shave, Slick, Hungry Cunts, Big Butt* and *Rear End Penetrator.* Below this lot are countless and nameless shrink-wrapped rags with black stars over the coarsest things imaginable right on the covers.

With so much product already out there it took me a little while before I understood any brilliance behind my idea and discovered where the real payday was. By then the 80's had come along and it was profit, profit, profit. There was business—Savings & Loans, junk bonds—

and culture—cocaine, clubs—and finally the thing that bridged them both was phone sex. Gooch, Larry, Rudie, and I were first. Each of us set up hundreds of lines and advertised them through our magazines. I was taking a million a month, net-net, after costs and taxes, for five years, until the field was watered down with copy-cats. It was a long and winding road to those days of hay. Serial struggle at times. Yet it all started in that brilliant, prick in hand, moment. I wonder if Ricky the climbing instructor's gap-toothed version was that moment when he saw Lauren.

I flush the toilet and look in the mirror. I see some squint lines around my eyes that give my face a negative cast. I should probably get some of those Botox injections that Lauren takes to smooth out wrinkles. A suntan mitigates them also, and I have plans to go to Florida tomorrow anyway. Shame about Yvonne though, I find a release in the morning before a flight when I'll be seated for a long time helps that old tickly prostate. Maybe I can work something out in the office before I go.

I think of my assistant, Taylor. She is young and suitably awed by my position. She's a thin little wisp. Flat-assed though, and no tits. Olive Oyle body. A turned up nose by the same doctor who did the rest of the South Shore of Long Island. I will, of course, keep things professional with her. I only need to learn expensive lessons once. More than fifteen years ago there was a young lady who offered her secretarial services to me by the name of Lauren Grubman, neé Payton.

She came along when I had just started doing well. The *Swagbelly* offices were over in Long Island City and I had just managed to take the magazine into the black. I had made over a hundred thousand the year before, for the first time. My whole life until then I thought a hundred grand was rich, that it would be enough. When I finally earned it though, I saw just how little it really was. I still had heavy debt on the magazine, and when I hired my first sex phone operators I used every personal dime I had at my disposal to keep my investors out. Best move I could have made. As it was, when the real money started rolling in, everyone I owed magazine start-up money to, even the ones I'd already paid back, tried to re-negotiate the terms. They wanted a share of the dirty-talk-jerk-off-over-the-phone business, but if they were too uninitiated to get in themselves, I wasn't about to start handing it over to them.

I opened some small offices on Madison Avenue. What I hoped was a classy front for *Swagbelly*. In fact, the place was called Swan Media—that's what I named the magazine's parent venture—and there was no indication, beside the stray statuesque model I might need to see personally in my office on occasion, that the operation had anything to do with pornography. I figured this would be my way into more money and bigger deals. I knew I couldn't expect big time players to come to Long Island City for meetings. Back then I employed an editor at *Swagbelly*. A puppet whose job I did for him, but at least it slid my name from the muck up the masthead a few spaces to Publisher. It was only an unfortunate lack of funds and foresight that kept me from hiring a beard publisher as well, as I have done since, to distance myself even further. What I needed next was the right executive secretary, a top woman, to add that *Town and Country* feel to my operation. When Lauren walked in the door, the interview process was all but over. I could tell she was what I needed on my side, maybe in that first instant I wanted her *by* my side too. Another brilliant moment? Love at first sight? Snap decision? Destiny? Biology? Regardless, she showed up bright and early the next day in a tan hound's-tooth check jacket, Hermès scarf around her neck, and knee-length skirt. She put a plant next to her desk, a Benjamin fichus I believe, and we were off.

At first I didn't come out and tell her what it was we did at Swan Media. I gave her bookkeeping, nondescript collectibles, and checks to handle, as well as some business letters. I set a small budget for her to work with, and the office soon gained a tasteful, welcoming feel. A Persian rug appeared in the reception area and the kitchenette grew well stocked. I often left my office door open and found myself staring out at her as she handled the phones and ran the place. She allowed no tawdry enticements in dress or manner. She was nearly asexual in her carriage, often wearing brooches pinning the throats of her blouses closed. Still, despite her hands and face being the only skin she exposed, I found myself magnetically drawn to her in a sexual way. Perhaps it was this counterpoint to the luridness of my business that pulled me to her.

The dirty work happened in the Long Island City offices. The photo shoots, layouts, and ads were all put together there. I had my first set of phone lines up and running nearby—twenty-five operators from a long, cold room, empty save for individual cubicles with phones, office chairs, and fluorescent lights. Open 24 hours. There was a table set up with coffee, and the women came in and out in shifts. Those were the days before many enterprising young ladies became independent contractors, and when it was still easier to run the phones from a central location. Before, too, the advent of the web and internet porn. Now things are mostly self-service and a telephone line and web-cam can be patched through to anywhere at all. I have a vision of a few sex phone queens sitting on the deck of their yacht, panting and moaning their customers to digital climax over cellulars and DSL lines. Back then, though, I was spending long hours with a few of my Long Island City staff, finding myself missing Lauren while coming up with the first generation of advertisements that have become so familiar today.

"Live XXX Hardcore, call and masturbate with me now," we encouraged. Call this number for oral action. Call this one for a horny housewife. Lusty lesbians available. Backdoor girls, leggy goddesses, dick sucking wenches, co-ed cunts, kinky nymphos, fresh and barely legal. Dial 1-800-prefix—lick, suck, cunt, clit, slit, slut, kiss, babe, hott, twat, whip, fuck, wack, obey, wett, tits, 4ass, hole, pink, kink, hard, load, spew, moan, cumm, rear, deep. It was difficult to think up new numbers and promises after awhile. We spun off into all kinds of odd combinations, like Norwegian double fucker, ballsuck fantasy, sex tramps, bang my black ass, Spanish tits and ass, Puerto Rican pussy, bizarre fetishes, bondage with Brigitte, party doll, come on my face, oil my ass, fill my hole, floppy tits, tiny tits, fuck my tits, leather, live, anal ecstasy, dick drooling tramp, cheerleader suck team, sweet virgin ball slurper, hump my rump, chicks with dicks, be my slave, I'll be your slave, do me, oriental orgasm, gutter sluts, Latin lickers, local girls, naughty Nina, bouncing Betty, munch my carpet, vacuum suck, I want my asshole fucked hard, please, long and slow, short and fast, bald beaver, greased hogs, I want two cocks, two-on-one blowjob for you, interracial fuck, nasty nurses rectal exam in room 3, hot sauce, spicy Asians, sleazy Swedes, cocksucking lesbo nuns. We really did a thorough job. Surprisingly, one of my most creative helpers was a fifty- year old woman named Vivian. She took it all as quite a laugh, and continued on late into the night long after I had left bleary-eyed.

A few months went by with me splitting time in Long

Island City and working closely with Lauren. I began taking her out to dinner after we worked late, and one night I invited her to a Knicks' game. We sat courtside and she opened herself to me about a guy she had been seeing in some fashion. He was a professional hockey player I'd never heard of who didn't see much ice time under his skates. She talked to me as a friend, as the boss she liked working for, but I realized my feelings went further. Even then I found it odd that though I spent half my day around shimmering, primed women who emitted allure and as pure a potion of sex as they could, at every moment, that though I pored over pictures of them in the most graphic poses, that though I had opportunity to witness as many photo shoots as I pleased, to create as much personal time with these women as I possibly desired, I instead found myself at a basketball game, craning for a look at the pulse of Lauren's briefly exposed wrist.

She watched the game, ballplayers storming up and down the court, hurling themselves at the hoop, and I watched the outline of her knees moving hypnotically beneath her pale ivory stockings. It irritated me to hear about this boyfriend of hers. He was some big Canadian farm boy with a mullet haircut and his speech full of "ehs." It was infuriating. I imagined she felt special sitting there at one of his games, similar to the spectacle we watched, seeing him on the bench, cheering for every breathtaking up and down the team underwent. Oh god, it could be so intense to have a personal stake in an exciting hockey game. She must have cursed that coach over and over for not having the foresight, the insight, to call her boyfriend's line. To put her man on the ice so he could be a big star, and he, he surely played for her, extra hard. Then there was the going out to bars with the team afterwards. The drama and consumption of a strapping bunch of pros, overgrown boys really, with money in their pockets, physically fit and physical, pouring back draft beers and hard liquor in tumblers. To be along with them at the center of attention. Manly energy. Never mind the nights he did not call, the road trips, no answer in his hotel room, and the mysterious infections. Never mind free-agency and release onto waivers, the Camaro he drove, re-constructive knee surgery, single syllable vocabulary, more penalty minutes than minutes played, and one goal and two assists for the entire season. Never mind it all, he took her breath away. I thought of Lauren, all these years gone by, with her latest sportsman. She was always so easily impressed.

After the game I decided to take her into my confidence. We left the Garden and got into the Lincoln Town Car I had hired for the evening. I was still two years from the twin turbo Bentleys then. "I want to show you something, Lauren," I said, beside myself at the sight of her crossed ankles against the carpeted car floor. I gave the driver the address in Long Island City. "Do you know what Swan Media does?" I waited for her answer. Her distance, her cool reserve provoked me. Over the last month I had completely cut out indulgences with other women, the models, and settled into a state of chaste torpor over Lauren.

"I know the company publishes an adult magazine," she answered demurely. I should not have been surprised, she was astute. I had no idea just how astute.

"You're right, Lauren. *Swagbelly* magazine. Have you heard of it?"

"I've seen the cover at the store."

"I do have other ventures though," I told her. We arrived at the run down brick building and went up to the third floor in the small elevator. I opened the door to the office suite housing my operators. "This is my little gold mine."

Perhaps I had become accustomed to the seething ambiance of sex that was such a part of my life. I suppose I had long ago stopped seeing and hearing the sights and sounds of my business, or at least registering them. The moment we walked through that door though, I realized Lauren did not understand what I was showing her and why. I perceived it anew through her fresh eyes, and my mistake was clear. There they were, the living end of all those advertisements that promised ultimate sexual fulfillment with rapturous beauties, and who were securing my future. The women who worked there were not all ugly. They were not all overweight. They were not all blotchy complected, unmade up, shabbily dressed, bearing facial hair and moles. They did all smoke. Every one of them had a cigarette going. Things were plenty unsightly. Extreme plainness can be one of the most disgusting things about reality. Snippets of half-conversations filled the air.

Ballsuck, cornhole me, I'll jerk you while I fuck him, lay your load on me, fuck me like the slut I am, I'm a bad girl, I'm your nasty nympho neighbor, I am wet for you, fill my slippery crack, bend me over, fuck my ass, make me beg, have you been bad, psycho bitch fuck hard, take me, I'll take you, suck, head, lips, come, pussy, cunt, cock, oh, ah, ooh, um, yeah, uh, gruh...

The short animal-like sounds wafted about on the cigarette smoke and filtered into our ears. Lauren blanched completely, almost collapsing, and I led her across the street to the editorial offices, which were empty for the night.

"I knew you published a magazine, but I...I thought you didn't have much to do with it." She seemed shocked, nearly devastated. I gave her a glass of water, and stroked her hair to calm her. After a moment she began to settle down. She even laughed a little about what she had seen, and her reaction to it. "I'm fine, Elliot, really," using my first name for the first time.

"Good. You had me worried for a minute there," I said looking at her. She had an odd expression on her face. One I could not read at the time. I began to feel something from her. I was not a man familiar with love, but I tried with all my heart, that neglected little organ, and with all my people and poker skills to understand what feeling it was that she was feeling. Was it repressed love? Physical need? Discomfort? Disgust? It could have been nearly anything. She was like a gyroscope, her exterior immobile, while inside she spun in a high speed centrifugal motion. I did not know what it was, but as long as there was something, some emotion, I had hope. I knew I could work with whatever it was, and turn it towards me. On an impulse I reached for her and kissed her. She did not protest. I had a moment's wild pictorial vision of my taking her bent over the desk. It did not go that far. I unbuttoned her blouse and exposed her alabaster breasts. She took out the stiff penis residing in my trousers. I tried to lift her skirt. She indicated we were not going to reach that destination. Before long I succumbed to her cool grasp and deposited a cloud of sticky semen onto the lap of her tweed skirt.

The next day I was in the office early, waiting impatiently for Lauren to come through the door. She was so different than all the models I had known, and from all the Jewish girls from Brooklyn too. She was of the greater world, and seemed of the top strata of that. I wondered if I possessed the dexterity to advance things between

38

us and I was eager to try. She usually appeared around 8:30, though her appointed time to begin work was 9:00. Both of these markers passed, and I grew concerned. Of course we were out the night before, so her being late was fully excused. I shuffled some papers around, and looked up at 10:15 to realize that she still had not arrived. I dialed her at home, hoping she had simply overslept. There was a degree of discomfort to be sure after our leap from employer/employee into the intimate. Even I felt it. There was no answer at her place, and I tried to kid myself she was on her way. By 11:45 I began to feel I had flushed her with my advance, that she had burst up from the hedgerow in a flutter of beating wings and, I was horrified to think it, I would never see her again. A moment's vision of her back in the arms of her hockey goon had me heartsick.

Downcast, I put the phones on voice mail, closed the office, and slumped off to lunch. An hour and fifteen minutes later I returned to the office. Standing in front of the locked door was a kid in battered tennis shoes, headphones, and fatigue pants cut into shorts. He had a canvas bag over his shoulder and looked like a messenger. I put my key in the office door.

"Mr. Elliot Grubman?" he said loudly. I could hear a bassy thump coming from his headphones.

"Yes," I said, as a sickly feeling was born in the base of my spine, in the direct vicinity of my rectum, at the formal way my name had been spoken.

"You've been served," he nearly yelled in the quiet hallway. He smacked my shoulder with a manila envelope that he let fall to the floor before he sauntered off toward the elevator. I looked at the spot on my suit jacket that he had hit, half expecting a large, smoking hole to exist there. I picked up the envelope, missing Lauren all the more. She rejected countless people looking for me, politely claiming not to be agent for me nor know my whereabouts.

Inside my office I opened the summons, and read its message with growing disbelief, admiration, horror, and fascination. Each sensation alternated in a throbbing rhythm, not unlike a salsa, in my temples. It was a civil action brought in district court, Southern District of New York, by one Lauren Payton, Plaintiff, against Elliot Grubman, Swan Media, et al., Defendant, charging physical and psychological abuse in a sexually harassing manner. It detailed my bringing her to the telephone room after hours in order to "shock and coerce her in an environment of explicit sexuality..." To my dismay, it continued to recount my "touching her around the face, neck, and legs, grabbing her and trying to kiss her, telling her he (that meant me) wanted to know her sexually, and ejaculating upon her person." The complaint mentioned the Human Rights Law, which "prohibits from exploiting a dominant position of power in the workplace by imposing sexual demands upon an employee." That to make any attempt to use the terms of employment to "coerce an employee, targeted on the basis of gender, to agree to participate in sexual activity is a form of sex discrimination outlawed by state law." It was all very edifying. I learned that proof of such discriminatory conduct on the part of an employer suffices to trigger liability under the Executive Law. When I read "proof" I winced at the thought of her semen crusted skirt being held up in court by some Perry Mason-like lawyer wearing rubber gloves as the jury gasped and shielded their eyes. Further, I was informed, "the employee need not prove that he or she resisted the abuse or refused to comply with the sexual demands." For citation of this little chestnut I was free to refer to Bundy v. Jackson, 641 F2d 934, 945. She was a prescient one, that Lauren. Really ahead of her time fifteen years ago. Shrewd, and fast as lightning with her counter punch. Any attempts to contact her were discouraged and should be directed to her attorney. For an hour I sat in my office, the glowing end of my smoldering Punch the only evidence of life therein. Then I picked up the phone and dialed my lawyer.

Leonard Loeb, my attorney, has horrible teeth and a plaintive, nearly beaten way of speaking, as if every single situation he faces causes him great degrees of grief. Once he sinks his teeth in legally though, those rotting, crooked, dun colored enamel placards of his, he hangs on like a terrier—a little, snarling, balding, litigating, Jewish terrier. "Elliot," he began, sounding as if he were in great pain, after I had outlined my situation.

"Yes?" I said.

"Elliot," he sighed. "How much money do you have on hand." I was embarrassed at the figure I quickly tallied in my head, increased it by 20% and answered, "About $55,000 cash. Without selling anything important."

"That's not enough," he let me know.

"The firm she's hired, they're low-rent hayseeds?" I hoped.

"Right," he said, "Mead, Luxor, and Hanrahan. They don't take cases indiscriminately, you know. They like to work on winnable, lucrative ones—and this could be a jewel case even for them."

"Leonard, you're making me uneasy," I told him. "Tell me you'll beat them up in court. You'll shred her on the stand."

"Court, Elliot? Oh we don't want to go there," he whined. At least he said 'we,' though. It made me feel a little better. I paid him $300 an hour back then. The call had already cost me $175, but I would have peeled double that in cash off my bankroll on the spot for that measly "we."

41

"What do *we* want to do then?" I asked, emphasizing the comforting pronoun he had just used. He said he would contact her attorney and try to arrange a settlement meeting that we would both attend. He hoped that her seeing me, and I was to be damn sure to act downcast and penitent, would weaken her will to go for blood. His idea was that she would not want to proceed with the suit if she felt I had taken it seriously, or at the very least she would accept a more nominal figure to settle the case. I, brash piss clam that I was, had my own ideas for the meeting.

I shift around in bed and cannot get comfortable. The mattress in my new apartment lacks a goose down pad like the one in my townhouse featured. Ricky is probably sleeping soundly on it now, having soaked it and my ex-wife with his sweat and jism. I turn on the television, still tuned to the Cartoon Network, to see some people in robotic armor flying around in outer space. I look at the phone and consider dialing Yvonne. Being with her makes me feel young and that's a good thing, except when I begin talking to her in that tone—part professor, part sadist—that I used throughout this evening and don't know from where it springs. I wonder at my son, lost up at boarding school, crazy ideas flying about in his head. It's after lights-out there, past time to call. I'm too confused anyway, using the phone is not an option.

I switch channels and come to a nature program about the great cats of Africa. It shows lions hunting in prides, cheetahs chasing down antelope, and then moves on to leopards. They are the most beautiful, with opalescent, heavy-lidded eyes and rippling coats that shiver on frames of pure muscle. Spongy, padded paws tread firmly across all surfaces. One walks smoothly down the

42

trunk of a tree and strides into high grass. The cat carries her head low beneath her shoulders. She does not seem hungry, malevolent, or excited. She patiently moves up on a herd of Thompson's gazelle, silently runs one down, and sits, her sides puffing in and out like a bellows, with her jaws around the victim's neck. When the young gazelle becomes still, the leopard begins to feed for a few moments before she will take the kill up into a tree to protect it. She starts eating at the rectum, the easiest point of entry, and moves on into the bowel cavity and intestines. Despite the cat's face being covered with blood, it is a scene of utter serenity. There is not an element of violence. The cat simply acts. Everything occurs without thought. This is what is behind the absolute grace of the great cats—remove thought, and instinctive movement, grace, is all that remains. Nothing gives human beings their inelegant and stumbling, almost soiled, aspect as does thinking. We people eat ourselves with our minds in a most unnatural way. Sometimes we can hardly manage to breath. It was the feline grace with which Lauren sued me, I see now, that created such an impression on me. Her actions were so unfettered by bad feeling or calculation that even her lawsuit, the most human of inventions, flowed like water. It would have been no surprise for me to see Lauren show up at the settlement conference with a leopard print scarf tied around her neck. She did not, however. She wore the classic red and green Gucci design. I suppose the double 'G' emblem is the human equivalent of leopard skin.

On the day of the settlement meeting, Leonard and I went to her attorney's office on Lexington Avenue. "Don't be nervous," Leonard assured me in the elevator.

I looked down on his bare pate, and said nothing. I am only nervous in a meeting when I do not have an edge, and I try to insure this is never the case. It certainly wasn't that day. "After all, it's only money," Leonard added.

I smiled thinly, my lips feeling like purple rubber gaskets. "That's all it ever is."

The four of us took our chairs in a small, glass-walled conference room and the meeting began like an opera—an opera with a confusing and unpoetic libretto too boring to repeat. Lauren, cold and stunning in a glen plaid suit, next to her attorney, buttoned-down collar, yellow rep. tie, and tortoise shell horned rims. He laid out the grievances, schedule of depositions, and court dates we would have to face in a Waspish *basso profundo*. In his own Brooklyn Semitic tenor, Len described the difficult, expensive, and embarrassing road ahead for their side based on the liberal discovery laws in New York, the publicity at our disposal, and the humiliation she would certainly face in open court. Humiliation, to which, as a man, I was apparently immune. As the lawyers talked and postured, I tried to catch Lauren's eye. I could not do it though, as she looked at her lawyer when he spoke, stared at a legal pad full of notes in front of her, peered out the glass into the law offices bustling around us, even glanced at Leonard when he spoke. She looked everywhere but at me. I was patient though. I fixed her with a soft, pleading stare. Finally she chanced a look my way, and I blinked slowly, bowing my head ever so slightly in pain and regret at the situation. She caught her breath a bit, and swallowed, and I knew I had her.

"Lenny," I said aloud, interrupting her man just as he had come to the numbers, "will you make a request to Ms. Payton's attorney that I would like to speak to her alone for a moment." I did not take my eyes off of Lauren.

Leonard opened his mouth as her lawyer blustered, "That's highly unusual—"

"It's okay, John, I agree," she cut him off. The two shysters got up uncomfortably, fearing they'd be squeezed out of the deal.

"I hope you know what you're doing," Leonard hissed at me as he shuffled out of the room. The two of them stood outside and both lit cigarettes as I let silence settle over us.

"Lauren," I sighed regretfully, "why are we here?"

"Oh, Elliot," she said.

"What is it?" I tried to soften my voice into velvet, to become piety incarnate.

"You...You shocked me that night, with everything. It was so graphic and aggressive."

"I am sorry."

"I've seen the women in and out of your office. I won't be discarded like—"

"That was not my intention."

"Well, what was your intention then?" She wrung her hands a bit. She was not used to high pressure negotiations and the proceeding was taking quite a toll on her nerves.

"Only the best, Lauren," I said as soothingly as I could. I reached into my suit jacket pocket and my fingers located the black velvet jewel box. "Marry me, Lauren. Forget all this and be my wife." I opened the box and slid it across the table to her. Inside was a 4.5 carat emerald cut diamond, F color, vvs 2. It was set in platinum. Those were the days before I could afford D color and flawless. It was plenty though.

"Oh my goodness," she gasped. She tried to gather herself with "Elliot, this is very fast...." but it was done. I waved Len back inside and said nothing. She'd closed the jewel box, but had left it sitting there on her legal pad. She whispered in her attorney's ear. He glared at me and then the box. He looked a bit like a hound who had cornered a fox and been deprived the chance to rip it to shreds, but he shrugged it off quickly, for he had seen it all before. Lauren and I left the two lawyers to settle up the paper work, and probably devise clever ways to pad our bills—bills which would now both come to me.

After that we were married. Some good, truly good, days came to pass. It is already difficult to remember all of it, especially the natural, unbound Lauren. The times of her moving gracefully and without thought gave way to hours of her sitting frozen in front of the bathroom mirror touching her face. She began referring to her slight laugh lines as 'plunging wrinkles.' She got her eyes done for the first time at age 33. Next, she wanted a cheek lift, and a tuck of her nasolabial folds. She received monthly injections of collagen in her face, wherever she perceived an imperfection. The shots developed fibroplasia, small scars, that served to fill in and smooth the look of her skin. She took other injections, of botulinum toxin, small amounts of the paralysis inducing bacteria botulism that acts as a relaxant on flesh, and is supposed to erase worry creases in the forehead. She became best friends with her dermatologist. 'Debbie,' she called her, and on alternating Wednesdays got glycolic peels and trichloracetic acid washes. I am in a state of wonder at the great dermatological compulsions Lauren suffers from, all the more baffling because I think she always looks great.

A stark question comes to me in the dark of my bedroom—did I bring her to this state? I reach out, to hold myself back from a slippery internal precipice, and come up with a handful of bed sheet. It feels coarse in my hand, as I await new ones from Pratesi, monogrammed

with my initials alone. No more "L" to go with the "EG."
The linen I lay on is temporary. From Bergdorf or
Schweitzer Linen. These sheets do not have the luxuri-
ous feel of Pratesi, which have a nap that is almost
suede-like. I sit up and switch on the bedside lamp, take
out a fresh pad of sticky notes from the drawer. "Thread
count?" I write, for under 300 per inch is too coarse for
me, and place it upon the pillow Yvonne would have
been using.

I walk out of my building at 8:05 in the morning and see
my limousine waiting in the circular driveway. My driver, Mamoo, puts me in the car with a "Good day, *sear*." He
is a jolly Samoan the size of a tool shed, and not a half
bad driver for a man who can lift a washing machine
and throw it into a dumpster, which is what his job was
before he came to me. I got him in the divorce and I am
very generous about lending him back to Lauren, of
course, as I can count on a detailed report when he
returns.

Once, when stepping from the limo, as Mamoo held
the door for me, an aggressive cracked-out homeless
man shouted a request at me for a million dollars. When
I ignored him he said, "How about $100,000 man, then I
be happy?" I still did not respond, causing him to utter,
"How about I take your life? *Then* I be happy." Mamoo
turned and ran into him, with nearly unbelievable speed
and menace. He was a blur of bulk. The Islander's belly
and chest impacted the frail and unhealthy beggar, sending his change cup flying and collapsing him to the
curb. It was terrifying to see a big man move with such
speed.

The car lumbers out from the driveway and we swing
into traffic. I appraise the dove gray interior of the Lincoln

47

and compare it mentally with limousines I have owned in the past. My first chauffeured car was a black Cadillac stretch. It was huge, comfortable, and intimidating. It got perhaps three miles to the gallon, and I cared not at all. Regretfully, Cadillac has discontinued anachronisms like her. Their new stretches are way too much glass, and far too light of fender. So now I am a devout stretch Lincoln man. They are battleships sluicing through Manhattan's crumbling roads and traffic bottlenecks. Inside tinted windows, vast banquettes of smooth leather wrap around me and there is a low hum of instruments. Glowing pin point lights hint at the placement of two telephones, a television, VCR, and refrigerator. Cut crystal decanters full of Cardhu single malt rest in custom designed holders, and monogrammed cocktail napkins wait beneath matching tumblers. The carpet on the floor is springy and new-smelling.

I am at ease as I ride, the limo as snug as a silk-lined casket, but as we pull up to my office building I see a large group of people milling about the front. It looks like a picket line, but they are mostly women and none wear the sandwich boards that come along with a porters, or other union wage strike. The car slows and I get a closer look at what the signs say. "Pornography = Rape," announces one, and I quickly realize this is not a strike, but a protest, and it is meant for me. I am aghast as I take in the NOW buttons pinned on many of the women and some of the men. Said women wear short-cropped haircuts and are plain of make up. Those with long hair have it plaited down their backs. Quite a few of the men wear chinos and sandals. One squat young lady in black waves a stick bearing a blindfolded Barbie doll hung by the neck in effigy. "What the fuck?" I say aloud, and then to Mamoo, "Take me around the corner."

He looks at me in the rearview mirror. "Yes, *sear*."

If I step out into that crowd, and they recognize who I am, regardless of Mamoo's presence, they will swarm me. The cardboard posters they wave rail against treating women like "meat." Ending "exploitation" in general is another common theme. I have a habit that crops up in certain stressful situations, which is seeing the outcome as if in headlines on the cover of a newspaper. *"Business Man Torn Apart By Angry Mob,"* is how this one reads. There is an accompanying photo in my mind, of me attempting to shield myself with my Asprey briefcase as they close in on me. Finally, the car clears the corner and the side entrance to the building is wonderfully free of people. Apparently the protesters are hostile but not thorough.

It is only after I step inside the building lobby, see things are in order, and hear the strains of light music playing in the elevator, that I become irritated. Pornography is rape, my ass. I have not taken anything against anyone's will. What have I done without willing partners? I know the argument; my magazine, my industry, me, we objectify women, make them seem *things,* not human beings. We stir the lusts of psychopaths, sociopaths, and misogynists and set them upon the female victims in society. I reject this. I think the rapist's parents, and the rapists themselves, have a hell of a lot more responsibility in it than I. Pornography is honest. It is the simple honesty of the exposed body, the acts between one, two, or more, put on view for those who are so inclined to look. It cannot be hidden. If it is taken off the newsstands in photograph form it will still be going on in real time in bedrooms, in bathrooms, in hotels, in the woods, in bus stations, in hospitals, in schools, in churches for Christ's sake. But there is less and less place for this honesty in today's mewling politically correct world.

I enter my office at 8:35, ruffled, and stop in front of Taylor's desk. "Good morning, Mr. Grubman," she greets me, and I cannot help but be briefly distracted by her erect nipples poking though the sheer fabric of her blouse.

"Taylor," I say, and regain my focus. "Call Dwight what's his name from Intercept about sending some men over to clear those dykes out from in front of the building." Intercept is a pricey but very effective security and executive protection outfit run by some ex-Secret Service agents. I first used them when one of my models had a minor stalking incident. They got a dossier together on the obsessed 'fan' and threatened him just inside the limits of the law. Made him disappear completely. "I can't have my loyal employees harassed on their way to work, now can I?" I smile broadly at Taylor, for today I am benevolent.

"Yes sir," she says and makes a note on her steno pad. "Have them put somebody on our door also," my smile snaps off, as I realize I cannot allow these protesters to get too ambitious and burst in with a vat of fetal pig blood to smear on me, or whatever they do to make political statements these days.

"This gentleman is C.B. Brancato, your first meeting of the day," Taylor informs me.

"He is?" I say, and glance over toward the waiting area. Sitting on the couch is a doughy, dark complexioned guy with stringy black hair in the process of migrating north from his forehead like a flock of geese. He wears a black leather jacket and his skin has a viscous sheen to it as if he has just worked out or exerted himself in some way, and I believe it must be some other way as his paunch seems a few years since serious gym work. I'm not sure, but I detect a slight unpleasant odor coming from his vicinity.

"You may have heard of me," he says, crossing toward me. "I'm a writer," he says offering a hand squishy with moisture.

"Really?" I rarely give recognition of knowing someone—even if I've met them a dozen times—and especially having heard of a person. Doing this keeps people nicely off balance.

"Have a seat," I point at my office, "I'll be right in." He walks in the direction I gesture and I notice he's wearing black suede clogs on his feet. I hate him already. I turn to Taylor and she answers my look.

"He writes the 'City Smut' column in the Post. We scheduled him to talk to you about writing a similar but more off-color column in the magazine. 'Star Sex,' or something along those lines." I can tell right away that Taylor is seeing the guy. It is evident by her demeanor—shy, hopeful—and the smug familiarity on his part. There is also the fact that he would never have gotten this meeting otherwise. I wish I had some irritating task with which to punish her.

"What time is my flight scheduled?" is what I have to settle for.

"3.30, La Guardia, Marine Air Terminal," she says.

"My luggage?"

"Federal Expressed yesterday." I always have my luggage sent by Federal Express when I travel, that way I don't have to carry it, or even see it, until I am in my hotel room.

"Fine." I shrug my shoulders and walk away.

Inside my office, the same smell I caught a whiff of in the reception area is present. It has a grilled polenta with gorgonzola character, and I blame Brancato for bringing it into my office. "So, Mr. Brancato—"

"Call me C.B." Broad smile. Space between his front teeth. "Love that suit. Brioni?" He is phony tough-guy obsequiousness walking. I act as if I discover the suit on my body for the first time. Though Brioni is not bad, I sneer.

"No, custom. What can I do for you?" I ask.

He makes his pitch. "I'm a writer. Like I said, I write a celebrity news column for the Post. You may have read it. I want to do a column for your magazine, but instead of the usual who is dating whom bullshit, and where they were spotted at dinner, I want it to be more hard hitting." He says the last excitedly, in a real cub reporter way. "I can deliver you twenty-five hundred words per issue of who is fucking whom, and how. Sexual proclivity, who goes for plate jobs, which famous actor or singer likes to hop around in Pampers and have girls fuck him with a strap-on." He pauses for a moment. "I know what you're thinking," he assures me, before I have thought a thing. "You're worried about libel. Don't be. I can deliver it all from reliable sources. I'm a *journalist* first and foremost."

"Not at all, I'm sure you check ten or twenty per cent of your stories." His dull black marble eyes, close-set like a hydrocephalic's, register my comment.

"I have multi-layered connections in *both* Hollywoods, East and West," he seems undeterred. "From time to time I will even have pictures of people we know as 'stars' *en flagrante*, heh-heh." Impressive. This guy is the Woodward and Bernstein meets David Halberstam of filthy gossip, all in one slightly odoriferous package. I look across my desk at him, as he looks back at me intently. Brancato prints things about people they want kept private, and though I may be a man of only a few mores, this happens to offend one of them. I wonder if he is leaving a slight imprint of greasy body musk on the $25,000 Frank Lloyd Wright chair on which he is seated.

"What is that smell? Are you wearing after shave?" I wonder aloud.

"No, just good old soap and water for me."

"It must be what you do then. You think of yourself as a writer or journalist of some kind, but "celebrity news," as you call it is the literary equivalent of flatulence. It stinks for a moment and then passes away forever." He is dumbstruck, but the street Italian in him takes right over.

"You comparing me to a fart? Listen man, I know people I can call. And you should fucking comment, in your line of work. Talk about frigging exploitive." So maybe I started, but he has now taken us into an area that particularly irritates me. In the months after Lauren and I were married, at her guidance and insistence, I had my name removed from the *Swagbelly* masthead altogether, and even scotched from the roles of Swan Media. She was quite practical back then. Despite these efforts, my profession has become known in certain circles and I have been rejected by several co-op boards, denied membership at countless clubs, and I believe, even my son was not admitted to a few private schools when he was younger. Add the fact that I am a Jew, and mine is more a story of places from which I have been barred more than one of where I have been. A dozen associates and myself had to put up several hundred thousand dollar bonds and build our own golf club on Long Island because the *goyim* pricks wouldn't let us into Shinnecock and the like.

Brancato is out of his chair by the time I say, "At least I pay my people for exposing themselves...And stay away from my assistant," I warn his departing back. I hear a quick, heated exchange between the gossip columnist and Taylor, and then the outer office door slams shut. I study the chair in which he has been seated, and it appears to be fine, no murky sheen like that of his face and hair. A moment later Taylor walks into my office with a stricken look on her face. "What happened?" she wonders.

"Very rude young man," I suggest. "Let's have the offices cleaned while I'm away this weekend." Taylor says nothing. What can she possibly say?

In the early afternoon I have still made no headway on the issue of my pre-flight release, and worse, have what started as a twinge but has now grown into a small pain in my conscience over what happened between Yvonne and me. I try her apartment, but she doesn't answer. I hang up without leaving a message, then meet my insurance consultant, Kenny Feinstein, to talk over some changes in my policy. Insurance is a tricky subject for me. You have a heart attack, even a mini, at 29, you can't expect to get much life insurance. I managed to secure a small policy after three years with no symptoms and no further treatment. Even then my blood pressure was high though, so Kenny had me take a nap on the couch in his office and had a doctor record my vitals there. "How was the blood pressure?" I asked upon waking up.

"Any lower and you'd be dead," they smiled over me.

There are other ways to protect what you have besides life insurance. We meet at the Friar's Club to discuss them. The food is dirt there, and the union waiters scuttle around like dandruffy crabs taking their leisure, but men love the place. We must find some woody comfort in the old wingback chairs. The club is strapped for cash and wouldn't think of giving me a hard time over my membership either. When we were married, Lauren would have received my assets had I died before her. Kenny had me buy a second-to-die policy on her that insured my assets after estate taxes for Andrew in the event of her death. Upon the divorce becoming final though, this policy was no longer appropriate, since the assets were not going to be swinging her way when I was done for. The fifteen million she has already gotten on D-Day was enough of a swing for one lifetime. Actually, it felt like a colossal yo-yo string with Venus attached to the end of it being ripped from my bank account and slung into hers. Like I say, even a hundred mil can be lost, and when Kenny runs through the numbers with me, this is nearly the sensation I experience.

"When you die, estate taxes are going to take half, no way around it. You can stash what you want in offshore accounts, and shelter it any way you like, but you better have some liquidity available or your son will be in a world of trouble," he tells me, and I suddenly feel it is the day of my death. I get the sense that I am dead already as we speak, and my ghost, fifty-percent less wealthy, is observing this meeting.

"The course I'm recommending is one known as 'Estate Preservation Tax Insurance.' It will pre-discount estate taxes in effect, and protect your liquidity." I wait for him to give some hint or indication of how much it is going to cost me, and admire the smooth delivery of his words, words that hang just on the edge between obtuse and perfectly understandable as he rapidly spouts them. I feel a little anemic as I re-evaluate my net worth and he continues. "We need to establish an irrevocable life insurance trust for you, outside of your estate, that will pay for this policy. It is the most cost-effective avenue toward paying your estate tax."

"Are you enjoying your lunch, Kenny?" I ask. Kenny is a trim, athletic looking fellow, with thinning hair and a snickering, rodent's smile. He eats with a jaw snapping gusto.

"What?"

"What are you eating there, Waldorf salad is it?"

"No, uh, Cobb salad..." He looks down at his plate.

55

"Oh, I thought I saw a walnut in there, like in a Waldorf salad."

"It's very good."

"Good, Kenny. Now what will this policy cost me?"

"$200,000 per annum."

I bring my lips together in an admiring snarl at the price of amortization. He, as my insurance agent, will be taking close to a hundred grand in commission this year, and another hundred over the next ten years. That is a nice diamond ring for his wife, a yearly trip to Barbados, a tennis court, a few years of college for his kid, a chunk toward his own insurance premium. This fucker could take a yacht around the Riviera this summer, with plenty left over, all for protecting me. I am one fat customer, and will he even pick up this tab for a couple of lunch salads? No, no, I'm buying. I am a lunch buyer now, in addition to a dinner buyer. I am the proverbial meal ticket. I have a sudden feeling that I would like to break the chain, and dodge a check one time. "I need this policy, Kenny, no doubt about it?" I ask.

"Absolutely."

"What about alternatives?"

"Don't die," he chortles. Terrific. Everybody has their shtick. There is Leonard Loeb, my attorney, when I ask his advice on my divorce settlement. "Stay married," he says, and now Feinstein. "No, seriously," he goes on, "it's the best way to secure the future of your money for your family." It's amazing. Now my money has a future, even beyond my own. Kenny pushes his plate away with some regret and reaches for his briefcase beneath the table, our having arrived at the business portion of our meal. He removes some papers and shows me where to sign.

"Call Stanley Grabow," my accountant, "and have him cut you a check," I say into Kenny's keen smile. "By the way, when will this be in effect?"

"The binder will be valid as soon as I return to my office and file it," he tells me, handing me an envelope with my copies of the documents.

"Good. You never know how soon I may need it. I'm going to Palm Beach today, to learn how to play polo."

"Polo!" Kenny is impressed.

"My friend Sandy Kleiner plays. He talked me into it. Just what they want in Palm Beach isn't it? Another Jew, playing polo..." Kenny stands up with me and pumps my hand with vigor. It feels like his is a tennis or squash player's grip. He can afford quite a few lessons now. I hand him back the envelope. "Have my copies sent to the office." I've nearly made exit from the club when the waiter cuts me off with a vinyl check wallet. It is the first time he has moved with alacrity since St. Patrick's Day. I hurriedly sign my name and membership number and leave. When I get outside I call Stanley Grabow and tell him not to send a check to Kenny Feinstein.

Palm Beach

It is twilight as I am driven along palm lined South County Road. We move freely along the street now, but come Sunday morning it will be jammed with Cadillacs, Jaguars, and wood-paneled sport utility vehicles. The cars are owned by the congregation of Palm Beach's grand stone Episcopalian church—sight of innumerable weddings announced in the society pages of "W." Suddenly, The Breakers Hotel juts up out of the flats of its golf course, the burnished pearl of the surf-pounded Gold Coast. She is white, with a terra cotta roof, spotlights thrown upon, and flags flying atop her. The place appears a great Mediterranean villa, but instead of housing the Medicis or Frescobaldis, it shelters the Barrows, the Beanstocks, the Smiths, the St. hyphens, and some Goldfarbs. They are vacationing hedge fund managers and their families whose ancestors were on the Mayflower, successful mid-western corporate leaders on golf junkets, and a breed of Jewish parvenu whose wealth or sensibility pushes them north from Miami, Ft. Lauderdale, and Boca Raton in search of *vrai* Florida. I am here, I did not succeed in my quest to unburden myself of semen before my flight. In my glum state after my meeting with Kenny Feinstein, I abandoned it altogether. Despite this, I feel good in the warm and humid Florida air, and I do have my list for later. I carry a two page list of addresses and phone numbers of past *Swagbelly* feature models who live in the South Florida area. I have already dated some on the regional list, and

I am on congenial terms with most of the others. There are only a few I would not presume to call. The master list, over twenty pages long, resides on the hard disk of my computer back in the office.

My chauffeured car takes me up the long, straight drive, and around the hotel fountain, depositing me at the front entrance. Gold braided valets greet me, which is the way I like it. I walk into the hotel's vaunted and vaulted lobby, where sounds are muted echoes like those of a mausoleum. The floor is blonde marble and covered in places by ancient Persian carpets worn thin by years of the well-heeled's heels. I am directly confronted by a stern sign announcing, "Jackets Required After 7:00." It is oddly comforting to me. The protection a good suit provides should never be underestimated. Old white couples, stooped and embalmed, shuffle blue-blazered across my line of sight. I approach the desk and begin the ritual of my check-in. I make the acquaintance of Will, the concierge, and win his immediate goodwill with a $100 bill slid across the desktop to him. As I'm handed the key to my suite, the quiet, soothing tones of the procedure are shattered by shouts of "Elliot? Hey-hey," and hail "hello-hello's." It is Sandy Kleiner and his family set upon me.

"Hello there, Sandy" I shake his hand. He wears bone colored slacks and a double-breasted blue sport coat with gold buttons, as if he is captain of some craft. On his large feet are driving moccasins, with small rubber nubs that run along the soles and up the backs of his heels. He does not wear socks and has the easy charm of a Tuscan wine aristocrat. "Hello, Jennifer dear," I say to his strawberry blonde wife, and give her a peck on the cheek.

"Moi, darling," she kisses me back from about six inches. I suppose that is as close as she will get, as Jen and Lauren have been, and are, great friends.

Sometimes I walk into a certain kind of place, an Upper East Side restaurant, or a charity function, and have the distinct impression that I know all the women in the room. Upon closer inspection, I may see that I do not actually recognize any of them in particular, but know their *type*. Then I know just how to speak to them, what to say, and just what they will say back. Jewish women from the New York area are so derivative in their manner, in their gestures, in their thought, dress, and speech, that they must all be copied directly from some all-powerful Central Jewess. For instance, if a young man, the handsome son of a friend perhaps, meets one of these women and is wearing a suit or sports a new haircut, she will definitely hold him at arm's length and speak upward, as if to God, "Gawgeous!" If a young lady is newly engaged, one of these women will most surely say, "So, let me gawk," and then trill, "Stunning!" of the engagement ring. A request for a particularly unpleasant favor is prefaced, "Be a doll and do this for me..."

And if a potentially tragic occurrence is spoken of, it will certainly be followed by, "..., God fuhbid." They will look for wood to knock on to prevent said tragedy, and if none can be found, they will knock, appropriately, on their head.

I took notice of this phenomena just after my divorce when I was talked into attending a middle-aged single professionals get together. It was held at a gallery called the Plaster House where they sell ionic columns cut down as coffee table pedestals and replicas of famous statues like "Winged Victory" and "Venus de Milo" made from plaster of Paris. I walked in and the place was full of men and said women drinking Chardonnay from plastic cups, eating cubed cheese, and trying to hide their fangs while they "mixed." I was glad I was in a suit, as all the men wore basic mid-life crisis uniforms of black cashmere mock turtlenecks, and black denim dungarees, sharply creased where their maids had ironed them. The women had pulled black leggings over liposuction, and sported severe eyeglasses, their heavy jewelry booty from previous marriages. For a moment I believed I knew most of the women as friends of Lauren's and that I had made a huge mistake in attending. After a moment though, I realized they were all perfect strangers and only *seemed* familiar. By the time "So, what's *your* story?" had been squawked at me for the fifth time, I suspected there must be a training center where these women go to learn The Personality. I began to notice the matrix of appropriate, uniform, responses to the many situations of daily life. These responses are strict, and must be adhered to with surprising formality. Now, as I am 'divorced husband of friend,' I receive "moi, darling," from Jennifer. Had I still been married to Lauren I might have gotten "Hello, sweetie," and a hug. Jennifer knows intimate things about me, from my ex-wife. Things perhaps more profound than I myself know, and in at least as much detail. She knows my habits, about the way I am in bed, facts about my body, information that no man would give his closest friend or brother. She also knows information about my business to the degree I have shared it with Lauren. Lauren was not born Jewish, and so is only an initiate in The Personality, and Jennifer is not a particularly bad case either, for which Sandy is lucky. Jennifer is merely a *sliver* of the Central Jewess. She could castigate me now with the slightest comment. "*So*," she could say, drawing out the word mercilessly, "I heard you saw Laur-en," for instance, thus referring to last night at Tre Fiori, and illustrating her knowledge of my just post-adolescent dinner companion and rubbing my nose in Lauren's 'date.' She says nothing though,

61

leaving it at the "moi,darling." I am grateful for this. In return I dote on her children. It is the least I can do.

At my knee are Sandy's and Jen's two blonde kids. A girl, about six, in a white dress, and a son, four years old, decked out like his father. "Hi kids, remember me? I'm Mr. Grubman..." The girl looks confused for a moment.

"You're Elliot," she says.

"That's right, honey," Jen says to her daughter, "Uncle Elliot."

Now the boy looks confused. "He's our uncle?"

"*Like* an uncle," Jen clarifies, "He was married to Auntie Lauren.

"You were?" both kids ask me, eyes wide with skepticism.

"That's right," I say, with a little tension in my jaw and voice. Functioning like a dog whistle, it is the pitch that stops kids' chattering.

"So, are you ready Ellie-o?" Sandy asks enthusiastically. He is referring to the polo clinic he has coerced me into taking. It is taught by a crusty, Irish ex-cavalry officer, and is purported to be the most condensed way to learn the difficult game. The reason *why* someone would want to learn it must be supplied by one's own self.

"Sure, Sandy," I say. While certain women can be classified in relation to the Central Jewess, their male counterparts fall largely and conveniently into one of two basic groups: *putzes* and *schmucks*. Strictly speaking the words mean the same thing, but these days they have a slightly different connotation. A *putz* is toward the goofy and good natured, the benign side of the spectrum, while there is more darkness, sometimes viciousness, or the potential for it, inherent in the *schmuck*. A *schmuck* can have some *putz* in him, but not the reverse. I am of course leaving out a few fellows with these classifications—the *good guys* and the *great men*. I don't know many. Maybe Rabbi Weiss and Sandy. I can easily guess into which category I fall.

"You want to join us for some din-din? We're going out for some din-din, right kids?" Sandy asks. The kids shrink into their father's thigh at the prospect of me coming along. "I've got a great spot right out front—" Sandy has an overweening concern with parking. Getting a good parking spot is tantamount to a major success in his life, while a bad parking situation can completely destroy his demeanor.

"No thanks, Sandy, Jen, I want to get up to my room and go over some papers," I beg out.

"I'll meet you in the lobby tomorrow morning then."

"Fine, Sandy." They leave, and I hurry off to my room with growing excitement. I am always anxious to view a new hotel room with all its inherent potential. That's the thing I love about hotel rooms, their *possibility*. I am yet to have a history in a hotel room, but the room itself does. I have a future in the room, an immediate, brief, and undecided one. A future in which anything may happen. It is like life in this way, only faster, and I can simply check out when I've had enough.

Do you know where to get a nice ripe pear, a pineapple, a juicy orange, a crisp apple, and a banana, at $300 apiece? Check into the Imperial Suite at The Breakers. It comes with a cellophane wrapped fruit basket—*complimentary*. They even attach a small gift card welcoming you to the hotel. I step into my room, which has been demurely lit by a reading lamp switched on in the corner, and see my luggage waiting next to a floral slipcover sofa. I heft one of my bags and feel it is empty. Good. In the bedroom I glance into the closet and see my clothes have been hung up. The bed has been turned down and there is a chocolate mint on the pillow. In the bathroom my toiletries have been unpacked as well. My sterling silver toothbrush rests in a rack next to a tube of gum-therapy toothpaste and a cup. My gray tube of hypo-allergenic creme shave is in repose next to my genuine tortoise shell razor. My alpha-hydroxy super moisturizer, after shave, and Clubman deodorant are in the medicine cabinet. I feel a slight shiver go through me at the sheer low-grade perfection of pre-arrangement to this moment. Then it is time to get down to business.

I switch on the television to CNN for background, sit at the desk with my list, and begin trying to remember exactly what some of the women on it look like. As I begin, they are mostly just names strung together to me. Eva Stevens, Mary Robins, Keisha Fisher, Marion James. I cannot place a face. Tiffany Thompson, no idea, Coco Tyler—a blonde I spent a weekend with in Martha's Vineyard. I won't call her. The list goes on. The most effective way to remember a specific model, I find, is to recollect her pictorial. Sometimes I can do it in surprising detail. Next to their real names on the list are the ones we used for their layout. Eva Stevens was called 'Tabatha.' I recall she is a well-dyed blonde with a page-boy cut, 5'6", medium sized breasts—non-augmented—butterfly tattoo on her shoulder. She is doing yard work when she begins to play with a water hose and her skimpy T-shirt and cut-off shorts become soaked and see-through, and then come off altogether. She has a peculiarly flat ass though. Next. Keisha Fisher, a.k.a. 'Valerie.' Simple black and white pictorial, a Herb Ritts simulation with no originality. Light skinned black woman oiled up on a chaise lounge, with some suffocating close-ups that look like topography shots of sand dunes. She has at least one kid, and I think I've heard something about her being married. Forget it. 'Sindy' and 'Suzy' are the monikers listed together next to the real names Louise Lynch and Diane Jacobs. The names are paired because they are lesbian midgets who posed together. At *Swagbelly* we usually stay away from oddities, but the payoff to this pictorial was their performance of standing blowjobs on a couple of regular-sized guys. It was quite comic and raunchy too. Nonetheless, I move on past the little pair. I come to a name near the bottom of page one, Lydia Barber. We called her 'Claudia' in her layout, not an inspired name change but enough to protect her real life anonymity. I remember the spread. Another lesbian duo, full grown. They posed as secretaries in an office who have at each other during lunch hour. Lydia has auburn hair, incredibly smooth skin texture, no nipple rings, labia rings, or tattoos. Shaved clean. I pick up the phone and dial. I never call in advance to arrange a date when I am visiting a city. Yet I am sure Lydia will drop everything and see me tonight. I've learned that this belief is the key to all phone sales success. After a few rings an answering machine picks up. Someone not being home is the downside to spontaneity. I hear Lydia's voice on a grainy tape asking me to leave a message. "Hello, Lydia," I comply, "this is Elliot Grubman. I'm in town, at The Breakers—"The machine is cut off.

"Hi, Elliot, what a surprise," she says, though there is no surprise in her voice.

"Lydia, what's doing?" I ask, turning around and watching Bobbie Batista read the news on CNN. "Are you still modeling?"

"No, I work in an office and I go to Florida Atlantic University. I have four more credits before I get my degree."

"Aw, that's a shame," I say, then think about how this sounds and add, "You have such talent, I mean. But that's great, about the degree, congratulations." What am I supposed to say? I forge ahead, "So, are you married, any boyfriends, anything like that?"

65

"No, Elliot. I'm single. Nothing like that," she answers.

"So, I'm in town for the weekend and thought of you. How would you like to get together and spend some time? Tonight." I let my voice go leaden on the last word to express inflexibility.

"Tonight? Hmm, I don't know. I'm so tired tonight," she says, and she sounds tired.

"Come on, Lydia, you're game." She's game, and I'm a closer.

"Okay," she says deadpan. "What do you want to do?" Such enthusiasm. I'm overwhelmed. Well, it is a start.

"You tell me honey, the only places I go in town are *Bice* and *Au Bar* and—"

"Uch, too stuffy—"

"Stuffy. Exactly. Too stuffy, that's what I mean," I say quickly, getting my 'stuffy' started before hers has tailed off. "Why don't you show me a fun place." With a woman half my age I need to walk the line between showing her elegance and boring her.

"Let's meet at Nouveau Martini, about 9:30." She starts to perk up, "You remember what I look like, don't you?"

I only physically saw her once or twice, two years ago. "Of course, I..." I begin to wonder if she's gained fifty pounds or taken a disfiguring wound.

"Don't worry, I'll recognize you." She hangs up before I can ask where this place is. No matter, the hotel's driver will know. I have an hour to kill before I leave. I look at the television, then the phone. I pick up the receiver and dial Dexter Academy, which is perhaps a mistake.

"Yeah?" a kid answers after a few rings.

"Who's this?" I ask sternly.

"Who's *this?*" I get back.

"Is this Lloyd Hall, third floor?"

"Yeah."

"Do you know Andrew Grubman?" I demand.

"It's study hours now, you can't call," he tells me.

"I've already called." Semantics can be a comfort. "Now, I'd like to speak to Andrew Grubman." I bet they don't give Vandever a hard time like this when he calls to speak to his boy, Cliff. I bet the decorous prick only calls during open phone hours though. He'd never want to offend the rules. No, I bet the Academy establishes regular phone hours based on his preference. That's the way it is for old boys like Vandever. "This is Mr. Grubman, his father," I add imperiously.

"This is the hall duty monitor. *Hold on.*" The line goes quiet as his footsteps recede and he leaves me swinging on the receiver. The hall is empty for a few moments, then I hear footsteps returning.

"Hello, Elliot, this is the hall duty monitor again. Andrew can't come to the phone, he's cramming for a History middie. Can you try—" I hear the sounds of a sneaker squeak on the floor, a half-chortle, the receiver clatters around for a moment before it is hung up. The line goes dead. I slam my own telephone down.

"Fuck," I say to Wolf Blitzer, who quips with Bobbie Batista on the television, one of the many that populate the suite. I redial, but now the number is busy. I feel a great unease inside at the state of affairs with my son and my ability to do anything about them. Things got rocky with us around the time of the divorce, when I wouldn't move out of the house until all the legal matters were hammered out. Len Loeb recommended this course, but Andrew blamed me for 'making everyone crazy.' Can you imagine? Our relationship has deteriorated over the past year, and the more I try to get a hold of things, the more he slips away. I take a stab at assuming a philosophical stance that will soothe me right now. Something far eastern, along the lines of *do that which consists in taking no action, and order will prevail*. My frustration won't let it set though, and it seems to slide right into some Schopenhauerian bitterness a lá *even he who has found life tolerably bearable will, the longer he lives, feel the more clearly that on the whole it is a disappointment.* That's the thing about philosophy, there's a good one to justify any thought or feeling, and you end up right where you started. I take myself into the bathroom, splash some cold, angry water on my face, and run a toothbrush around my mouth. I straighten out my suit and go downstairs to arrange for a car to drive me to Nouveau Martini.

A blonde-haired Australian kid named Johnny drives me there in a stretch Lincoln limousine with a Breakers placard on the dash. Johnny volunteers conversation on the local surf, the real reason he has come to Florida, in case I was under the impression he had come to work in a hotel. Several well-lit mansions pass by outside the car windows as we make the short drive to the restaurant. There is such a calm to the Florida night beneath the bent palms, that the empty part of me wishes to continue driving around aimlessly in suspended hope.

"Can I ask you a question Mr. Grubman?" Johnny inquires, glancing back at me in the rear view mirror.

"What's that, Johnny?"

"Give me a tip on making a million, would you? I figure if I ask everyone I drive, I'm bound to pick up a good one."

"That could work, Johnny. Let me think..." I contemplate telling him of my brilliant moment, but it's an ungainly thing to explain quickly to a stranger. Besides there is plenty more to it than just that moment. I've done the phone lines already and the market has tightened up now. I could suggest he open a web-site, but tightened market applies there as well. 'Buy low and sell high,' comes to mind, but I imagine he gets that seven times out of ten. I consider "Neither a borrower nor a lender be." I say that though, suddenly I'm a world class *yutz*.

"Make your fortune how you will," I find coming out of my mouth, "I can't help you with that. But try this for keeping it. Rule number one: never get married. Rule number two: never have kids. Rule number three: if you break the first two rules, never, never get divorced." His eyes dart up to the rearview mirror again as I speak, and as I finish I see the flicker of disappointment in them. It is not what he is looking for.

"Thanks, sir. If you need me to do any more driving for you during your stay, just let the desk know. Here you are." He steers the car over to the curb in front of a nice little restaurant-bar, with a screened-in verandah. I am half expecting a blue neon sign with a blinking martini glass, instead there is a small brass name plate next to the door. "I'll call if I need to be picked up tonight, but my car is being delivered first thing in the morning," I tell him. I keep a townhouse off South Beach along with a gleaming white antique Rolls Royce Silver Cloud. Taylor has arranged to have it driven to Palm Beach for the weekend. "Here you go, Johnny. Thank you." I hand him a fifty. Maybe he'll start his fortune with it.

Inside, I have a fifty dollar conversation with the maitre d', who seats me in a comfortable armchair made of wicker, and takes my order. At his suggestion I try a variation of the bar's namesake. Why not? The martini has made quite a comeback. Its popularity and *rightness* rivals that of the recently deceased cigar chic. It arrives shortly, a *Martini Français*, made of ice cold vodka and Lillet instead of vermouth. I glance around at the other patrons. Only a few wear suits, and I am the oldest person in the place by ten years, but it is not some college bar thankfully. There is a degree of sophistication to some of the tanned, mostly young faces around me. I browse the wine list, to kill time. There are some decent California cabernets, an overpriced Opus One, but nothing from France, so it's just as well I'm having the cocktail to soothe my nerves. Not that I'm actually nervous per se, I just have nerves. When I was a young man it was much worse. I found it bothersome to be so stricken then, and I wondered when I would grow out of the edgy feeling. I used to suffer that trinity of dry mouth, clammy hands, and cramping stomach. Now I embrace the slight tremor and flutter that accompanies these moments prior to my meeting a new woman. It makes me feel like I'm alive. I'm not embarrassed to admit there is a part of me, smaller some times than others, a part that refuses to die, that clings to the hope that the next one will be the ultimate one. The woman so beautiful, perfect, and radiant, who feels I must be the one for her, that the remainder of my life will be forever changed to a condition of peace and happiness. I have the sneaking suspicion that despite my profession, and my wealth, I might just be a poor romantic at heart.

Mild disillusion quickly wins the day as I see Lydia arrive and pick her way through table and chair toward me. I do not feel my soul set aloft on the wings of angels. Lydia does look lovely though. She has grown more slender since she posed, and her hair has been cropped down into a flippy boy cut that has become popular due to an actress on a hit television show wearing it that way. I'm guessing Lydia has not changed after work, for she wears a Key Lime color business suit, department store level, and unfortunate white pumps. Her bag is a Luis Vuitton copy, and if she paid more than $40 for it, she was beat. She carries the outfit though, somehow, thanks in part to a plunging neckline on her white blouse that has certainly been lowered a button since the office. A lot of heads turn as she moves through the place, a place that has its share of good looking customers. When a woman of Lydia's level enters a room, people notice. Men may actually become aroused, while women often have to settle for analyzing her beauty's minor limitations in classicism and how these flaws may keep Lydia from Supermodel status. I rise from my chair in greeting.

"Hello, Lydia," I effuse, leaning forward and kissing her. She lets her kiss linger on my lips, more than friendly, and her well-tended hand rests intimately across my tie. My stock in Nouveau Martini has just risen from aging loner/barfly to mysterious and fortunate *homme*.

"Elliot, what a nice surprise, babe." Lydia has not even a grain of the Central Jewess in her. She is, of course, not Jewish. As there is a paucity of Jewish men in the N.B.A., there is a similar lack of Jewish women on runways and magazine pages. I don't even know why. Is it genetics, morality, or something else that keeps them from joining their counterparts, those tall and fickle Christian flowers who fill the profession? There is a big name beauty or two from Israel in the trade, I guess that counts. I retake my seat, and Lydia sits down right next to me, pulling her chair close. The waiter is already upon us. "Whatever the gentleman's having," Lydia says of my drink, "and bring him another." She turns to me. "I almost called you about a month ago..." she begins. I have started to become flattered when I look into her eyes and see that we have already commenced the negotiation.

"Really, Lydia? You should have. I would have loved to have heard from you."

"Seriously? I was afraid you wouldn't even know who I was, like you'd only remember 'Claudia,' but not Lydia. Something *horrible* like that."

"Don't be silly. How could I forget the real you?"

"Well, it has been a few years..."The drinks have arrived and we pick them up. I mumble something about past times and the future, and a certain someone being unforgettable. We clink glasses.

"What did you want to talk about?" I wonder.

"Oh, nothing really. I just needed some financial advice, you know, tuition was due soon..."

I purse my lips in a knowing yet caring way. "How much advice?"

"I owed like $1200, just short term, but it doesn't matter. I managed. I always manage."

"That is no problem. For your education, you can always call me," I shrug.

"Really?"

"Not a problem. Anyway, what have you been doing? You look great."

"I've been dancing to keep in shape. Ballet and jazz—" She is shy now, just for a moment. This is her personal thing, what matters to her.

"*Obviously* you've been dancing. I was just going to ask 'what type of dance have you been studying?'" Big smile. From both of us. Our drinks are already low. We're off.

We drive back to The Breakers in her Lexus SC 400. It is a sporty car that handles well. It must cost $40,000. She says its her 'brother's.' I drive, piloting by instruments, relying on the speedometer to convince me I'm going below the local septuagenarian thirty-five miles per hour, as I seem to have given up my perception of velocity upon my last drink. I change gears when the needle on the tachometer tells me to since I cannot hear the engine over the music Lydia plays. The song is a neo-disco

72

epic, some diva wailing that she's 'every woman,' while Lydia sings along with her. I park the car alongside the hotel in the lot, foregoing the lobby and valet parking for a smaller entrance that opens with a room key. I don't need to make a pageant of myself for any somnambulist hotel guests milling around downstairs. As we elevator up to my room, Lydia leans against me, a litany of smells. There is her flowery hair spray, the clay-plastic odor of her lipstick, the acidity of her Cartier perfume, and some sickly sweet vanilla scented body moisturizer. My arm is around her waist as we both play our roles. We can be seen acting them out in fine hotel elevators around the world. I am the worldly, moneyed gent exercising his youthful streak, drawing from his great surplus of personal freedom, along with her, the lovely and vivacious daughter-aged cohort, well-schooled in the art of *companionship*.

Turning the corner from the elevator on the way to my room Lydia slips out of her pumps and walks down the plushy carpeted hall carrying them. "Oh, the Imperial Suite," she says, while I work the key.

"Of course. It's a one room hotel for me." I swing open the door and feel a sense of satisfaction at how impressive the suite must look to Lydia. There is a large, overstuffed couch with marble coffee table before it that dominates the living room. Small side tables with cabriolet legs flank the sofa, and oil paintings hang on the walls in ornate gilded frames. Large urns holding lilies and begonias stand in corners and on shelves here and there, while no less than five balconies overlooking the ocean wrap around the room. It is a set up fit for an emperor on campaign. Lydia takes off her suit jacket and steps out of her skirt, leaving only her blouse to slightly cover her sheer bikini underwear. After her past profession it is no wonder modesty is not a great

73

commodity for her. Even so, I am surprised at her casualness as I marvel at the shape of her from behind. Why should I be surprised though, the way exposing oneself has become such a virtue these days? Tell-all books, actors 'coming clean' in interviews, countless talk shows full of the inner secrets of everyday folk and celebrities alike. What an array of topics too. My boyfriend/husband beats me, then sleeps with my sisters, my husband is not the father of our child, I left my wife for her mother, I sleep with my stripper-daughter's friends, children who abuse their parents, slob makeovers, unfaithful and ashamed, unfaithful and proud of it. The topics are all so unusual and yet identical. They are all about revelation. I watch with a bemused feeling of shock and yet without surprise at once. Then there are gossip columns like that swine Brancato's, to reveal the few scraps that people choose not broadcast themselves. A woman like Lydia removing her clothes, shaving off her pubic hair, and spreading her legs wide in a national magazine is hardly revealing of the *person* at all in comparison. Soon people will have camera crews in their bathrooms to film them raising the toilet lid and displaying their morning bowel movements for all of America to see.

I've made myself feel a little queasy as Lydia crosses the room to a large country French armoire housing the stereo. A scowl comes to my face when I think she will blast her disco music like she did in the car, but she tunes in a more sedate soul station. A black man's bass-register voice croaks expressions of love. Turning back to me Lydia gives me a deliberate smile as her hand goes to her blouse buttons. I see her flashing eyes, her toe-nails painted coral pink, and try to make sense of everything in between while she crosses the room toward me. She puts a hand against my cheek, then helps me

74

out of my jacket and tie. As she peels back my shirt and exposes my body I become painfully aware of how many days over the past weeks, months, even years, I have foregone the gym for other priorities. The lean layer of muscle I used to wear around my chest has slid down to my waist and thickened it greatly. The slight grid of my abdominals is a nostalgic memory of my late 20's, like a gentile's commemorative shot glass or spoon collection is of a past vacation. My nipples ride the slope of my drooping pectorals and point hairily toward the floor. Yet this does not seem to daunt Lydia. Somewhere within this fact lies one of the primary reasons I have such esteem for women. Yes, esteem them, I surely do, for the way they maintain their autonomy, even in acts of compliance. It reminds me of Marie Antoinette, how she was purported to have acted the perfect lady and queen during her imprisonment in the Conciergerie, right up until her beheading.

It is not long after Lydia has reached her knees and begun attempting to pleasure me when I realize I am not up to it. I look down past the swollen sphere of my stomach at the top of her beautiful head and catch a golden glint as she turns to the side. I see a small, gold crucifix she wears hanging from her necklace. Suddenly I have visions of Lauren, newly pious, kneeling and taking the Eucharist. I see her and Ricky, proudly watching Andrew's conversion in a dark and gothic cathedral. The strangeness of things Christian washes over me. Midnight mass, choir practice, ham dinners, censers, plastic slipcovers, tuna casserole, mixed breed dogs, ambrosia fruit salad. A thread of disappointment starts to unwind deep within me, as I have gone to so much trouble to arrange this moment for myself, and now I know it is not going to work for me as it is conceived. It is too standard, and in the sexual arena, the formula of the standard minus emotion does not often equal satisfaction. I am not sure about what I want instead though, and do not want to waste all I have endeavored to plan. I cast my eyes about the room and see the fruit basket. I gently disengage Lydia and go to it. With a great wrestling and crinkling I strip the cellophane and root through the basket's offerings for the banana. It seems there are always snippets of dialogue during sexual scenes, but my participation in them is automatic, my speech even more clipped than usual, and they are such that I cannot really register them even as they take place. "What do you want, baby?" I have just made out Lydia asking me, for instance, "Do you want to take a Jacuzzi?" There is a Jacuzzi in the suite's master bathroom, but Lydia has yet to go in there, *tonight*. "Don't touch my balls," I seem to recall myself instructing. I slip into the bathroom to locate my small bottle of aromatherapy botanic oil. When I return to the living room, Lydia is reclined on the couch. I take the banana, peel it, oil it a bit, and begin to slowly fuck her with it, and fondle her body. It slides in and out easily, without losing its shape, the outer, velvety layer merely becomes a bit slicked down. I am delighted as the banana did not at first appear firm enough for penetration. I look down at my penis, which is definitely not so. Lydia and I could do a perfectly legal pictorial right now, as I hover well below maximum tumescence despite her rubbing me with a handful of the oil. Ah, the silly indignity of the penis that fails to be hard, it makes me wish I am wearing a suit. This banana thing is not something I've ever done before, and it does not excite me sufficiently that I'll be doing it again. Lydia purrs enthusiastically, but things just don't gel. I am not an authentic fan of ersatz erotica. I am not a genuine degenerate.

Perversions are just a fallback for when the normal fails me, or perhaps, I fail the normal.

Eventually the banana begins to break down and grow mushy in my hand. I carefully withdraw it, and Lydia and I cease our fondling and caressing. She excuses herself to the bathroom and I am left alone bare-assed on the couch, wondering how many bare asses have sat here before me. The smell of overripe fruit is heavy in the room. A moment later she returns, cozily wrapped in one of the hotel's white terrycloth robes. Before she can cozy up with me, I stand and collect my suit pants, putting them on. I am not in a frame of mind for cozy. "Lydia, you are remarkable," I say as breathily as I can. "Oh, and before I forget, for your tuition." I break twelve $100 bills from my roll and slip them into her purse. I dig for the most chipper tone of voice I can find. "So, what does your day look like tomorrow? I have to be on a horse first thing..."

Her face falls and she is off the couch as I reach for her. She grabs her clothes and is back in the bathroom again. I go and tap on the door and ask what's the matter to no answer. I have clumsily hurt her feelings in a dark unspoken way that I cannot understand and that she cannot or will not explain. Perhaps I was to invite her to stay the night. Or to give her the money more surreptitiously. Could she actually be disappointed that we didn't have sex? I don't know, but it leaves me feeling bad, frustrated, and foolish. I go about the room picking up. I deposit the banana, its skin, the rest of the fruit basket, the depleted bottle of oil into a wastebasket. Finally she emerges from the bathroom dressed, tired and pale looking.

"Good-bye, Elliot" she says and kisses me with surprising passion. There is nothing like hurting someone to move them. Just as I begin to respond, and I feel stirring in my trousers, she breaks off.

"Stay..." I chance. It comes out sounding like "Don't."
She shakes her head and picks up her purse.

"Drop this down the end of the hall, will you?" I hand
her the wastebasket. She pulls the door shut behind her
with force and I am left alone, oily-penised, in my suite,
which now feels seedy despite being deluxe.

The Polo Clinic

Next morning I receive my wake up call at 7:30 and I'm in the lobby to meet Sandy by 8:00. I just cannot wear a suit to a polo clinic, so instead I am dressed in cream colored trousers and a yellow polo shirt. We walk out of the lobby and around the corner of the hotel toward the side parking lot. Sandy carries a bag of polo gear, I am empty handed as I have yet to buy mine. Sandy has rented a Lincoln Continental for the week, and his head turns with slight regret as we walk past it toward my Rolls. He has gotten another excellent parking spot. Once in the car, Sandy directs me onto the road heading inland toward Wellington, where the Palm Beach Polo and Country Club is located. I am aware of the eyes of other motorists upon us. The area is affluent and the streets are full of Mercedes gullwings, ancient Corvettes, and Ferrari Dino's, but the rounded fenders and gleaming chrome grillwork of a 1940's Rolls Royce gets the attention of even the most jaded or unconcerned driver. Next to me, Sandy is busy with a list written in felt pen on a piece of yellow legal paper. His handwriting is hieroglyphic. "Here's what you'll need to buy before we play," Sandy waves the list. He has played polo for seven years, today will be my first time, yet he is the excited one. "They should have the boots we ordered last month. You need jodhpurs, spurs, knee pads, wrist band, gloves, aahh..." Sandy says 'aahh' when he thinks while he speaks. "...aahh helmet, a mallet, no, a few mallets." I look over at Sandy, his hair shining

79

silver in the morning sunlight. Sandy is one of those guys who has previously done the first marriage and kids thing. In addition to Jennifer and his young children, he has a few older kids, nearly grown, decals of the colleges they attend affixed to the rear windows of his cars. Sandy is successful, he made between several hundred thousand and a few million a year leasing commercial real estate through the 70's and 80's. When real estate died in the late 80's he switched into leverage buyouts, and when that crapped out in the early 90's he moved into mortgage banking and complex financing deals. He takes cash flow hits each time he changes areas, but somehow hangs onto the lifestyle. With all the kids, wives, houses, secretaries, and cars he maintains, running around on a horse is the only place he can find a moment's peace and freedom. We drive in silence for several miles. The only kind of silence there is between two middle-aged Jewish businessmen with plenty of overhead—a noisy silence, filled with the nearly audible separate conversations going on in our heads. Estate taxes, life insurance, hookers and hotel rooms, cigars and cognac, mutual funds, flaccidity, capital gains taxes, property leases, pictorials, Yvonne, Lydia, Lauren, horses, waistline, hairline, public offerings, tuition bills, Andrew, Rabbi Weiss, bar-mitzvahs, baptisms, subscription revenues, cholesterol level, Rolls' oil level, quarter page advertising rates—

"Hang a right into this shopping center," Sandy interrupts. I make the turn, and see a store called The Tackeria right in front of me. Suddenly I feel a fluttering sense of apprehension across my lower abdomen. I have no interest in hurting myself, and merely making a fool of myself is enough to cause me to cringe. The idea of hanging off a galloping horse in order to hit a bouncing ball has just become an unpleasant reality. I have my cellular phone and I can instantly invent a reason to beg out of the clinic and even helicopter off the polo field importantly right before we start to play without losing face. I look to Sandy.

"So am I ready for this? I haven't ridden that much lately..." I'm not much of a rider at all, truth be known. Lauren started horseback riding after we bought the place in Greenwich five years ago. I took a series of lessons from her teacher, some ex-Olympic champion in dressage. I did it mostly to see what kind of a fellow was spending so much time with my wife. By the time I figured out he was a definitively gay fellow, I had learned how to ride a cross-country trail and go over small jumps with relative competence. I haven't done it much over the past two years though.

"Elliot, you're going to love it. It's like golf on horseback, and the horse is 80% of the game, maybe more for beginners." This is Sandy's way as a friend. I am lucky to have him. This first year after my divorce, it has been the same deal as for a first year widow—all my 'couple' friends take me out to dinner, they speak to me in hushed, hopeful tones, and encourage me to try singles get togethers for middle aged professionals, to meet someone. They do it with an element of mourning too, to "recognize" the loss I've gone through. They even pay the check one time. Then they forget about me, unless a few of them happen to get divorced too, in which case they want help getting dates. Since I haven't yet coupled back up officially, I'm no good to them socially. After a few months, after I learned the drill, I skipped all those and just stuck to the models. Sandy is different though. He is the only one who called me on Rosh Hashanah to wish me happy new year. I pull up in front of The Tackeria. "Let's get you suited up," Sandy says energetically, slapping me across the thigh.

The saddlery shop is made small by all the merchandise hanging on racks and shelves, by beautiful hand-tooled English polo saddles on wooden saddle trees, and horse blankets stacked in piles. The air is earthy with the smell of new, clean leather, saddle soap, and creosote. I find myself lost in a maze of bridles and bits of every size and style while Sandy conducts our transaction with the man behind the counter, an old rural sort with wiry hair and a scythe of a nose, dressed in a button-down oxford shirt, old jeans, and dusty cowboy boots. During the next quarter hour, as I am bedecked in the appropriate wares, I am excited by the smell and feel of the leather and metal items.

"Beautiful," I say of the semi-custom boots I try on. I was measured for them in New York last month, so they fit well. My new white trousers are not cut as wide as Patton's, but have a nice bag to them just the same. Sandy has the rest of the things I need on the counter, including heavily padded leather knee guards, snazzy leather gloves, and a sharp looking white helmet with a metal face guard. I pick up a pair of point spurs. "I need these Sand-ino?"

"Not really. They help you turn the horse at high speeds, but we won't be going that fast this weekend."

"I'll take 'em anyway," I say, throwing them on the pile. I like to provide myself with every advantage. "What else can I get?"

We cut the air with long, leather handled whips—I select a yellow one—then we spend a little time flex testing bamboo mallets. Sandy suggests two at different lengths to fit horses of various size. I take a dozen, including one experimental unbreakable graphite job, and a nice leather stick bag in which to tote them. All totaled, my bill comes to over thirty-two hundred dollars.

"Check or plastic?" the old coot asks me.

"I've got greenbacks," I tell him, pulling out my roll. If I travel for a week or more I bring twenty grand cash, minimum. For weekends, ten thousand. Including last night's festivities I'm thinning down to under fifty-five hundred.

"Frogskins? We take 'em," the clerk says, and goes about bagging up the remainder of the purchases that I do not have on, including the slacks and shoes I am no longer wearing.

Our arms full, Sandy and I return to the car and make the short drive into the little world unto itself that is Palm Beach Polo and Country Club. Where there once was only swamp now exists perfectly conceived roads connecting aesthetically pleasing houses and club-houses. Low slung three, four, five bedroom houses with slanted, sun blocking terra cotta tile roofs, spring up and abut golf course and polo field alike. The developers dub them with whimsical titles that correspond to their prices. There are Tennis Lodges at the bottom of the scale, Golf Cottages, Tennis Bungalows, Polo Villas, Polo Island Estates, Eagle's Landing, Fairway Islands, and Oaktree Estates, to name a few. To buy them costs two, three, four hundred grand, right up into the millions depending on the size, level of luxury, and amount of land. It is a colony of seclusion for the wealthy. "Nice isn't it?" Sandy says. "The whole place is near bank-ruptcy."

"That so?" I say, trying to shake a sort off horsy drawl I seem to have picked up in the polo shop.

"Near belly up," Sandy says, unable to do so himself for a moment. "We ought to put together a consortium and make a bid on it." Sandy is constantly thinking of ways to combine his sport with his business—a risky proposi-tion. I know a guy who owns race horses, has even won the Belmont Stakes, and has still never realized a profit from them. "Would you ever consider getting involved in something like that?" Sandy wonders.

I think the real estate is over-inflated, and there just aren't enough people around with big money to float a place like this. It's not like you can pack in a giant paying crowd for a polo match either. I know what I need to know. There are few necessary topics I don't know about, and fewer still of which I cannot speak knowledgeably. Yet on another, more practical level I feel I only really know my business, as seedy as it may be, and plunging into other ventures is not something in which I have great confidence. When you become wealthy there is such a thing as too much opportunity. I'm not in the fish business, and I'm no real estate developer either.

"You say it yourself, Sandy, the thing about horses is they never stop eating and crapping, and you never stop paying." Sandy laughs, his loose chin flesh bouncing freely, and directs me to the main clubhouse where the clinic will begin. As I park the Rolls I catch a glimpse of vacant grandstands flanking an expansive emerald polo field, the grass manicured like a golf green. I can't help but think of where I am, and from where I've come. Eastern Parkway to Palm Beach. The thought of owning a single one of these bungalows would have been a flight of fancy when I was twenty, now Sandy is talking to *me* about buying the whole shooting match. I'm here to learn polo, while I used to play stoopball and stickball. I used to make a living hustling basketball and bowling. I told Sandy about it a few weeks ago when I signed up for polo. "What was your average?" he asked of my bowling. "A few points higher than whoever I was rolling against," I said to him. Sandy shook his head. He just shakes his head when I tell of my past and the way I scraped and hustled. Sandy is not first generation money, and does not know about scraping and hustling. His father had a company and Sandy worked there for ten years before going on his own. Sandy has his job and he works hard, no doubt about it, but that's not the same as scraping and hustling. Hustling is putting together a two-on-two or three-on-three pick up game, losing once and getting down seven points in the second, doubling your bet, and then winning best two out of three. Scraping is having ten bucks to eat with for the week, turning it into twenty and betting that. I know, as we walk into the club, the walls lined with photographs of sweaty and handsome four-man polo teams clutching silver cups and trophies being awarded to them by celebrities, princes, and queens, that most of the men in the pictures don't know what it is to scrape. I know I will always be a hustler, and that even my hundred mil, less fifteen to Lauren and forty more in taxes after I'm dead, has not erased the haunting sensation of scraping from my past.

Inside the main room of the club are six men, about ten years shy of my age, who stand loosely ringed around a table. On the table is a mock polo field resembling a board game. The men listen to a stout, bald man who barks out polo strategy in a nearly unintelligible Irish brogue. He is Colonel Darby, formerly of that elite fighting force the British Cavalry. The students wear white jeans and polo shirts, while Darby's britches *are* as baggy as Patton's. I'm simultaneously jealous of him and aware that as a novice I cannot carry off the look. Darby's voice is sharp-edged and spouts from between cracked and brown teeth. He begins and ends most phrases with "Right, men!..." in a way that reminds me most unpleasantly of the army. In his left hand is a swagger stick, and with it he moves around model horses numbered one through four on the simulated polo field table top. Darby is teaching the proper formation for a knock-in and keeps referring to it as "the crooshed darmond formation." I am bewildered by what he instructs and what a 'darmond' is, until I realize from the position of the horses that he is saying 'crushed diamond,' as in shaped like a baseball field. For the next three-quarters of an hour Darby makes many unfamiliar references to types of penalties and shots— nearside forehands and backhands, neck and tail—and concepts like 'shutting the back door,' and 'respecting the line.' He makes constant references to his "book on the subject," which I have not read. Along with all the instruction come comments and chortles from the group, some of whom are friends, all of whom seem at least acquainted. There is a tall, broad-chested fellow with a deep quaking voice and a cadence like John Wayne's. His name is Guy, and he is straight ahead American as a beef burger. He asks pedantic questions—questions I can already answer after my brief initiation—that Darby seizes on with gusto. Darby pushes the horses around with his swagger stick like a demented croupier. There is another fellow named Jay, who is short, round, and fuzzy, with white hair, a shocking white mustache, and watery eyes. He is the most *successful* of the group—whether he is richer than me I cannot decide. I glean his position by the deference he receives from the others. There is one called Simpson, his last name apparently, who is the youngest, under 40 years old. He must be a junior partner of Jay's, for the way he looks to the older man before he speaks. Simpson packs alternating qualities of arrogance and deprecation, as if he is constantly catching himself at fault and reminding himself how to act. There is a small, lean guy with the finest set of polo clothes and manners amongst us. He has silver laced black hair, side-parted, and obsidian black eyes. He is referred to as Kingsleigh, but I take it as his first name. The evidence seems to present he is the *wealthiest* of those assembled, but hasn't done much to earn the money. I'm confident that when I learn his last name I will recognize it as an aristocratic family's. Not saying a word, but following the instruction with his eyes, and a cigarette on his lips, is Randy. Jay and Simpson comment to him about certain situations in games they've played in the past, and I discern he is a low-level professional hired to play for them. I will watch out for him on the field, for he'd be happy to make me look bad or maybe even hurt me to gain the win for his bosses. The last man is one who would have given me pause when he was young, but looks beyond much conflict now. He is a trim, very tanned man named Larry. He doesn't have a sunbather's tan, but an outdoor person's. He is dried out a bit and has deep crags and crinkles across his face, especially near his eyes. He has the look of one who has seen terrible things, something so bad that nothing else in the world will flap him ever again, yet he cannot quite get over it either. The look in his eyes reads as exhaustion on the surface, but he is not simply tired. I have seen his look before. He has been in a war, Vietnam I figure. For a second I also wonder what the group might think of me.

After the lecture we go outside to the field where we are divided into two teams—myself, Sandy, Kingsleigh, and Larry, on one, while Guy, Jay, Simpson, and Randy form the other. The Colonel has all four players on each team hold onto a rope while we scrimmage around with small hand mallets. The idea, more than scoring on the makeshift goals that have been set up, is to keep the ropes taught in a way that dictates proper spacing on a polo field. This is apparently one of the most important and difficult things to achieve when playing polo. I personally do not like running around a field in riding boots and hanging on to a rope like a grammar school kid on a field trip. Sandy is very enthusiastic about the drill however, shouting pointers nearly as often as Darby. Sandy has taken the clinic before, and is mostly here to accompany me. After what I've seen so far, I can't believe he is doing it again, for me. We move about, two strings of softening-around-the-middle wealthy men, snaking up and down a field, chopping about our ankles after a small, white ball.

By the time the South Florida sun is beating down on us and polo shirt armpits are sweat soaked, we move on to the next drill. Off to the side of the field are eight mock horses awaiting us. Our mounts are wooden barrels with legs at horse height, tacked up with real polo saddles. We are forced aboard with mallet in hand and given buckets of balls to whack around while Darby hollers refinements to our swings. "Nice and slow garddarmnit! Its the farce o' the harse not yer harm that sends the ball..." My spirits lift as I begin to connect with the balls solidly, sending them flying about the field, until I think about doing it on a moving horse, which settles me back into my saddle. Poor Jay gets a little excited too, and leans after a ball placed a bit far away. He slips off his wooden horse and crashes to the ground. Randy is off his own horse in a flash to attend to his boss, who comes up smiling and laughing at himself, brushing at the grass stain on his shoulder. I admire a rich man who doesn't take himself too seriously. I consider myself one, often right up to the point I find I'm acting the fool and not laughing.

"Great, isn't it, Elliot?" Sandy calls out to me.

"It's terrific, Sandy," I say. At last, it is lunch time, and we are called down off the wooden horses.

We sit down for lunch on the terrace of the player's club. My shirt now has a stripe of sweat down front and back to match those at my armpits. I regret not having a change with me. The only one of us who doesn't look damp is Kingsleigh. His grandfather probably didn't sweat a drop or muss a hair at Bull Run either. Several handsome young men with unkempt long hair eat lunch at tables around us. The air is laced with their heavily accented Spanish. Darby tells us they are young professional polo players from Argentina, who receive high salaries for their skills. They are millionaires before they are twenty years old in their country, and are treated like rock and roll stars. I wonder if earning a million dollars when you are twenty is the same as finally earning it later in life. Perhaps without the struggle, the significance isn't there. I'm sure there are pressures in the lives of these players, trying to stay on top and win, but do they really appreciate what money means? I look at them for another moment. They wear espadrilles on their feet, they tuck their pants into their socks to fit more easily into polo boots at game time. With pastel sweaters over their shoulders, the sleeves wrapped about their throats, they make it pretty clear—a million is sweet no matter when or how you get it.

The lunch served is roast baby pig with fresh herbs. I corral the waiter by the elbow and ask for something else. I don't do pork. I'm not religious about my diet, but swine makes me uncomfortable in a more societal way.

"I'm sorry," the waiter says, not sounding particularly so. He refers to his duplicate pad. "It seems your group is offered a set menu today." The waiter is about seventeen years old, and evinces no interest in satisfying customers. The idea of customer satisfaction relating to tip size doesn't occur to him, perhaps because this is a private club and tipping is not allowed. His insouciance bears more resemblance to that of a rich kid's though, the way money doesn't seem to *interest* him. Only rich kids can afford this disinterest. He is a bit chubby, his skin buttery looking, and he wears a pooka bead necklace. As he stands in front of me, bored, his upper lip sweating, I get the impression his wealthy parents have forced him to work as a waiter on weekends in order to learn how *tough* things are out in the *real* world. As if the Palm Beach Polo Club's dining room is that. I am on the verge of pulling out money in order to get what I want, but instead appeal to Darby. Meantime, Sandy slices into the tender white meat along with the rest of the guys. Darby shrugs at the kid-waiter, and waves with his fork that whatever I want should be brought.

"I don't eat pork. Bring me a shrimp cocktail," I tell the waiter.

"Air ya ko-shire er somethin'?" Darby asks boisterously.

"Shellfish aren't kosher either," Jay volunteers.

"I don't keep kosher, I'm just a cultural eater." There is a momentary air of confusion at the table over me and my ways, but I'm not in the business of clearing people's minds or explaining myself.

The meal progresses, and Darby picks up his oratory on the intricacies of the sport of polo. "Yuh've gut ta think three moves ahead, like a chess plair." The birdlike sounds of cellular phones' chirping occasionally cut into Darby's talk. At any given moment at least three of our group conduct the conspicuous too loud half-conversations unique to cellular phones. It must be difficult for Darby to teach people like us this sport. Yelling at pimple faced recruits on a parade ground, you can hope for some results. Take a bunch of middle-aged men, men who are successful and thus think they *know how things are done,* and it is rare to find someone to be taught. Darby doesn't flinch as he is interrupted though. Worst case, some executive doesn't get better at polo. Not like a buck private catching a bullet or stepping on a land mine. Soldiering, learning, they are for the young. Forgetting, that's what your fifties are for. Forgetting disasters, disappointments, and failures. It's the only way to get on with it. Remember it all when you're eighty, if you make it. Old Larry needs to know this. When I was in the army, in 'Nam, I was in the rear. I never saw combat. I was the smart Jew who got himself a supply job. Da Nang airbase was as close to action as I ever came. I saw some atrocities though. Body bags and massacred corpses. But if a guy can't forget, he'll never make it. Right, Old Larry? He sits there in sunny splendor following the cordial polo talk, all the while his eyes flickering to some inner memory movie of tragedy.

As coffee is served by our young aristocrat waiter, a professional practice game commences on the field not twenty yards from the terrace. My gaze lifts over the table and I take in the sleek beauty of horses against the manicured grass field. For a moment I witness the grace and skill of expert equitation and mallet work as the players warm up. The men are agile and light upon their mounts, the horses compact and responsive.

"Look at 'em," Darby says, "see 'ow they put all their weight on da right laig when they hit?" The other guys in the group coo their appreciation for what they witness. As the players raise up from their saddles and take arc-like swings, sending balls sailing hundreds of yards distant, my original impression of polo is confirmed. It is an effete game, and like ballet, or jai-alai, something I cannot, and do not want to master or even learn. Then they begin to scrimmage. With some organized confusion the two teams form into rough lines at mid-field and the ball is rolled between them. The action travels down field toward us, the teams in an approximation of the positions we have learned. The riders are incredibly natural as they steer their charging horses, focused only on the ball. The rhythmic patter of hooves on the soft ground is punctuated by equine snorts, the snick of mallet on ball, and shouted Spanish. "*Dalle, dalle,*" one them calls out. Suddenly two horses come together at the shoulder with force. There is the solid sound of ton on ton flesh and the high clink of stirrup irons meeting.

"Look at them ride," Kingsleigh says, full of admiration, "the way they become one with the horse..." I glance around the table and a few in the group raise eyebrows at the comment, Larry and Randy in particular smirk at the grotesque romanticism. The ball rolls into the corner of the field. There is a small fence there to which the riders come precariously close. One horse actually brushes the sharpened wooden pickets. His rider elbows an opponent trying to gain some room. I suppose the idea *is* to become one with the horse, but it is the utilitarian aspect of the riders that strikes me. This is what makes them *professionals*. The one who gets to the ball first reins hard and causes his horse's tongue to pop out pink against the bit. He uses his horse as a tool. The ball moves up field, and a defender tries to close the distance between himself and the play. He switches the reins to his right hand along with his mallet, freeing his left hand to whip. And whip he does, bringing it three times quick, the sound of it cutting the air viciously. Some of the horses wear red, hairless spots on their flanks where rider's heels have bitten into them. Beneath blinding sun polo is boot and spur, leather and metal, glove and whip. The gentlemanly superficies surrounding the game have so far concealed it from me, but now I see the true nature of the game, which is to gain ascendancy over horse and opponent, to dominate man and animal.

"Let's ready airselves, men," Darby calls out while the lunch plates are cleared. "When they are dune, the field is airs." We begin to strap on our heavy knee pads, there is the ripping sound of Velcro being secured on wrist band and glove. Helmet chin straps are snapped and tightened. As a group we walk to a pony line where horses are being readied for us by several thin, teen-aged South American grooms. They help us aboard and pass up our mallets and whips like immigrant vassals. We are white collar knights.

"Ready for battle, everyone?" Guy quips, the word 'battle' rolling low in his throat like a belch. For a moment there is a painful sensation of group embarrassment. We are actually going to play polo, but what are we really playing at? Larry sniffs sarcastically at the exaggeration. "Battle? You ever in the service?" he asks Guy.

"Yeah, I was stationed in Canada," Guy answers. I'm sure this will ruffle Larry, that some tension is coming. This provokes a fist fight in men ten years younger. Let it go, Larry, I urge under my breath. Then Larry shrugs and laughs.

"Hell, you're smart. Smarter than me."

We begin with drills and schooling of the horses. We are forced to ride two, and then four, abreast, to stop on command, to perform caracoles to the right and left. Darby gives us help with our riding, demanding a toe pointed here and a heel dropped there. Finally we play our scrimmage, stopping often for instruction. Darby joins in the game now and then, moving the ball along with a long distance shot when we lose our momentum. My horse is a small bay mare who runs after the ball without my steering her. It feels we are flying on the breeze as we thunder along and I swat at the ball. We are a team within a team, my mare and I. I find myself trying to become one with her, to communicate my will to her. Only when I am out of the play for a moment do I see how slow and ungainly we are compared to the professionals who played before us. It doesn't matter, after the heat of this game I will never pick up a golf club or tennis racquet again without a sense of boredom. We rotate our positions so everyone has a chance at all aspects of the game. Although the ball peskily hops over my stick near the goal several times, I am most comfortable playing at number one, where my responsibilities are to charge up field ahead of the game to receive a pass, and hopefully score.

I am like a baby at this game. My limitations and trouble controlling my horse frustrate me. The fickle, hopping ball irritates me. I swing mightily at the ball and miss, time after time, only beginning to learn that a polo ball cannot be hit when swung at mightily. As we ride I become incensed with the other team when they have the ball. When they score it unleashes a wave of pure molten hatred inside me. I urge my pony on, and my vision of the field becomes tinted red. I wish my mallet were a pike. I want to impale those I ride against, to fell them from their horses and trample them beneath my mare's hooves. I bump with my opponents whenever I can, throwing my elbows fiercely as we ride side by side, trying to unseat them. By the time we finish it is difficult to determine who is more lathered, me or my horse. My heart is going at it hammer and tongs in my chest and the humidity makes me feel I'm in the neck of a tea kettle. I wonder for a moment if I shouldn't have called Dr. Bobby Gold and cleared this with him, but I don't feel any pain in the chest. I've considered going out in the sack, but going out in the saddle doesn't seem an unglamorous alternative.

We ride off the field, the horses' heads hanging low in exhaustion. There is some manly gloved hand shaking as we exit. I climb down, stiff-legged, from my horse. On the side of the field is a video cameraman next to his tripod- mounted camera. He is introduced as "Ron," and it seems tomorrow morning before our final scrimmage we will review the tape of today's game for instruction purposes.

"Let me ask you something, Ron," I say quietly, hooking his elbow and walking him away a bit. My horse's reins are in my other hand, and she comes along with us. "Does anyone buy their own copy of the video? Because I would like one."

"Well, no one has, but sure, I'll sell you a copy."

"How much?" I wonder, preparing myself for a negotiation. "Well, the tapes cost me $3.99" I nearly shake my head at his lack of guile. I slip him a hundred dollar bill.

"Keep the camera on me tomorrow morning. Make me look good, okay buddy-buddy?" I turn back to the others, who are filing toward a low slung barn with their horses in tow. I look around for a groom to pass my mare off to, but see no one. Nice service. I trail along toward the barn after the rest, stumbling a little in my stiff new boots and I am hit by an increasingly seldom occurrence in my life: an idea for a *Swagbelly* pictorial.

Horseplay

–Well swept stable. Afternoon sun. The elegant squire, in from his daily ride of the countryside is sweating lightly. Katie, the groom, fresh and natural, an outdoors girl, meets him in the breezeway in front of the stall to take his horse. She has worked the manor since childhood and has always been a bit afraid, but fascinated, and yes, excited, by the squire. As she takes the reins from him, their hands brush, and her breasts heave against her tight white T-shirt.

–Katie's bashful smile turns wicked as she allows the reins to fall and leads the squire into the stall. She brings the shaft of his riding crop up between her legs. The squire, a man of the world, arches an eyebrow. Taboo begins to crumble in the face of lust.

–Katie bends over and teasingly directs a light whipping across her taut buttocks. The squire sheds his tweed jacket. Katie's neat ponytail is undone, her tawny hair ruffling in the breeze. The clean straw on the stall floor is fragrant.

–Denim shorts and riding breeches are slung over the stall's Dutch door. Katie eases her T-shirt over her head. The squire cups her nubile breasts.

–With a leg thrown up over a saddle resting on a sawhorse, he kneels behind her, burying his handsome face in the creaminess of her tender thighs.

–The young barn girl faces her master, inserting his stiffened tallywhacker inside the lacy band of her panties.

–The squire, standing tall, folds his young groom over a hay bale. She takes his engorged meat thermometer as he rides her home and...

I seem unable to concentrate sufficiently on this pictorial vision. This has never happened to me before. These fantasies used to visit me constantly years ago, with me starring in the role of the squire and the like. So I am a bit concerned as I hand my horse over to the young blonde barn girl. She wears dusty jeans, a dirty T-shirt, and is extremely overweight. It is an unsightly reality, perhaps that is the problem. Regardless, the group, standing outside the barn drinking Mexican beer, distracts me.

"We're going to the Outback for happy hour, if you and Sandy want to come," Simpson invites us. I decline, and so does Sandy. Sandy does not drink, while I am not a beer guy. I am not much of a bar guy. I am a not a happy hour guy. I am not a man's man type of man. I prefer the company of women. There is something about being in the company of men that tends to make me uncomfortable. Because I am large with money and success, they look to me too much, they listen too closely. They seek hints. If men are talking politics and I say for instance, "The Democratic party is dead in this country," silence will fall as they try and analyze my statement, as if it must mean more than it originally seems, and that there is some lucrative clue hidden amongst my words.

"Right then, men," Darby shouts, "we'll see each other tomorr' marnin' at 10:00 sharp."

"Come on join us for some beers, Colonel," Guy drawls. "No thank ya'," Darby smiles, "the wif' won' 'ear of it..." His refusal is met with groans of protest from the group. I prefer to think he merely doesn't want to fraternize with the enlisted men. He begins his chest-out strut away when I trot a few steps after him.

"Meet me for dinner at The Breakers tonight, Colonel. I'd like to talk some business with you."

"If it's business then I'll see ya' at narn." I suppose he means 9:00. A few of the group who have caught the exchange look on me with jealousy.

Back in my suite, I check and find I have no message waiting for me from either Andrew or Yvonne. I call in to my office and my home machine and there is no word. I absorb this, and the cold air of the suite, then take to the phone and work my list with grim determination. I leave messages for Jodi Denby, Petra Kamen, and Donna Fulton. Clarissa Williams has unbreakable plans, but I am welcome to call her again. Sandra Menendez's number has been changed and her new number has not been published at the request of the customer. In the end I cannot find anything, and wonder if somehow Lydia has put out the word on my performance. Has she gotten in touch with Yvonne? Perhaps there is an underground network of *Swagbelly* girls who have experienced me and banded together to protect others. Its just as well, for as I stand from the chair from which I have worked for the last hour, I find I can hardly move after all the horseback riding. What the air-conditioning in the Rolls began, that of my suite has finished. I am stiff as the proverbial board. My lower back feels hard to the touch and I have lost the ability to bend over at all far. I recognize muscles I've never before considered. My mallet hand is nearly immovable, my right forearm feels wrapped in vise-like tefillin. My trapezoids are clenched from reining my mare, and the cords connecting my legs to torso are taut and angry. I gingerly unbutton and remove my riding pants. The insides of my calves and the backs of my thighs are bright pink with broken blood vessels,

99

and rubbed raw of hair. The frigid air of the suite chills the abraded skin. I walk into the bathroom to prepare the Jacuzzi before rigor mortis sets in, and it is this that gives me a miniature terrific idea. Not a brilliant moment, just a great little thought: in-room massage. I pick up the phone and dial my friend Will, the Concierge.

"Will?" I begin.

"Yes, Mr. Grubman?"

"I've had a hard match today at the *polo ground*," I smirk to myself. I fancy that one hundred years ago the same conversation could have taken place, Will's ancestors a family line of concierges...But of course one hundred years ago the only horses my family knew were the ones the Cossacks rode over them back in Russia. Things change though. "Anyway, Will, I was wondering if you could arrange to have a *masseuse* come up to my room—"

"No problem, Mr. Grubman," he cuts in.

"A *masseuse*, Will, a *woman* who is very good at what she does, you know? Someone outstanding at total body relaxation, Will." I absolutely insist on receiving a massage from a woman, because I invariably gain an erection during one. In almost every case the masseuse is kind enough to offer me a hand release. As I am a bit old-fashioned, perhaps even prudish, playing out this scenario with a man is not inviting to me.

"I see," he murmurs.

"A strong handed woman, Will," I say.

"Yes, I can certainly arrange it, sir," Will tells me, sounding uncomfortable, and rings off. My next call is to room service. I order several bottles of medium quality red wine—a Jordan Cabernet, a Castelgiocondo Brunello, and a Latour Grave. Though its not really part of my heritage, when it comes to drinking too much, maybe its never too late to become a *shikker*.

Finally there comes a knock at the door. Firm, yet not invasive. I love that breathless moment before opening the door on a whore. A lot has been said about whores, and I could say plenty myself—sweeping things about their kind and their kindness, their refreshing honesty, the comfort of their frankness, the freedom of the transaction, the intense need for desire without love after all the love without desire, the satisfaction that comes from commanding them like a king to coddle me like a baby—but I am not inclined to think it through to some profound end, I'd rather just give myself up to this day's offering. Today, of course, it is merely a masseuse and not a hooker, companion, new woman, or any variation thereof. Strangely though the sensation is the same. It doesn't matter what she might look like either. Just as any man who has endured a hospital stay considers what it would be like to sleep with his nurse, so it is with a masseuse.

The woman at the door is plain, athletic, and vigorous looking. She holds a small shoulder bag and carries a folding massage table in her left hand. Her auburn hair is pulled back tightly and she wears a sweat suit of shiny blue crinkled material. She extends a red knuckled hand in greeting.

"Hi, I'm Mary, here for the massage you ordered." Her handshake leads me to believe she can give Kenny Feinstein a real test on the squash court. "Where shall I set up?" I usher her into the living room, where there is plenty of space for her table. I excuse myself to the bathroom, where I scald myself with a hot shower, and emerge wrapped in one of the hotel's white terrycloth robes.

If I had been doubtful as to Mary's qualifications as a *total* body relaxer upon first seeing her, I am more convinced when I see her again. The living room lighting has been dimmed and a soundtrack of ocean waves plays on the stereo. The massage table awaits me with a white sheet over it. On the coffee table next to Mary's open shoulder bag are a collection of oils and creams, as well as several odd shaped and powerful looking vibrating devices. Mary has shed her sweat suit and wears a lycra bodysuit and brief nylon shorts. Her fitness is confirmed in her well muscled legs. Her nipples stand out against the bodysuit, thanks I am sure to the air-conditioning rather than seeing me in a robe.

"Care for a drink?" I offer, filling up my glass with cabernet.

"All right," she allows. We touch glasses, and I look away so I do not have to witness the boredom in her eyes. "With towel or without?" I ask.

"However you're comfortable," Mary answers, putting down her wine glass having neglected to taste from it. I finish my glass and drop my robe. Mary averts her gaze, holding open the sheet for me. I climb onto the table and she quickly covers me with the light linen. "How do you want to start, front or back?"

"Back is fine, babe" I say, arranging myself. The wine has loosened me apparently, and I find my own last word odd. I fall quickly silent. I feel foolish for speaking to her so familiarly, and I am glad I am face down and do not have to look at her. I am not much of a chit-chatter during a massage anyway—I find it as conducive to conversation as being in a dentist's chair—and this seems fine with Mary, who silently goes about her work. She uses a light sesame oil, and begins manipulating various parts of my body in a soothing, undulating rhythm. Her strokes take me back over the course of my three-blowjob record of infidelity with Lauren. The first time was late in the first tri-mester of her pregnancy. It was a difficult pregnancy with lots of vomiting, cramps,

102

and backaches, and we had not been together sexually in many, many weeks. We had been in Florida then too, at William's Island Spa. I received a massage, and when I rolled onto my back so the front of my body could be attended, Vera—Vera was her name, a young woman from Cuba—offered me a hand release. I managed a *No, thank you.* Then she said *You want me to suck your cock instead?* I didn't speak the word *no* again, and so she hopped to it. I gave her $500 afterwards, I felt so guilty, as if the commerce would minimize the transgression. I sat in the steam room and Swiss shower for an hour trying to wash the wrong off of me. Did Lauren suspect anything when I went back to the room? I still do not know. She was so wrapped up in the misery of her body, I doubt it. But on what sub-sonic level were the waves connecting us damaged? The destruction of the relationship began somewhere.

Mary really digs at my lower back now. She is into some deep tissue work there, her hands laboring over small grape-like knobs of lactic acid, freeing them in burning surges. My eyes are closed in the half light, the sounds of pseudo-ocean come from the stereo, drowning out the sound of the real ocean beyond the windows. The smell and texture of the exotic oil, the feel of Mary's taught limbs leaning against and across me as she throws her body into her work—it all should, but does not, have a stimulating affect on me. She rolls me over and instead of a proud and dramatic obelisk, my penis lies dormant under the sheet like so much other balled up sheet. I think perhaps the wine is responsible, but I drank enough wine, not too much. It certainly is not Mary. She has her head thrown back, chest out, her eyes closed, a mermaid on a prow, as she works my abdomen. Her hands move as if she conducts a symphony. Nothing. What brings the erection? If not a beautiful woman lavishing attention directly on the penis, if not a healthy, albeit plain, young woman attending to all other nerve endings? How, sometimes, is it just a sunny day and bang, stainless steel in the trousers? Why is it always and forever Lauren and her reserve that sends the blood? What is the nature of desire? The nature of desire is a mystery. Although I have built fortunes and roamed the earth in order to lay claim to answers, although I have allotted resources and created elaborate settings in which to play out my fantasies, although I have raised to an art form the search for qualified technicians—the essence of those fabulous contractions between prostate and urethra eludes me. Now even my starting point, my given—a steady hard-on—seems to be in doubt. I have been scaled down to tiny doses, but I will now pitch out any and all anti-hypertensives that may be in my possession, I hear they can have this result sometimes. I watch Mary for a moment. She opens an eye a slit and catches me staring.

"Are you the regular masseuse here?" I ask.

"Not exactly. Will calls me from time to time when there is a certain, special client..." She glances at my groin suspiciously.

The massage finishes in polite fashion. I am relieved that she does not suggest any of her vibrating tools. I am silent back in my robe, holding a glass of wine in front of me as she packs up her wares. I thank her profusely and overpay her with $100's in my embarrassment. She clatters out the door with her table under her arm and her bag over her shoulder, and I am left in the solitude of my suite. Some would suggest I am with all these women because I am afraid of being alone. They would, however, be wrong. What do I have to be afraid of? I'm not with all these women because I am afraid of being alone, because I remain alone when I am with them. It is just less boring than being truly alone—only slightly at times—but still less.

In the morning it is only sheer force of will and an old naproxen I find in my toiletry kit that enables me to make it back to the Polo Club on time. The surfaces of my inner legs are pink as raw veal, and my taut back screams at the idea of taking the saddle again. It whimpers at even the thought of sitting in my Rolls Royce. The day is scorching by 9:30 in the morning, the humidity a soggy ninety percent. I sweat Bordeaux by the time I reach the hotel lobby and thank myself for at least not completely finishing the Latour. I find an inscrutable Will at his desk with a message for me from Sandy.

"E.G., Waited for you and called—no answer. Driving myself over to the club. See you there—S."

I pilot myself to the club in the Rolls, which I cannot get down to a cool enough temperature. The merciless flat, intersecting county roads are confusing. I become lost in the badlands of Wellington, and arrive late.

The group is awash in chuckles and mirth over something when I get to the clubhouse. The video of yesterday's scrimmage has just been shown, to the great entertainment of all. A chorus of greetings is thrown up at me, shouted right into the bags under my eyes, as I enter the room.

"Hey, Ell-erino," says Sandy, "you almost had that one at the end there yesterday." I treat my friend to a glare, courtesy of my evil hangover. I am not pleasant most mornings, and this is an exceptionally bad one. Sandy

105

sits there gleaming, his silver hair puffed up by a blow dryer and lacquered into place. Some of the others still look cool and slick from their morning showers while I feel flat and groggy. Simpson and Guy start in about the hair of the dog, and Jay gives me a sympathetic smile. Next instant, silently corrected, Simpson gestures toward a pot of coffee in the corner. Randy's red eyes tell me he was up to what I was last night, probably harder, but he is younger than me. He cups a cigarette to his face. There in front of the television is Darby, pink-cheeked and scrubbed, as if our dinner had not taken place.

I made it down to the dining room a little after 9:00, lit from the red wine, discouraged, but relaxed despite myself, after the massage. The Breaker's dining room is a rococo affair done in sickening pastels. Darby was standing there waiting, hands clasped, in his tweeds and regiment tie. We sat down to vichyssoise, lobster salad, and tornadoes de bouef. "So what da ya think of the sport a' king's so far? Ya play like a damned crazy man."

"Do I? Well I thought it was a game of skill, but it seems like one of aggression. I have to admit, I love it."

A few violins, a viola, and cello, began playing in the dining room and provided an odd counterpoint to our conversation. Most around us were families, or couples out for a romantic evening of dinner and dancing. The men were the stiff, suit clad Wasp prototypes I model my own suit wearing after. The kind who will wear a suit to a pool party. The women, with their straight hair and tiny twig noses—the young ones were slip dress and strand of pearl blowjob debutantes, the older ones were wearing short skirts too, but bigger pearls.

"It was originally a game o' war," Darby went on. "Ya

don't have to be outwardly cruel or vicious, but it don'
hurt to let that out on the field once in a while. Every
man 'as a corner in 'im full of violence. That's what
makes polo everyman's game."

"And women?" I wonder.

"Less women have that side to 'em, but those who do
are often on the polo field." Our plates were cleared

"What does a man need to get into this game,
Colonel? Besides a big wallet." His laugh filled the spacious grooves between his teeth.

"You need half a dozen good ponies that have played
the game before." Suddenly, when it was brass tacks, the
brogue thinned out considerably. The Irish stew he
shouted around the field must have been for show.

"I'm sure they're cheaper by the dozen," I said.

"A dozen it is. From the Argentine preferably. They
make the best beef, and polo horses. And wives. Mine's
from down there."

"I see, and here I thought they were only good at har-
boring Nazis." He looked at me quizzically for a moment,
then went on.

"You'll need a dozen saddles, bridles, assorted bits, stable sheets, buckets, brushes, clippers, halters, stabling,
shavings, feed, vetting, shoeing, worming, turn-out facility, grooms, grooms quarters, trailers, vehicles—" His
method seemed to be that of overwhelming me with
the details, and it was effective.

"What I need is a manager to handle the details for
me, isn't that right, Darby?"

"Per'aps."

"Do you know a man like that, one who could play on
my team and show me the ropes?

"Per'aps."

"What's the rate of pay for someone like that?"

"Five thousand per month, more if we play for a cup,

and five figure bonuses if we win," he told me in, flat, unaccented language.

"Where's the best place for me to play?."

"You live in Manhattan, don't ya? So Connect-i-cut, or the 'amptons, for the summer, then back down here next winter." The Hamptons already contain at least one polo playing publisher with a penchant for models. So does Greenwich though. Sandy plays in the Hamptons and that's where my golf club is. That swung it.

"Let's make it the Hamptons." They were just going to have to make some room for me.

"South'ampton it is." We shook hands and toasted our new marriage. I wrote out a check for $250,000 for starters. It's hard for me to decide what constitutes a bargain. I once paid fifty grand to play a round of golf with Arnold Palmer. Even still I was impressed with the cost of this game. Apparently, to mount up a top team for a single tournament could cost a million, so I was just getting warmed up. We drank Irish Mist and shots of Bushmills eighteen year old.

"How did you get into your line of work anyway, Darby?" I asked him.

"In the h'army, they had a team," he said, hand on check, the brogue creeping back in.

"Army sure wasn't like that in my day," I said.

"It got inta me blood so much I had to stick with it when I got out."

"Seems risky."

"It's a tight dance, making a living from what you love, but it's the only one I know. What do you do fer a livin'? I think it's fair ta ask..."

"I publish *Swagbelly*." I said unguardedly.

"The nudie magazine, is it? Haw-haw, then you know what I mean," he said and raised a glass to me. The conversation went somewhere from there, somewhere drunken and philosophical, and far more difficult to recall.

After my cup of coffee, I still have plenty of headache left, but it is time to adjourn to the field to play our final scrimmage. My team is Sandy, Kingsleigh, Larry, and myself, and we lose. During the game Kingsleigh proves to be a detriment. He rides elegantly and hits lovely shots once in awhile, but is constantly too far ahead or behind the play as it turns and careens around the field. He seems unwilling to bump hard or ride anyone off the ball. He never gets a penalty whistled against him, but he's useless. Sandy plays position number four, a defensive role. He shuts the door on their offense, more often than not hitting a good back shot. Larry and I are left to score, which is appropriate. We ride into the teeth of their defense. Larry does it with resignation, and I with fury. I get a lot penalties called on me for crossing the line in my aggression. The other team cannot convert on most of the penalty shots though, so at least we keep it close. In the final chukker, Randy, that prick, hooks me on an easy shot on goal, and then right before the bell I get free. Just as I go to put the ball through the goal to tie the score, my unbreakable graphite mallet cracks in half, and the shot trails wide to the right. I'm seething when the final horn sounds and it is over.

As I ride off the field I no more want to shake hands with the others than I want to take a climbing lesson from Ricky. I force myself into some grudgingly social nods. I guess that I have an overly competitive nature. I remember one time I had a running race against Andrew. It was to the end of the block on Sutton Place. He was about ten years old, and we winged down the street stride for stride, the kid faster than I originally thought. With each step I tried to let him edge ahead, to win. But my legs had a mind of their own. I was not able to force myself to really slow my stride, to lose. Finally Andrew, his own will to win intact, actually surged ahead and won by a step. Did I tank the race? I still don't know.

Waiting on the side of the field is the cameraman. I ride over to him.

"So, did you get it all on film?"

"Oh, sure," he says.

"Have my copy at The Breakers by this afternoon, would you?" I ask. Jay rides over and hands Ron a business card. "Heard you're selling the video. Send me two copies and a bill," he says and rides off.

"See that?" I tell the cameraman, "I'm giving you business. I should get a commission." He looks uncertain until I start up a hacking laugh, and ride off toward the stable. I hope the video will be some consolation for the loss. I wouldn't mind Lauren somehow seeing it, seeing me in action.

Finished riding for the weekend, I peel my sore legs out of the stirrups and swing myself off my mare. I hand her over to the groom, and I am ready to say my good-byes. I figure I will be back at the hotel by lunch time, where I will relax by the pool for the afternoon before my plane back to New York, when I hear about another polo match. It seems the group is going down to Royal Palm Polo in Boca Raton, about thirty minutes away, to watch a high-goal professional game. My interest is piqued already when Sandy starts lobbying me to go. "Come on, Ellerino, these guys are fabulous. Wait until you see high speed polo."

"All right, Sandy," I allow, "who'll drive?"

"Naw, come on, the clinic has a mini-bus. We'll ride down with the guys."

"Fine, Sandy," I agree, doing what I nearly never do, which is hand over my autonomy in a situation. My mistake is not immediately clear.

The ride down to Royal Palm in the comfortable, air-conditioned mini-bus is full of good natured chatter about business and the game, which serves to take the sting out of the loss. It is my first polo game, and not a particularly significant one. I tend to learn as I go along, so I am not sure why I expected it to be any different in polo. Still, as I listen to these men, these *guys*, around me talking about the turning tides and highlights of our just past contest, it is mostly mild contempt that I feel rather than any particular *bonhomie*. The fact that Guy for instance, who sits sipping a purple sports beverage, faces the same challenges that I do as a neophyte polo player, or business person, does not give me the feeling of sharing a common bond. Rather, I feel distaste at how undistinguished I am for my company. Jay and Simpson sit next to one another, carrying on separate cellular phone conversations. Darby and Randy discuss polo in the front of the bus, and Larry seems to be lost in the boonies somewhere on a long past reconnaissance patrol as he stares out the window. Certain experiences are so confounding that one must replay them repeatedly in search of coherent reason for their being. The trouble is, the replay almost certainly mixes matters further, usually irrevocably. This is the beauty of Sandy, on my right. He thinks in the present and the near future, and doesn't dwell on his past. His first marriage, his own childhood, are second rate movies he walked out of in the middle and cannot quite remember how they went. He travels light.

"I hired Darby. I'm gearing up to play this summer," I say to Sandy. This kind of talk is right in his wheel house.

"Fabulous," he says, "I'll get someone else from the

club and we'll play as a team." He is thinking of a summer full of sunny days, galloping about a field, making the polo ball a priority. If I ask him about something else, his father's death when he was a younger man, or his divorce, he gets a glazed look in his eye much like Larry's and answers vaguely, with appropriate pain and gravity in his voice. "Tough, real tough stuff," he says, and then "ahhm," as he begins a further thought that goes, that must go, uncompleted.

Royal Palm Polo Club is in full pageantry as we arrive. Fine cars troll slowly along the sides of the field as a nice crowd gathers for the game. The stands are an ocean of color courtesy of the spectators' clothing. Most are casually dressed, simply enjoying a day, while some make an occasion of it and sport blazers, their women in elaborate hats and dresses next to them. The match is being held to benefit a foundation that supports a degenerative muscular-skeletal disease, this made clear by a tote board next to the scoreboard. On the scoreboard the teams are listed, eight South American names. The score reflects a close game being fought. The thermometer on the tote board only shows a lukewarm level of contribution mercury. As a group we walk up to the ticket booth and can hear a British announcer over the public address system calling the game and cajoling for donations. It is only when we take our seats in the bleachers that I can make out the far side of the field, lined with wheelchairs occupied by palsied and sickly people. Amongst the adults, are smaller wheelchairs holding afflicted children whose skulls are nearly denuded of hair. My throat thickens as I see how they sit there and watch the exciting game, one that they will physically never be able to play. The kids seem taken by the spectacle just the same—the young players in sharp uniforms, color coordinated with their horses' leg wraps and saddle pads, are quite a sight. Orderlies in white institutional clothes hover about the children, and help them with cotton candy, hot dogs, and soda. The inside of my chest goes wooden as I imagine my own boy similarly infirmed. I want to do something for these children, but simultaneously feel weak, sodden limbed, and helpless. I sit and gaze at the game in silence.

After three chukkers of play the score is tied at 8, and the half-time tradition of divot stomping ensues. The spectators flow down from the stands and onto the field where we replace sod torn up from hoof and horse-shoe, and put it back into place. Some healthy children run about kicking a soccer ball, using the break in the game as an opportunity to annex the field. The more ambulatory members of the charity group are led onto the field's edge and instructed by volunteer profession-al players in hitting balls with miniature mallets. One of their shots hops over my foot, when nearly one hundred yards down the field I make out a bent, yet familiar fig-ure climbing up out of a wheelchair. She is not another invalid child, but one of the stricken adults. An attendant helps her get situated with a pair of aluminum Canadian crutches. Suddenly, I feel conspicuously dressed, my polo clothes nothing but a foolish costume. To my hor-ror the woman starts walking haltingly toward me, and grows more familiar as she draws closer. She is Barbara Schafer. Barbara who was once beautiful, and vibrant, and new, slants in front of me, now desiccated and drawn. She is the woman I nearly married over thirty years ago. If I had, there would have been no Lauren in my life.

"Elliot," she says, as she reaches me, and the word vibrates in her throat. Her voice sounds like an oboe with an improperly placed reed.

"Barbara," I answer, coincidence and improbability colliding painfully in my head. "How are you?"

"Hanging in there," she smiles, and coughs. It is a wet sound, lodged deep in her frail chest.

"What are you...Why are you here?" I stammer.

"I moved down with my parents ten years ago."

"How are Lou and Esther?" I cling to polite niceties.

"Dead five and seven years respectively. I stayed anyway. The last thing my joints need are cold winters."

My hands move about and my mouth gapes silently in a feeble attempt at condolence. A memory washes over me, one that I'm unable to reconcile with what is now before me. It is of Barbara and I, so many years ago, naked and locked in a lover's embrace on the cold tile floor of the kitchen in her parents' apartment. Her ripe body buoyed me from the unforgiving floor. We were silent, almost without movement, not wanting to wake her parents. She looked up into my face, a supplicant, and asked if she "should let herself?"

"Oh, yes," I breathed.

Later, giddy in our intimacy, we made our way to the boardwalk for the sunrise. Cold sea air in our faces, I fashioned every important promise I was later to break. The sun rose, shining on her full lips...

"So you play this game now?" She gestures toward my whites and boots. I feel idiotic for their cleanliness, their *newness*. I toe a piece of torn up turf, place the soil part down into the hole from whence it came, and press it back with the sole of my boot.

"I've just begun."

"It suits you. Publishing magnate and now equestrian."

"I'm no magnate. So, how do you feel?"

"Degenerated. The pain has started to get bad," she begins unsentimentally. "The wheelchair is as of last

114

year, crutches the year before that. Physical therapy almost every day. I got used to the hands a long, long time ago." I steal a glance at her bony hands gripping her crutches. They are devoid of extra flesh, her fingers like weakening slender talons. The metal hoops on the crutches cut into the slack skin of her forearms. There is silence between us.

"The checks come, Elliot."

"Good," I say, embarrassed.

"Every month."

"Yes?"

"Year after year...They help," she says evenly.

"I'm glad," I breathe. I wonder for a moment if this is all, if this is the way it can be for a bit—nearly pleasant, conversational, and no more—if we can then say good-bye and I walk back to the bleachers and watch the second half of the game unscathed. The possibility of it hangs there for a moment right in the face of logic. No, it is of course not possible.

"I would have rather had you with me," she says simply, someone with less time than most, who no longer waits to say a thing. "But you disappeared."

"I...I'm sorry, Barbara. For so many...You have to understand...I'm sor—"

"I hope you are," she says, fixing me with a smile unique to any I have seen for its severity, "Perhaps it will help you start to become human." The smile remains on her face, gelid in disappointment and struggle. In a bare instant I am aware of all that life may give or take away, and how much lies in the province of health. She turns slowly on a crutch, and begins an excruciating, tottering journey back to her wheelchair at field's edge. Her gait is hobbled, nearly crippled, and I am paralyzed. I cannot move or speak as I watch her attendant take her crutches from her and help her sit down.

115

The British announcer pipes up over the public address system, urging people off the field so play may resume. Her attendant leans down and snaps her footrests into place. He eases her small feet onto the metal paddles, and I feel something crack within me at the sight of her slumping into that chair. It is an audible and sickening sound, like a compound fracture, and it may as well be my femur snapped and gone jutting through my pant leg for the pain it brings. Cotton-footed, the crowd floats back to the stands. Players on horses re-take the field, hitting their looping warm-up shots. I want to stay where I am, to lay down in the soft, short grass, and let eight charging horses trample me asunder.

"Please clear the field...Sir, will you please clear the field," the British announcer continues, talking, I finally realize, to me. I feel the eyes of the crowd on me standing there, and at last I start to walk. One creaking, oaken foot in front of the other, I plod off the field. A minor round of applause erupts from the crowd as I finally get out of the way.

I continue, drifting past the bleachers and where my group sits, past the concession stands, past the donation table, and pony lines, on toward the mini-bus. A sepia tone of sorrow glows within me. Sorrow, one of the prime emotions I try to avoid. Sorrow, roasted over the embers of regret, with a dash of the irrevocable.

Arriving at the bus, the driver opens the door for me and I climb aboard. He has an obscured view of the field from where he sits in his driver's seat eating a sandwich. I can still recall my time with Barbara. I remember it fondly for its purity. She was the first woman I loved, and the life I began with her seemed the one I was *supposed* to lead. She was a good girl, from a good, poor, family. She was so kind and pretty and interested, just like her mother, I could not help but love her. I went to temple with them every Friday night. I was in and out of community college then, and there was even talk between us all, serious amongst her family, that I might go on and become a lawyer. Barbara spoke encouragingly about how she knew that one day she would see me trying cases in court, defending the weak and poor against the system.

But what did I, and what do I yet know of the poor? Only that I didn't want to remain amongst them. Back then I was taking pre-law classes during the day and bussing tables at night at Lundy's. Each night, along with the other bus boys and porters, I put in long hours taking deliveries, sweeping, mopping, putting away food, cutting, chopping, squeezing and preparing fruits and vegetables, gutting and cleaning chicken and other meats and fish, washing dishes, and polishing every surface in the restaurant. We would lay out crates of garlic on table cloths and step on it gently to break it from its cloves, then peel it by the bucketful, until we stunk of it relentlessly. Sundays at 11:00 p.m., after the dinner service, we worked through the night, scrubbing the thick grease and filth out of the kitchen, and then the chemical stench of ammonia began to overwhelm even our garlic scent, until I grew dumb with misery.

Despite this, I tried it anyway, for a little while. I tried for Barbara, and for what she wanted me to be. I was to finish school, get a job, struggle, and marry her. We would live with her folks for a year or two, have a baby and move into our own place. I would then get a better job, a bigger place...It went on. The picture was clear. The only problem with it was that I was young, and I did not want the horrible, multi-layered challenge of responsibly facing a difficult reality. I did not want strangling routine. I wanted money, other women, at least for a while, and a life that was just *bigger*. Finally, along came

117

her diagnosis, and for me, the army. Herein lies a fact, of which only myself and the United States Government are aware, and that is: I was not drafted. I enlisted. I went to war with North Vietnam voluntarily. It was easier than breaking things off with Barbara Schafer. When every other *shayner Yid* from Brooklyn got married, had a kid, and tried to stay in school to avoid it, I chose the welcoming embrace of the U.S. Army. And when I got back, I did not come home to her.

Even though I never saw combat, I used the trauma of war as my reason for not calling when I returned. I used the fact of my not being up to the task of good husband as a salve to my own conscience. When that failed me, I substituted that what she really needed was money for treatment, and that I'd be better able to provide it working on my own. And if loneliness of any kind threatened me in weak moments, I countered it with my imagined picture of her face, crumbling in disappointment, when I told her that I wouldn't ever be taking the bar.

In a moment of clarity, right here on the frigidly air-conditioned mini-bus the truth comes to me: what I want, always wanted, and always will, is to become rich enough not to have complicated feelings. Feelings are fine. Some, like pride, nerves—as in facing a bet or a new woman—triumph, simple loss, fear, even love in its basic form, for mother or son, that is all fine. But there are other feelings, dark, disordered and tyrannical ones, like regret. The devastating desire to have time or an action back. The inability to escape a memory at once bitter and sweet. These are feelings I will gladly do without. Or being prisoner to a poison love. Being inexorably drawn by something, (what?), to a certain person, despite the rational knowledge that it will lead nowhere but my own frustration, and perhaps destruction. Again, no thank you. These tricky, hydra-headed feelings—fuck them. Forgetting all about them is the only smart play to make, if you can afford to. How rich will I need to be to succeed in this? I once thought, briefly, $100,000. Then $1 million, then ten. A hundred million wasn't it either, but I'm getting closer, I swear.

In my agitation, I turn to the bus driver. "What's your name?" I ask him. He has a long, wiry pony tail and similarly rough beard, red, brown, and gray in color. He wears a T-shirt, shorts, and sandals.

"Kurt," he says, now finished with his sandwich.

"I need to get out of here and back to Palm Beach, Kurt," I tell him. He says nothing in response. "I will give you $500 cash to drive me straight back to The Breakers." I figure I will leave the Rolls where it is and have it picked up later, so long as I can get away.

"I can't do that," Kurt drawls, a phrase I particularly loathe. I can call the hotel on my portable phone, but even if I make the same offer to the young entrepreneur, Johnny, it will take him forty-five minutes to reach me. I don't see any taxis around either.

"How about straight back to the polo club then?" I try.

"I wouldn't be able to make it back in time for the others, sir. The rest of the group would be waiting around when the game ends."

"They can wait, Kurt. I'll give you all the folding money in my pocket to do it for me." I hesitate to talk in these terms, because making people aware they are prostituting themselves can cause their reluctance in doing so. It drives up their price at least. Nonetheless, I take out the previously referred to money so Kurt can appraise the thickness of the wad. It must run $4,500. Such is my desperation.

"I can't do it," he says. "This is my job."

I just do not understand people who are inflexible for

no good reason in the face of money. "You'll always be a bus driver then," I tell him with venom, and sit back to wait.

New York

Back in the welcoming black air of New York, the streets shine after an evening's freshening rain. I am met by my car at La Guardia's Marine Air Terminal, where I land in the Gulfstream III that I lease. During the flight, Nancy, my usual hostess, served me shrimp cocktail, lobster salad, fresh turkey and chicken, which went untouched. Nothing like an individually catered meal served on a private jet. I moved up to the plane about seven years ago. I considered buying, but didn't want to end up with aging equipment, so I leased. This is the dating philosophy of most wealthy men I know. Flying in a private jet costs perhaps twenty times what first class does, per flight, but the convenience and luxury cannot be measured. I am driven on to the runway, I get on the plane, and we go. No waiting for a take-off slot, no boarding by rows, no luggage, no crying babies, no obese person sitting next to me—no people. I will not go back to flying commercial. Should I lose everything, the absolutely last thing to go will be the plane. Despite this, I did not eat on board this trip, preferring to wait for Tre Fiori. I look forward to being in the familiar dining room, ordering a plate of *al dente* pasta with tangy, heavily garlicked pomodoro sauce. I look forward to seeing the dependable Rez, to leaving the tangled realm of my past behind me and getting back to the world of the cut and dry.

It is past 10:00 on a Sunday night when I arrive, so only a few tables remain occupied. Still, the staff are

121

happy to see me back in Tre Fiori. Rez jumps up from the table where he sits in the back smoking a cigarette and drinking white wine. He fairly rushes up front to greet me. "How are you a-Mr. Grubman, so nice to see you," he gushes.

"Fine, Rez, how are you? I'm just back from playing polo."

"Mah-no, Mr. Grubman. Polo!" I am pleased at how impressed he seems. "I don't believe it, *con cavalli*, on horses, no?" He seats me in my usual corner table by the window. I nod across the way to one regular customer I see often at Tre Fiori. He gives me a wave as if shooing a fly. He is Judge Frusciante, a tiny and wizened retired circuit court jurist. Standing with him are a few of the waiters and busboys. He barks his expertise at them on every subject. Most of the good, class Italian restaurants around have their own judge in residence. At Gino it is Shelley Banker of Supreme of New York who hangs out, holding reluctant court at the bar. In Girasole they have Evan Crane, also of New York Supreme Court, retired. He has lunch and dinner there every day, and sometimes breakfast. It is not often that there is more than one judge in residence in a place. Not enough respect to go around that way, I suppose. Judge Walker, who used to sit on the Appellate bench, First Department, does not have a regular haunt, he is only consistent in never picking up the check. Then there is Judge Freman, Civil Court of New York. I am not sure where he eats, but he is so slow with his docket and motions that the service in Bouley must seem pushy to him. And at Tre Fiori there is Judge Frusciante.

As I am seated, Rez tells me the specials of day. The pasta is a fettuccine with salmon and caviar that sounds heavy. "How is the pasta today?" I ask.

"Very nice and rich," Rez says.

My brow creases. "I want something light."

"Its-a very nice and rich and-a light too," Rez's words smooth my brow back out.

"Okay then, Rez, I'll have an insalata Tre Fiori, chopped, the pasta special, and a bottle of Reinina," I say. "Very good," he answers, and with claps, snaps, pops, and whistles to the staff he conducts my silverware, bread, mineral water, and wine into place. I taste the Brunello, and a full glass is poured for me by Piro, a small, old waiter with thick glasses and a confused expression on his face. With his heavy eyebrows and strange animation, he looks like an automated puppet. He waits for my approval on the wine, although I have already nodded after my first sip. "You like-a the Reinina, hah?" Piro says, somewhat rhetorically.

"Yes, very much," I answer.

"The Reinina is-a good, hah?" Piro smiles. I say nothing and he goes away.

My salad is delivered, peppered from a mill by the precise wrist twists of Bruno, the food runner. I am then left alone to eat, and the motion and commotion of travel begins to wear off. Instead of leaving them in Florida, it seems my heavy thoughts of late have stowed away with me on the G3. I should have ordered Tignanello or a simple Barolo, because the Reinina with its light body, brings me back to the last time I drank it, which was the past summer, and the final family dinner here at Tre Fiori. It was to be the dinner when Lauren and I finally broke word to Andrew—*don't cry, don't cry*—that we were getting divorced. That unbearable occasion comes back to me vividly in the mysterious, dark textured flavor of the Reinina.

We sit down at the table, Lauren and I exchanging wide-eyed, loaded glances about who should say what and when. It seems the time to order comes quite quickly, as the service is very attentive in Tre Fiori. *Don't cry, don't cry*. The food appears almost instantly. *Don't cry, don't cry*. Then Andrew spills his Shirley Temple, a pink stain of grenadine spreading across the table cloth. *Don't cry, don't cry*. Before we know it the mess has been cleaned up, and dessert has been ordered and served. *Don't cry, don't cry*. The tension builds, the silence's own momentum somehow sustaining itself. Before we have said anything about it, Andrew blurts out, "Are we getting a divorce?" He has obviously over-heard the talk, but has no idea what it means, for he asks the question innocently like he might of any type of acquisition, like a new pet or a Range Rover. Lauren and I look at each other desperately and search for an answer, *don't cry, don't cry*. In my mind I beg him not to cry as he tries to put it all together. "Don't cry, don't cry, don't cry," I plead silently with my boy, because if he breaks, then I might too. Lauren says something about her and daddy not being happy together, but we both still love him very much. It's not your fault, but Daddy and I can't live together anymore. He is confused— *don't cry, don't cry*—he really doesn't know what's going on and what it all means. He has a strange look on his face, like a dog when they think you've thrown a ball for it to fetch, but you've palmed it instead. A kind of understanding comes over him, that melds into an expressions of pain—the shocking kind of pain like touching a hot pan, when the nerves aren't even sure if the burn is hot or cold. Then his face falls from kid hap-piness to tired agony, falls in a way that makes me won-der if it will ever lift quite completely again. While I observe this though, I must have stopped my telepathic "don't cry, don't cry, don't cry," for just a moment, for Andrew begins to, silently, as he eats his chocolate gela-to. His face angled down, large, silent tears splash into

124

his dish. Nobody says a word. I clear my throat harshly and put my arm around him.

"Ice cream is made of ice, cream, sugar, and rock salt, along with flavoring, son. In this case chocolate flavoring," I say, apropos to nothing, wanting to offer hard information on at least *a* topic. I feel our table is a life raft taking on water.

We are a bent over, exhausted trio as we climb up from our chairs, clinging together, moving to the door as one. This is the keening moment of our family. We are more tightly pulled together than ever before in this instant, but will fragment further in every future moment. We have eaten two salads, three spaghetti pomodoros, a few sodas and desserts, and of course the Reinina—I leave what must be $500 on the table, such is my distress. Two days later when I go in for lunch, still in a daze, Rez begs me to take back three hundred dollar bills.

"Please-a Mr. Grubman, it's too much," he pleads.

"No, no," I refuse, not even sure why he is doing what he is doing.

"There is no check for you today," he says at the end of my lunch.

"Thank you," I say, and leave $100 more on the table.

My pasta arrives, steaming, and I come out of the memory. I am peppered again, and lightly parmesaned. I am given a large, shiny spoon with which to twirl. The flavor of the dish is extraordinary. I'll be damned if Rez isn't right, it is nice, and rich, and light also. I look up and notice Piro leaning over me, so close his glasses are nearly misted from my hot plate. "You like-a the fettucine, no?" "Delicious," I say through a mouthful.

"The fettucine is-a good, hah?" Piro asks.

"Unreal," I say, becoming annoyed. My terseness

125

discourages the diminutive waiter, who at last leaves me in peace. As I eat, I play with the caviar in my mouth. I enjoy bursting the tiny eggs between my teeth. The thousands of eggs on my plate are merely a fraction of the amount produced by female sturgeon. They have large caverns within them lined with the roe. They lay them out and the male fish spray them with their milt. It is so unlike human reproduction, where there is a single shot each month. Sure, there are millions of sperm going after the egg, but it still takes one dead-eye. Thirteen, fourteen years ago, Lauren and I had plenty of trouble conceiving. We tried for several months before we went to doctors to get to the bottom of things. While I thought it would have something to do with her, much to my surprise, the diagnosis was oligoasthenospermia—low sperm count.

The count was low, but not impossible. It would take some technique and close attention paid to her ovulation, but things were not hopeless. Before we figured it out, plenty of tough times came from our early failures. Those were good days in the business for me, and I suppose I put more time and effort into that, than having a baby. Perhaps I even turned to work as an escape from the home troubles. Lauren took to sitting around the house in a depressed stupor. After awhile I had enough money to move into our first townhouse, off Park in the 60's. It was a beautiful three-story place with wrought iron balconies, front and back staircases, and a small elevator. The floors were black and white marble, the ceilings high and decorated with elaborate mahogany moldings. She perked up for a few weeks when we moved, then slid back into the doldrums. We decided her project would be decorating the new place, and one day I came home with a shopping bag full of cash for her to do it with. She just sat there. I dumped it on the old coffee table we had taken from our other place. I began to play around with the bundles of cash. She didn't even smile. She was not impressed. She wanted a baby. That was the crux of it, although we only fought about other things. Six months later the house was decorated, the bag of money spent, and a few more bags along the way, and I had never had a single meal cooked by her in the newly appointed kitchen. Sure, we had a chef four nights a week, and usually went out the other nights, but I felt neglected, taken for granted. I thundered my outrage over some take-out Chinese slop.

"I built this, this...empire for you, and I can't even get a decent meal here!" I sputtered at her one night. She raised a glass of white wine to her lips in response.

It was around this time her hockey player began calling again. I'm not sure how he got the telephone number. He never called during the day. It was always around 4:30 in the morning. That was when the bars closed where he lived, Lauren mentioned, the idiot's witching hour. He was good enough for some more battling. She accused me of meddling and being controlling after he called one night.

"She was just on loan to you from a brighter future, so why don't you skate off into the sunset," I yelled into the phone, and then berated her for the guy's very existence. Afterwards, of all things, Lauren became insecure about my past.

"Why were you with her?" she asked me of a past girlfriend, "did you think she was so smart, or funny, or pretty, or what?"

"No," I said, and foolishly went on, "it was nothing so substantial. I found her sexy and exotic, I suppose..." Big mistake. My description "haunted" Lauren for months I found out only later when she admitted it to me in tears. She was always so "plain and blonde" that "exotic"

127

women maddened her. From that moment on, I qualified "but none were as sexy as you..." or the like. I always say that now, no matter who I'm with, no matter who or what they are asking about in my past, and it has never once been a lie. The past is faded, and my memory is not nearly as vivid as my imagination. Finally, when it seemed things were slipping away, we conceived. She brought me to orgasm one rare wine-soaked and peaceful night. She directed the result into, and then inseminated herself with, a device resembling a turkey baster.

"What was that thing that we used actually called, honey?" I asked her in New York Hospital, giddy with good humor on the day of Andrew's birth.

"That was a turkey baster, Elliot," she told me, the baby in her arms, finally in bliss.

I push back from my empty plate and note the Reinina is two thirds down. Like a Cuban cigar, excellent wine has a sort of third stage, when the complexities of flavor and character build on that which has gone before and take the drinker or smoker to new heights of pleasure. I consider seeking this in the Reinina when Judge Frusciante, the old goat, sidles over to me. He has a crown of white hair encircling his bald pate, and a few meager wisps pasted across it. He has a penchant for color coordinated dress, wearing shirt, tie, blazer, slacks, and even shoes in different hues of the same main color. When the color of the day is red, it is difficult to take. Today he is pink. A fuzzy lox-colored golf sweater over a flamingo sport shirt, and rose double knit slacks. His shoes are not actually pink, but the off-white plastic comfort variety common to folks over seventy and most store bought dolls.

"You look upset Grubman. Problems?" Frusciante asks me in his gruff balsamic voice.

"Yeah, sure, problems," I answer him.

"Work?"

A turn of my head tells him that's not it.

"I notice you're here alone. Where's that young one..."

A wave of my hand tries to steer him away from this. Instead, it brings forth a conspiratorial nudge from Frusciante and a gleam comes to his yellow eyes.

"There are drugs, Grubman. Performance enhancing drugs."

"Sure, I know," I sigh, too weary for denials. "I can't take Viagra. Blood pressure."

"Nah, not sildenafil citrate. That's kid's stuff," Frusciante scoffs. "I'm talking about alprostadil. Twenty-five units of that, a mere quarter cc, and you're like a piece of iron. You're back in business," Frusciante howls in his gravelly voice, then treats me to the Italian gesture for iron-like penis. He holds his arm out, hand in a fist, and grips his forearm firmly with the other hand. The action creates a slapping sound. I'll admit it, I'm intrigued.

"That's taken orally then?" I ask, trying to impart a casual air, wondering if it's a comparable alternative to Viagra that my doctor failed to mention.

"No no, that must be phenoxybenzamine you're thinking of," he is unsure for a moment. "Alprostadil is by injection," he adds wolfishly.

My face pinches involuntarily. "Into the penis..." I say grimly.

"'Intracavernosal injection' is the medical term. You do it yourself, before the, heh heh, act. Here." He thrusts a worn business card into my hand. I find myself looking around furtively, as if people in the restaurant may be aware of what we discuss. I glance at the card—Dr. Meshulam Schlenger, M.D., F.A.C.S., Specialist in Erectile Therapy.

"Don't fear the technology, Grubman. This is the

golden age of penile hemodynamics," Frusciante says fervently, whacking me on the back with an arthritic, claw-like hand, before shuffling out of the restaurant.

Old as he is, there is a sort of youthful quality about him, it is true. I picture him, skeleton-like, poised for sex, bloody hypodermic in his fist, his wrinkled face flushing in paroxysms of pleasure. On the other hand, I do remember an article we ran in *Swagbelly* a few years back before Pfizer's introduction of the big 'V,' which delved into the subject. It described an array of semi-rigid prostheses, malleable plastic implants, inflatable prostheses that were engaged with a squeeze pump mounted near the testicles. There were vacuum devices, clamps, electrical vibrostimulators, and surgically implanted water pumps, not to mention dermal fat graft widening, and lengthening by ligament release. The piece chronicled the scientific assault on an age old problem, and I, naturally, was all for it. If not directly for myself, then at least for my customers. Sex is good business for me, and if these implements keep my subscribers humping away for an extra ten or twenty years, then great. I edited the section on potential problems myself, muting their severity. There were many though. Everything from accidental inflation, accidental deflation, blockages, punctures, leaks, strange noises, pain—even gangrene of the penis. Jesus, a gangrenous penis, that's the last thing I needed. What a fate.

It has drawn late and the place is empty, so I beckon Rez to sit down with me. I am not sure exactly how to begin, but I don't want to sit too long saying nothing. "You know I love Tre Fiori, Rez," I say sincerely.

"Good-a Mr. Grubman, I am so happy."

"I want to be more closely involved with it, you see."

He looks at me semi-blankly, suspicion only starting to stir.

"But you come-a almost every night."

"I want to buy it, Rez." He looks dumbfounded for a moment. I have a fleeting thought that he has been waiting to hear this, that maybe I can get it at cost, like my polo video tape.

"Ma-no, it is not for sale," Rez says politely.

"I see," I say. I do not like to hear something is not for sale. I detest it in fact, nearly as much as hearing someone say, "I can't do it." I fix Rez with my eyes, looking for an angle. "If someone offered you a sum of money that made you a rich man—"

"I don't understand."

"—so you could retire."

"Retire? No, you must-a work."

"Very admirable, Rez. Okay, say you won the lottery. What would you do then? Go to Europe or Bermuda maybe? Take it easy? What would you do?"

"How much-a I win?" Rez asks, warming up to the talk.

"You name it, in the millions," I say.

"I don't know, I would take off two days a week...and stop by for only two or three hours-a every night, you know, not-a work every lunches and dinners. I would come in and say-a my 'hellos,' you know, like a *padrone*." I consider what he has said for a moment.

"Listen, Rez, I'm offering you that chance. You could be that rich man, and still work as much as you want, take more time off, but with me as the owner, or *owner-partner* if you like." I am already thinking about going through Tre Fiori's financial records and seeing how many times Lauren has taken Ricky here on my money, and how far back the practice dates.

"No, no, please, that is not the same," Rez protests.

131

"Things will be just the same as now, only better. Talk to your partners, I'm buying in," I say. I have never treated Rez to my firm tone before. He pushes back from the table, a bit stiffly.

"No, please-a, Mr. Grubman—"

"I don't want to discuss it any further right now, Rez, but I'll see you soon." I get up and stride out of the restaurant that will be mine.

I take out my key and open the door to my apartment expecting to hear the sound of the television, and to see the sight of a penitent Yvonne waiting for me in bed. All is dark, and silent, however. I check with my answering service. There are a set of messages regarding business left by Taylor, and one from Andrew's school letting me know that their father's sports day begins tomorrow at 9:00 a.m. I am surprised that there are none from Yvonne. For a moment I feel a creeping thread of concern over this, that perhaps our little act is over. I'm surprised at the scope of the hollowness that the beginning of this thought brings on.

Beneath my arm, I carry a thick envelope sent over from the office by Taylor and handed to me by Tommy the doorman. Inside it are the blues for *Swagbelly's* next issue. While I rarely contribute editorially to the magazine anymore, it is a tradition verging on superstition for me to go over all the shots before the next issue is released to press. This month we have a mock Olympic nude sports pictorial—naked track and field, skinny-dip swim meet, Greco-Roman in the buff, etcetera—a few couples' segments, two lesbian runs, and several solo shoots. I grease pencil a few shots that I don't approve, ones in which the models' eyes don't engage the camera. I've found over the years, and it is one of the things

132

that allowed my magazine to succeed when so many others failed, that a model playing to, or questioning, or seducing, or challenging, or even repelling, the camera, and thus the viewer, is what makes the difference. It creates a bond with, maybe even haunts, the man thumbing through the magazine in the newsstand or his bathroom. It still has this affect on me. In this quiet apartment I do not quite feel at home in, as I look into their eyes, I cannot help but contemplate the whole lives and sets of aspirations within the quivering tender flesh of the models. The market is saturated these days with beautiful young women willing to display themselves, and the rate of pay out there reflects this. The money can only translate to the most basic comfort in their lives and no type of security. Many models also dance at strip clubs, act in porno films, sell pictures on the web, run phone lines, or all of the above as supplement. It is no part-time windfall. It is work, hard, dirty work. This truth, as it glints tiredly from behind the seductive expressions, the pouts, and amorous eyes is a disturbing proposition. I replace the photographs in the envelope and toss it into my black crocodile Asprey attaché. I go into the bathroom to assess the truth behind my own eyes with the help of the mirror. What I actually end up doing is checking my suntan. My face has received some color beneath my polo helmet's brim, as have my forearms and neck. I have a farmer's tan. I am a silly melange of taupe and paste shades, but my crow's feet are muted at least. Then, in the mirror, I catch a glimpse of the toilet paper holder behind me. It is now re-loaded with a fluffy white roll. The sticky note I left instructing this has been re-affixed on top of the tissue however. Same with the towels on the rack. I feel a surge of irritation within me, and rush into the bedroom. In my sock drawer only brand new socks remain...along with my note. In the closet my suits are now hung with perfect care, *around* the sticky notes. What could possibly be the reason for something so *ridiculous* as leaving my notes where they were? It could only be the maid unnecessarily bringing my attention to the fact that she has ministered to my requests...or, or it could be a subtle message of mutiny. A mocking response to my instruction. Either way, I am not pleased. I think for a moment then draw a new package of sticky notes. "Remove," I write on one, then another and another until I've written it perhaps thirty three times. I place my new notes over the old ones. I do this in the bathroom, in my sock drawer, on each one along my closet rod. At last I sit down on the bed, nearly winded from my anger. I note by their crispness that the sheets beneath me have been changed. I see the note I left on the pillow regarding this. I crumple it up and throw it across the room. I pick up a fresh liter of water from my night stand and drink. It is this side of me that drove Lauren mad. I know this because it drives me mad too.

Throughout the night I repeatedly wake up and check for the automatic night-woodenness that visits the male member several times during sleep. On this night there is none for me. Each time I awaken, I seem to have visions of a skeletal, decrepit Barbara limping across the inside of my eyelids and upon investigation inside my pajama bottoms, my heart pounding, I discover only a clammy, recoiling worm. By the time I get out of bed in the morning I am an exhausted, nervous wreck. I finally decide to relent and call Dr. Gerry.

Dr. Gerry is my lanky, Harvard-educated, occasional psychiatrist. He has a heavy black mustache that walks the line between bushy and droopy. He dresses in slacks, shirt and tie, though no suit jacket, and keeps a sloppy office with mountain ranges of toppled books and sliding glaciers of papers strewn about the floor. His office is in a limestone townhouse off Fifth. Dr. Gerry sits with one foot pulled up beneath him in his desk chair, and often chews on a pen as his patients speak. I saw Dr. Gerry a few years back when Lauren started in with, "I'm concerned that you'll develop a cancer after suppressing your feelings for so long."

"What about my heart attack? Wasn't that enough?" I asked her. "Its different," she said, unwilling to elaborate. So my friend Dr. Bobby Gold recommended the guy to me. Dr. Gerry. I had a couple of sessions to placate Lauren, to show her that I was interested in *getting in touch with my emotions.* Dr. Gerry is a good man. Smart, tough to fool, quiet, interested, a Jew. I had a few intriguing conversations with him before I became self-conscious and broke off, for I must admit I am not comfortable with the idea of visiting a psychiatrist. They *seem* sympathetic, but unlike a friend they will not even listen if they are not getting paid. They are paid friends, with diplomas and prescription pads, and I am not wholly convinced that Brett, my licensed personal fitness trainer, isn't more effective in his similar role.

Nonetheless, by 9:00 a.m. I am sitting in... in Dr. Gerry's small, old-magazined waiting room. I suck on an atrocious Styrofoam cup of coffee and soon hear the door to his interior office open. A patient comes out to where I await my appointment. I experience a ridiculous flash of something near jealousy, or at least a feeling of commonness, at the sight of her as it is brought home to me that I am just another patient with problems, waiting to go in and unburden them. With the

mixture of anticipation and dread, it does not feel
entirely unlike waiting for one's turn at a brothel. The
patient is in her mid 30's with wiry black hair. She
wears a flowing floral skirt, and a long, loose gray cardi-
gan sweater. She carries a woven Kenyan bag over one
shoulder and a has a handful of knotted up tissue. "Is
she crazy?" I immediately wonder, examining her slightly stunned face. "From precisely what emotional mal-
function does she suffer?" I see her look back at me,
thinking perhaps the very same things. We are not friendly toward one another, no loose smiles are exchanged,
nor are we scornful. We are precisely neutral. We are
held in a state of intimate mental *détente*. She walks out
of the waiting room to the more open air of the street,
while I stand and head toward the hyperbaric chamber
of Gerry's office.

Dr. Gerry and I do not exchange greetings. He offers
me the chair with a wave. He remains seated but leans
forward, scrabbles around in a pile of paperwork at his
feet and comes up with a Manila folder. Like a Japanese
businessman he leaves the onus to talk first on me. Like
a better Japanese businessman, I wait him out. Finally, he
speaks.

"Do I have your current address?"

"You have me on 69th Street?"

"Right." It is my old address. I hope he will send some
correspondence to the townhouse and Lauren will see
that I am *in therapy*. That might make her stop and
think for a moment.

"That's it."

"Office phone number still the same since last time?"

"Yes."

"Still married?

"No. Currently in a state of interregnum." He makes a
notation on my file.

"What's been bothering you?"

"Well, I've been having performance problems."

"I see."

"Yes. Not at work."

"With women?"

"Yes."

"And you feel it is a mental/emotional issue? Have you seen your physician?"

"I think it is emotional, yes." It is stuffy in the office. A feeble window unit wheezes semi-cooled air from the corner.

"Because more and more these days physical causes are behind impotence." The *word*, the one I had hoped irrationally to avoid, jumps out at me. How I wish the word was even slightly different. Like 'impudence,' for example. If that were the problem, it would be a completely different situation. Then we could deal with matters like lack of respect. Or 'imprudence.' If that were the case, we could focus on rash or unwise behavior. Instead I am faced with the *word*, and all that it encompasses.

"Have you exerted yourself a good deal physically lately, or received an injury?"

"Well, I took up polo quite recently." For a moment I entertain the wild hope that perhaps I came down wrong on the saddle or pulled something that can be repaired surgically. I would prefer a clean surgical procedure to this, but then I must offer the truth. "I did have this problem before that though."

"I see."

"Yes."

"Have you been masturbating?" Dr. Gerry asks me in the direct way doctors have that is supposed to prevent embarrassment by virtue of its frankness, but instead increases embarrassment.

137

"Yes," I admit, "I have been masturbating, but not in the past several weeks. I haven't been with a woman successfully since seeing my ex-wife in a restaurant with her new boyfriend. I think this is—"

"I see. We'll get to the wife in a minute. Do you use artificial stimulation? Devices or visual aids?"

"Like pictures? I do use pictures."

"I see."

"Yes."

"You know I'm actually in the process of a book in this area. Pornography in society—the movies, the magazines, the strip clubs, the prostitution—it is all leading to a desensitization of natural sexual stimulation in the individual. That is my theorem anyway."

"So?"

"You must stop masturbating, at least to visual images of these 'imaginary' women. It raises sex too close to the surface. It becomes too shallow an activity," Dr. Gerry tells me. "You must re-develop your sense of actual fantasy, if you'll permit the oxymoron. If you must, visualize real sexual situations that you've experienced before, in order to re-create stronger cords attaching the sexual experience to a deeper place inside you as a person."

"When you say 'imaginary,' I think you mean women in graphic magazines?"

"Correct."

"But they're not 'imaginary women' to me, Doc. I know them. Maybe they're imaginary to you, or the average guy. But I'm actually encountering my difficulties *with them.*"

"Oh," Dr. Gerry says, and then falls silent, deflated. He seems both annoyed at being corrected, and yet impressed. He is either envious or his book has not yet progressed to this point. The silence lingers.

"What about your parents?" Dr. Gerry wonders. Great. Oh boy. I'm past fifty years old, does he think I'm going to talk about my mommy and daddy, leave his office with tears on my lapel and feel better?

"My father died just before I turned thirteen," I begin. Since I'm here I may as well try. "We had an argument one morning, and my last words to him were me calling him a prick. Then he dropped dead at work. Massive coronary, anterior wall, right ventricle. Bad vessels run in my family."

"What were you arguing over?" Dr. Gerry inquires.

"I don't really remember," I tell him.

"*Don't you?*" he says in that knowing way that is so maddening. I don't budge. "And your mother?"

"She's dead as well. Lymphoma. Awful. I didn't see that much of her during her last ten or fifteen years. She was cooped up in one those Collins Avenue mausoleums in North Miami. I wanted to do more for her, but the condo was what she wanted. She mahjongged and early-birded her way into her own sunset. What a great lady she was. Dinner on the table every night for my first eighteen years, and she never said a bad word about anybody in her life. I would have never made it through her funeral if it weren't for valium."

"How did you *feel* about her?"

"What are you getting at, Doc?" I ask. "I mean, was I not just pretty explicit?"

"Well, Freud would say it all goes back to your childhood. You were jealous because you expected your mother to love only you, but then you figured out she was boffing your old man...That's what Freud would say."

"Who else have you got?" I wonder. This gets a laugh from him.

"Hey, *you* try figuring this stuff out..." he says.

139

"That's why I'm paying you," I say. I think about the fight with my old man. I do remember it, Dr. Gerry is right about that. He had been cheating on my mom. He had girlfriends, and beside that on Friday afternoons they had hookers come down to the store where he sold suits. They would take turns with them down in the stockroom. He was so weak with his indiscretions, he made me sick. I told him so. I told him I never wanted to be like him. He smacked me across the face, and then I called him a prick.

"Tell me how you got into your business then. What made you choose your line of work?"

"Dr. Gerry, you have a real hard-on for pornography, if you'll excuse the wordplay." This time he is not amused. He gives me a patient, urging stare that tells me if I don't answer he will think I am evading. "It isn't a business for everyone, but it can be lucrative."

"Yes, well you could have become a stock broker or an arms-dealer, they are lucrative fields as well, but you didn't, why do you think that is?"

The information, presented in this particular way, has the effect of a double slap to my face. I actually feel my cheeks tingle. "I don't know," is my answer. If he says *don't you*, I will walk out, I promise myself. But his mind is built like a racing frigate, and he tacks slightly on me.

"Do you recall your first experience with pornography?"

"Uh, yes, I do." I say, suddenly flooded with the memory. "It was a Saturday afternoon. I was about eleven years old. It was my cousin Heckie's bar-mitzvah. The party was being held at his house, in the backyard, and me and another cousin, Mickey, disappeared from the party and went into the basement. We explored all over the place. We were half-looking for something to do, half-looking for something to steal. They had a big house, and every corner we turned seemed new and exciting. We came across a small room with a Bell & Howell Super 8 home movie projector set up. There were cans of film all over the place. Heckie's father, my Uncle Alan, was upstairs filming the party. He was the family shutterbug. Mickey and I were looking at the cans, and we had no hope of putting one on the reel and spooling it through the machine. Except there was already one on there. Mickey went ahead and clicked the projector on."

"What was there? What did you see?" It is as interested as I have ever seen Dr. Gerry. I have him on the edge of his seat.

"It was a grainy, badly lit, black and white movie that was sprayed out on a sheet tacked to the wall."

"Yes."

"It was a dark haired woman with pointy tits and hairy armpits. First she fucked a dog. He looked like a cross between a Great Dane and a black Labrador. He mounted her doggie style."

"Naturally," Dr. Gerry says. I cock an eyebrow at him, but his expression is completely blank.

"Then the scene cuts to her and a horse. A small Shetland pony. She climbed underneath him and fucked him too. I can't remember if the dog or the horse climaxed." I pause a moment in thought.

"Go on," Dr. Gerry urges me.

"So then the scene cuts again—inelegantly. No transition. She is suddenly bending over with a towel on her back and a guy is leading a pig over to her—"

"A towel?"

"Right. I guess so the pig's hooves won't cut up her back or something, I don't know. That's about it." I shake my head at the memory.

"Did she fornicate with the pig?"

"Probably. We heard my Aunt Grace calling for us so

141

Mickey and I shut off the projector and ran out of there."

"I see," Dr. Gerry says, and then chews on his pen. "Do you think this event affected you deeply?"

"Hell if I know. There wasn't much to it. It's not like I looked over and saw Mickey jerking off and was traumatized. I don't even think I was aroused—more horrified and amazed. I just remember thinking that we were very sneaky and that the film was the most fascinating thing I had ever seen. It might still be. I think that this woman nearly enjoyed what she was doing, and I was astonished at the *range* of...of humanity, I guess."

"Hmm." Dr. Gerry hums. I seem to have him stymied. I check my watch involuntarily.

"So where does this leave us?" I wonder. Dr. Gerry quickly explains that I need to strive to feel good about myself, in a profound way. This good feeling shall come from a place deep inside myself. Like a natural spring. He apologizes if it sounds mystical. He will teach me how to do this during hour after hour—special hours that last only forty-five minutes—of appointments at $325 a pop. He will teach me how to know myself in a deeper way, and along with this knowledge will come acceptance. This acceptance will give me peace of mind I have apparently never known. There is one question I have for Dr. Gerry that I will leave unasked—what if I already know what lies deep within myself, but have begun to suspect it is unacceptable?

"About your billing...Do you have insurance?" Dr. Gerry asks, taking off his clinician's cap and putting on his businessman's.

"I don't want records of this," I say. That's just what I need. As if I don't have enough problems joining clubs

142

and social organizations, and with the protestors for that matter. "I'll pay cash." I peel off three hundreds and a fifty from my roll and toss it on the coffee table between us. Dr. Gerry seems surprised. Perhaps he's never been paid this way before. After he swipes up the money and puts it in his pocket, he crumples up the medical bill he had been writing out and tosses it toward his trash can. I am almost reluctant to leave, I have so many other issues that we haven't gotten into. Things about sex, specifically between Lauren and I, which seem so pertinent to my problem. There was a whole corrosive phase between her and I that I need to discuss. When we were younger and things were out of control and exciting. There were long nights using stimulants and talking dirty. We explored just past the fringes of normalcy, into the incoherent worlds of fetish and domination. Something about those flights left me broken and uncomprehending upon my return to domesticity, while she made it back intact. Since then, sexually I have been like a diabetic with her, while to her I am something slightly rotten. I swear her skin tastes like confectioner's sugar, her sex a rhubarb crumble. If this is not love, I do not expect to get any closer to it in my life. I am afraid I am not quite normal for all the effort I expend on achieving those manna-like eighth of a second contractions, the surging of the seminal vesicles, and delivery of vas deferens. I have these problems, and now the defection of my sex drive and my son...It all seems much more important than my first porno film, but how to spit it all out escapes me. I make an appointment for the same time next week, but as I leave I don't have much confidence I'll be seeing Dr. Gerry again soon.

Outside on the street I am exhausted. Shrinking is hard work. I know I must look decimated like the woman with the Kenyan bag, but on the half-dozen block walk home I must gather myself for my drive to Connecticut, to The Academy.

The Academy

My car, one of my black Bentley Turbo Rs, has been brought around to the front of my building at 10:00 sharp for my drive to Andrew's school. I slip my gym bag and my briefcase into the passenger seat and set out on my drive. The Dexter Preparatory Academy is located outside Darien, Connecticut, about one hour from Manhattan. I cut cross-town and get on the West Side Highway, joining the light traffic flowing along the Hudson, ultimately merging onto the Huchtinson River Parkway. I drive myself today, eschewing my limousine, both for my own solitude and because Andrew prefers me to act the regular guy around his peers. The city fades behind me as a deepening infusion of spring-green trees fills my windshield. It is a bright day, the sun beaming from an unbroken sky, and the fine car leans into its work as I wind along the curving road. I settle back into the Connolly hide seat and try the office on the car phone, but I cannot get a clear signal beneath the heavy canopy of foliage that arches over me. In silence I ride along with my thoughts—passengers I increasingly prefer to leave behind these days. I wish I could perform the kind of escapism at which Sandy Kleiner is so adept. Without aid of pill nor powder, without sip of wine nor other alcohol, without smoking, Sandy manages to disconnect himself from reality almost totally. He converses, he laughs, he seemingly listens, but nothing really registers beneath the surface. I could tell him of my divorce, I could tell him I am going bankrupt, I could tell him Andrew, a twelve year old, is getting married, without Sandy stirring, and then in the next breath shout "horse," or "chukker," or "polo," and watch for the sudden interested enlargement of his eyes that would reveal him. I haven't enjoyed that kind of dislocation since the late 70's when I frequented a certain type of party that was popularly thrown in spacious Soho lofts. Bad art was often displayed as the excuse for the gatherings, and I am guilty of purchasing too much of it. Vodka and Chablis were served, but only as a seemly and legal cover for the cocaine and Quaaludes which were omnipresent. In those days my magazine was thin and printed in color on news stock. The models were thin also, more so than today, with less up top. A dark tan line contrasting with white breasts where a bikini top had covered them, and a more liberally haired snatch than the tiny patch or clean shave popular today, was that time's zenith of sexiness. Darting schools of these young ladies populated the lofts, their pointy noses leading them toward line, wallet, and bed. The suppliers were curly haired gentlemen in their thirties, with large zodiac medallions and heavy rings. Men with not-yet-pendulously-flabby stomachs and sweaty faces, wearing huckapoo shirts open over jungly haired chests, and hip hugging denim jeans. Bushy mustaches were prevalent as were woolly sideburns, and we let ourselves believe it was we who were desirable, and not our Fire Island houses and Mercedes convertibles and money. Now we have grown, our bellies and our prosperity, a whole generation of us, and I am no longer under these illusions. Now I *know* it's the Bentleys and mansions. I can accept this. Maturity is a wonderful thing.

My exit looms ahead and I turn off the Merritt Parkway. I guide my purring black machine through wooded hollow and on toward the school, driving half by memory, and half in obeisance of the directions Taylor has typed out for me. One wrong turn down a dead end lane, one straightening out, and I crest the hill that holds The Academy. The school is a cluster of limestone buildings with clinging ivy crawling up the walls on a journey that is already more than ten decades old. It seems I have suddenly driven into a medieval cloister, such is the architecture. The buildings are gothic in style with elaborate friezes and inspiring mottoes carved in Latin over the entryways. Set off around the grassy environs are athletic fields and a small amphitheater. Three residence halls and the dining hall outline a grass quadrangle laced with footpaths and off to the right is a parking area filled with expensive automobiles. This school, and a few others like it, is considered amongst the finest private schools in the country for young men. It is spoken of as a place where a classical education can be gained of the type not often seen in the crass suburban sprawl of the United States these days. It evokes even a Europe of a past era, when art, history, learning in general was considered important as enrichment rather than as tawdry necessity. I know what Dexter really is though, it is a whetstone. Attending will keen Andrew's edge in life. With even average grades he will go on to an Ivy League college, and will become long-time friends with the scions of important, landed families—the Binkies, Bunkies, and Kirbies, of his age, who will take over the reins of industry and wealth from their fathers. He doesn't have to like them, nor they him, for he will have known them for years by the time college is over. Then he will be 'Grubman from Dexter,' 'Andrew Grubman who went on to Cornell,' or the like. He won't be an interloper, he will be 'old Grubman, our kind of guy.' He will have been around forever as far as these people are concerned, and even the Semitic timbre of his name will have given way to familiarity. He will not be scrounging for a job after graduation like most mortarboards, he will be weighing his opportunities, *deciding* which one to take. This is the big difference between from where Andrew and I come. Samuel Tilden High School back in Brooklyn, where I went, did not provide this edge. It is true I have made a fortune, more even than most of these old families have managed to hang on to of their own inheritances, but Andrew will not be on the fringes, he will be somewhere better—he will be installed.

Small flags designate where we fathers should park, and strung up between a pair of old maples is a banner of welcome. I shut off the Bentley and climb out, taking my gym bag with me. Not far to my left is the school's chapel. It is officially non-denominational, but for all intents and purposes it is a Protestant house of worship straight down the line. I had to send a letter to the dean excusing Andrew from the services they hold there just to insure he didn't come home singing Christmas carols at Winter Break. I walk along the crunchy gravel trail toward the middle school boy's dormitory. Several groups of fathers stroll around with their sons. Some are gripped in the heady nostalgia that comes from having attended Dexter themselves when they were whelps. I nod to a few of them I happen to recognize and they nod back. We don't know each other formally, we are not friends, we just see each other around. We eat in the same restaurants, end up in the same hotels on vacation, and I've been an occasional guest at some of their golf courses. If Jewish adult magazine publishers were admitted, I'd see them around the tap room of the University Club too. I *could* buy my way in there, I know that, but it isn't worth it to me. I can only go so far in terms of acceptance. For Andrew though, Dexter is money well spent. Memory is short where wealth is involved.

I find my way into Lloyd Hall, my Ferragamo heels knocking against the worn stone floor of the corridor. Information pertinent to scholastic life is posted on a notice board next to a trophy case full of cups, trays, and plaques all engraved in commemoration of the school's victories in various endeavors. They have been frequent champions in crew, in oratory, in lacrosse, and squash. There is not a single award for stoopball. I climb three flights of stairs on a pair of stiff post-polo legs and come into the floor lounge, where sons and dads mill about. Down the hall, a white towel over his shoulder and toilet kit in his hand, I see Andrew just leaving the bathroom. I am simultaneously gripped by happiness at the sight of him and concerned over his slumped posture.

"Hey hey, buddy buddy," I shout, starting toward him.

"Hey, dad," he says back, extending a hand toward me. I walk through it and wrap him in a hug.

"Hey, dad? Not too enthusiastic there, pal." I slap a kiss on his cheek, and it seems to make him distinctly uncomfortable. With my kissing another male, I must look like an Israeli rug merchant to these ram-rod spine frigid gentiles watching from the lounge. I see Andrew glance over my shoulder toward them. Several sit in adolescent size club chairs, and I hear the word 'scandalous' drift over from one of the WASPy windbags there.

"What's the matter, boy?"

"Nothing," Andrew says. I look at him through narrowed eyes. Nothing indeed.

"Grades okay?" I wonder.

"Yes."

149

"Are you feeling well?"

"Yeah." Andrew has bright a gleam to his upper lip. It stands out in a way that is unfamiliar to me. He looks the same, yet different. I cannot place why. Then I realize it—he recently started shaving. I swipe his lip playfully. "What's this, huh?" Andrew flushes crimson and walks me to his room without taking his eyes off the floor. Andrew closes the door behind us and throws his kit on the bed. On the other bed, about three feet across the tiny cell-like room, sits a small, silent kid. He must be Trevor, the roommate. There are mirror-image writing desks against opposite walls, both loaded with reference books and anthologies of American Literature. I look around and see a small television resting on a stool.

"Where's that VCR I bought you, buddy?" I ask. "I want to show you a video of me playing polo."

"It's been stolen," Andrew tells me glumly.

"Stolen?" I look at the television again. "They left the T.V. though?"

"No. It was stolen out of the lounge. A few of the guys on scholarship don't have televisions or VCRs and they can't watch except in the lounge, so I put it in there," he says.

"Well that's brilliant, Andrew. Now the VCR is gone. You see?" I dislike my critical tone. I know how deeply it cuts him. He's a sensitive kid. It just leaps out when I hear something like this though. I try to soften it up. "You have to be more responsible with your property. I hate to see you taken advantage of." I reach for my money. "How about if I give you money for a new one, how would that be?"

"It'll go back in the lounge, dad" Andrew says quietly but firmly.

"What?"

"I can't let a crime change the way I act when doing

150

what I think is right."A mature voice of conviction issues from my young son, who goes shy once again as he falls silent. It sounds as if he is quoting someone, but not from something he has read, he is too sure for that. I wonder from whom he has heard this, who taught him. I am conflicted over Andrew's integrity and his naiveté. I want to show him my videotape, but need to teach him a lesson. I put the money back in my pocket.

"Well son, I can't just buy another VCR to get stolen. That's known as throwing good money after bad. Sometimes we have to suffer for what we believe." It is important to me to have a voice of influence over Andrew when I can. He, however, purses his lips skeptically. He comes dangerously close to disrespect. It is not like him to act this way, and I am beginning to become exasperated.

"Andrew, what is the matter?"

"Dad, do you not know, or do you just not care?"

"Know what, Andy?" I ask, growing worried. Andrew picks up the *Post*, folded back to page seven, from his desk and hands it to me. It takes me a moment to apprehend what is there on the page in greasy newsprint. As I do, the room becomes close, the free air seemingly sucked out of it, and the words swim in front of my eyes.

City Smut, by C.B. Brancato:"Elliot Grubman, ghost publisher of raunchy rag *Swagbelly*, and millionaire about town, has recently been soothing the sting of his $15 million divorce settlement with a string of nude models. Meanwhile, his ex-wife Lauren has been consoling herself with mountain man Richard "Ricky" Jones.The hunk is a private climbing instructor and fitness trainer in Aspen. Word has it that Grubman's taste has gone

151

dangerously young these days, as his latest courtesan is rumored to be a mere fifteen years old. No word from Lady Lauren as to what she plans to do with the ex-couples' $10 million antique-filled Madison Avenue mansion, only that Elliot is not welcome there."

I am light headed with fury as I fold the paper closed. The invasion causes me to shudder with frustration and helplessness. I look at Andrew, whose face is tight with comprehension, I believe, and humiliation. I must think of something to say, but nothing that has come before this has prepared me to speak to my son on such a subject.

"You know it isn't true," I say to Andrew, my vessels scraping with angry blood at the inaccuracies this slob Brancato chose to print. I try for a disinterested factual high ground. "I mean, the house is on Park, that part is obviously wrong, his numbers are way off, and just so you know, Yvonne is turning twenty this fall." My words sound weak to me, petty excuses in the face of major charges. But what are the charges? I haven't even done anything to feel guilty over. Divorces happen and partners move on. On a rational level I do not have anything to be apologetic over...it's just that look on Andrew's face. That look of collapse.

"This is yellow journalism, son. Jesus, these guys find a few facts so things appear truthful, then they make up whatever they want and feel no remorse about printing it. It's libelous. You know what that means?" I ask him. Andrew says nothing in response. "You know what that means?" I ask again.

"Yes, it's like slander, only written," the previously silent roommate peeps. Christ, I've forgotten he's even there.

"Exactly. Good, good. Kid...Trevor, right? You're Trevor?"

"Yes, sir."

"No, no, call me Mr. Grubman. Nice to meet you, Trevor."

"Nice to meetcha, Mr. Grubman." He stands up and shakes my hand, a very formal little chap.

"You can't believe everything you read in newspapers like this." I wave the offending daily and then throw it down on Andrew's bed. "You can't take this stuff seriously," I say, trying to believe myself. I realize that Andrew and I have never had a direct conversation regarding what I do. He knows to say I am a publisher when asked what his father does for a living. Maybe he even knows his father publishes an "adult" magazine. I do not know how he feels about it at all though. I begin to suspect it is not something he takes pride in, and if it is not surprise he is suffering from, it may well be shame. This pierces my sonar and I veer from the topic like a bat.

"You going to play a little basketball with us, Trevor? We're going to play a little basketball, right? Where shall I dress?" I ask blithely, lifting my gym bag in a show of my readiness. I seek reprieve by change of subject. "Come on guys, we don't want to be late."

"Not me, sir. I'm playing baseball with my father, so I'll see you." Trevor may not be well informed as to what is going on, but he is as aware of changes in atmospheric pressure as anyone, and he lunges for the door in order to escape. He leads the way out into the hall. I begin after him, but Andrew does not budge. I turn back to him.

"Come on, son, let's go. We'll talk about it later." He walks forward miserably. I put a hand on his shoulder, which he tries half-heartedly to shake off. I keep it there.

I am beset by great inner tumult at this latest turn of events, as my son and I trudge into the gymnasium. If there is anything I detest, it is being on display for people's hungry eyes and gossip-slobbering tongues. It makes my temper flare scarlet and bright. There was a choice of sport for this day—soccer, baseball, or basketball—and I told Andrew to put us down for basketball, as it is one of my strongest. I had been hoping to show him some of my skills, to impress him in the way that a father can only through athletics. Now I need to wow him more than ever thanks to this item in the paper, though I am not at all sure it will work. I will have to play like Earl Monroe rolled into Wilt Chamberlain to succeed now. I am sure all the other dads, and even some of the sons, will know about the story. My legs are still quite stiff from riding as well, and the fathers, already on the court warming up—a virtual morass of traders, raiders, and corporate law partners—are in their late thirties and early forties, some ten to fifteen years younger than me. Fathers, wearing slick blue and red Italian tennis suits, along with their sons, in school uniforms, grab basketballs off racks and pop jumpers into the clamorous air of the gym. Andrew shows me to the locker room where I change into my gray T-shirt and gray sausage-leg drawstring sweat pants. My basketball attire is strictly old school. While many of the others wear three-quarter and high-top basketball shoes with Velcro closures and soles injected with shock absorbing air or gel, I prefer canvas low-cut sneakers of the same make I wore in high school. They were becoming difficult to find some years ago, until recently when they came back into fashion with the young generation. Now, besides the black that I prefer, I can get them in all the colors of the rainbow and every conceivable shade in between. When I located a store that sold them in

New York I bought twenty-five pairs, so I am covered should they go out of style again.

I step onto the court gingerly, trying to get some blood flowing in my legs, feeling a little self-conscious about my common attire and my recent notoriety. I park myself under the basket and collect a rebound off the rim. I put the ball up from two feet, banking it off the backboard and through the hoop. I always take a lay-up before any other shot, that way I am sure to sink the first one. I collect my own rebound and dribble outside. I loft my two-handed set shot, which is unlike the modern jumper. I suppose it is a little quirky looking, my hands up, forming an upside down heart on the ball. My form gets a snicker from a few of the others doing warm ups, despite the fact I swish it from fifteen feet. I don't look like Michael Jordan or John Stockton with a basketball in my hands. I probably look more like a squirrel doing a chin up, while lots of guys these days have all the professional moves during lay-up lines and practice. They learn the look from watching highlights on sports channels and sitting court side. They take a thirty-footer and chastise themselves for missing, as if they can hit it on a good day. My shot falls during the game however. I can drain it with sneakers squeaking on the court around me, and a hand in my face. Not many others on the floor can make this claim. I get only one more practice shot before a whistle is blown, and everyone is forced to congregate at mid-court. The whistle blower, named Coach Klapper, chooses up teams in a brisk, unapologetic gym coach manner. The lateness of my selection, as well as the short, bespectacled guy who is triaged to the other team opposite me shows what Klapper expects of my game.

Introductions are made around on our squad, and positions are given out. We have a guy on our team named

Sterling, who is the self-appointed captain. He is a young, healthy father, overconfident and take-charge in manner. He makes himself point guard, and puts his son, J.P., at off-guard. Andrew and I are placed at forward, and Randall, and his boy young Randy, two beanpoles, will alternate time in the middle depending on who, kid or adult, is playing center on the other squad. The game starts with Randall winning the tip, and then Sterling brings the ball up the floor. As he dribbles with his right hand, he signals with his left hand held high, two fingers up. He is calling a play, as if we are professionals with an elaborate triangle offense to utilize. He must be in the midst of a Kobe Bryant fantasy. Sterling picks up his dribble and pump fakes passes around the floor before having the ball picked cleanly from his hands by Fenton, a father on the other team. Fenton is tall, lean, and strong. During shoot-around I heard someone mention he played college ball at Penn, and he indeed wears a UPenn Basketball T-shirt. He goes up for an easy lay-in, and it seems he can nearly dunk. Fathers on the sideline jeer Sterling's loose play.

"Was that the offense you called for, Sterl?" one of them yells.

"Aw, I was just calling for a wheel," Sterling answers. He is the type of player who believes anger compensates for poor play, that his ire creates the illusion of competitiveness. Then, turning his discomfort on us, chastises, "Don't you guys know the wheel?" Even Coach Klapper isn't immune. "Don't you teach 'em the wheel offense, Klapper? And how 'bout a foul, he got me on the hand there."

We run up and down the floor for awhile, and my legs finally stretch out a bit. The kids scrabble around with the ball, and keep the game fast if not graceful. In fact I'm breathing hard before very long at all. As I suck air, my face becomes heated and my hands begin to tingle. I think about calling for a substitution, but I don't want to disappoint Andrew. I manage to make a couple shots, one turnaround in the lane, and a fade away using Sterling as an inadvertent pick. I look for Andrew to pass to every time down the floor. I want him to score, but he doesn't move around much to get open on offense. He actually allows his man to stand right next to him, as if he'd rather have company than get the ball. I make a mental note to teach him about this, while trying to keep us within a few points. Because of my baskets, the team sees I can play, and my assignment becomes defending against Fenton. As I square up with him, trying to deny an inbounds pass, I realize he is truly a giant. Nothing like D-ing up a guy to appreciate what 6'5" means in basketball terms. My low defensive crouch and busy hands succeed in keeping him off his mark, while I drill a few set shots over him.

Height notwithstanding, I am succeeding in my personal battle with Fenton, and I believe I am actually winning over Andrew with my play. He has started to run the floor with more enthusiasm and his face relaxes into a smile. This is when I realize I have another problem on my hands. I do not feel at all well. My stomach is very acidic and I feel I might vomit. The horror and embarrassment attached to this vision may be all that keeps it from happening. My man Fenton goes up for a shot in the paint and I strip him of the ball. I dish the outlet to Randy breaking up court and we tab an easy basket. Andrew moves to give me a high-five when my sight starts to go spotty, then comes blinding pain that shoots down both arms and up the center of my chest. I can see the blonde wood of the floor, its deep grain, lacquered to a brilliant shine. I have a thought about how nice a gymnasium this is. It is of quality but old. Nothing compared to the new gym that is being built. The floor in there will have the Dexter insignia at mid-court and be of an even lighter wood than this floor, which I can see very closely...

I am hesitant to speak of my proudest memory. I usually keep it a secret because of how petty it may seem to others, and how juvenile. Most men list the birth of a child or some great achievement in business. Mine, however, is a mere physical fitness award. I am not sure why it comes to me so clearly now. Back in high school, at Samuel Tilden, there was an end of year ceremony when awards for excellence were given. Varsity letters were granted to those who had played on the teams, as well as academic citations in other classes. The whole school assembled for the event. In order to receive any particular award one needed to have earned 'A's' in the class during all four terms of the school year. I figured I had one coming in Phys Ed., though I didn't get along well with Coach Kuhn. Kuhn was a heavy drinker, and a volunteer fireman in the neighborhood. I didn't play football so he considered me a candy ass, and since I was a Jew, well that made me close to a leper in his eyes. Kuhn was not above public anti-Semitic comments. Actually the word 'kike' was such an essential component of his vocabulary it seemed nearly a nervous tick. He would foul a ball off his shin demonstrating a batting stance, "Son of a kike." Stub a toe, "Dirty kike..." Forget something, "What the kike?" and the one for every occasion, "For the love of kike..." This was reason enough for me to hate him, and I did, but I loved sports. Gym class was the highlight of my day. My attendance in his class, and my skills, were impeccable, and I had earned my 'As'.

On the day of the ceremony, Kuhn called the names, about fifteen or twenty of them, of those who had qualified, and the students went up on stage with him to receive their awards. The proclamations were written in calligraphy on thick parchment paper with the school's seal in wax and were tied with a ribbon. I wanted one badly, and I was stunned not to hear my name called. I knew how well I had played baseball, basketball, and soccer, how well I had performed in track and field. I played hard every day, as if it mattered. It was the only way I knew how. And now I was being skipped over by the bastard because he had it in for me. As Kuhn came to end of the names, in his halting awkward way of speaking, he said, "...and there is one more award I would like to give. One who stands out from the rest. To the finest athlete of the year, who distinguished himself above all the others, Elliot Grubman." I was dumbstruck. The auditorium actually applauded. It must have killed that Jew-hater coach to give me that award, and that, in the end, was what confirmed for me just how well I really had played ...

I wonder how it is I have had the time to think about such trivialities, and suddenly I can sense people all around me on the court. Hairy legs tower above me and large sneakers move at my eye level. Several pairs of hands lift me up and carry me somewhat roughly inside the locker room. On a bench in there, with a wet towel across the back of my neck, I begin to come to my senses. I shake it off and get my breath back. I take a drink of water from a cup offered to me, and feel the redness start to leave my face.

"I'm alright, I'm fine," I say, "Just winded." Several of the guys whack me on the back, and give me encouragement. "There ya go," they shout. "He's okay. You're okay," they tell me. "Give him some air," they tell each other. "Give him some room," they advise. I wave off offers to get a doctor, then look over and see Andrew seeming very concerned. I shine him a little smile. "Did we win?" I ask. The others laugh at this and, the drama ended, the crowd breaks up and fathers and sons begin to strip down for their showers. Sweat suits and shorts and jockstraps are pulled down and suddenly I'm surrounded by a group of uncircumcised big-penised Philistines, and their young, striding to and from the showers. The small locker room fills with steam and mirthful shouts. Despite their age, the men are more than happy to participate in the timeless joking and grab-assing common to locker rooms. The snap of coiled towels on wet buttocks registers in the humid air. I hear one voice telling a joke from the fogged over showers. "What's the difference between a golf ball and a clitoris?"

"What?"

"A grown man will spend fifteen minutes looking for a golf ball." Wild chuckles. Young laughs join in falsely, uncomprehending and wanting to know what's funny about that, but afraid to ask. I do not laugh at the joke. I do not even smile. I do not participate. I could. I know them all: "What's the difference between P.M.S. and Mad Cow's disease?"

"Absolutely nothing."

Or: "What's the best part of a blowjob?"

"Five minutes of silence."

I could go on. I hear them all from my bond broker, Jeff Lipsky. He and all his Wall Street buddies and their jokes, it's a wonder they find time to churn an account. I never tell a joke such as these, and I never laugh when I'm told one. I decided a long time ago that being in my business I could not afford jokes demeaning to women.

160

From the showers I make out "...twenty percent off." Knowing guffaws. It is the punch line to a joke having to do with Jews and circumcision. Then a young voice, tentative at first, but growing in giddy confidence can be heard. "I went to the wailing wall last summer, but they made me leave..."

"Why's that?"

"I brought a harpoon..." He receives some encouraging laughs, some "haw-haw, very goods," from the older men. I shake my head and endure a morose moment at the atmosphere to which I've delivered my son. I think to the future, when it will all have been worthwhile. In my youth I played on many teams full of this type of *goyim* asshole. Ruddy cheeked and strapping they were, and as unstrategic as they were physically gifted. Oh, how they tortured me. Sure there had been plenty of Jewish assholes around too, but naturally none of them had attacked me based solely on my being Jewish. There were countless fights after a game or a play that wasn't 'nice play,' but 'nice play...for a Yid." The worst of them resented the Jew driving in the winning run even when I was on their team. It was insane. It was never the actual religion—nothing much significant ever happened to me in a synagogue but this suffering that brought me close to my Judaism.

"You didn't have to play so hard if you were feeling sick," Andrew says sensibly.

"Was I playing hard?" I ask. I realize I have only one speed in sports and other contests, and that is: all out. Me and my Hebie friends back home never had the luxury of playing for fun. Others around Andrew and I are mostly dressed by now, and begin filtering out of the locker room. I stand up unsteadily, and peel off my gray T-shirt gone black from sweat. Andrew and I shower alone and in silence. I notice he has the sproutings of

161

some dark hair around his *schmeckel*. My own has gone gray, in grave contrast to the orangey-brown stuff on my head, and I look forward achingly to getting back into my suit.

"What now, son? Lunch?" I wonder aloud, zipping up my slacks. As I slip into my jacket I feel it is the suit that actually climbs on me, so well does it fit. I am feeling much better already. It is amazing what stout armor a well cut suit is. I knot my tie just as the headmaster, one Winston Pratt, walks into the locker room wearing his blue Dexter blazer with the school escutcheon—a gold stitched amalgam of swords, books, and crosses—sewn proudly on his left breast pocket.

"Hello, Dean Pratt," says Andrew. Pratt is a large man with white hair squared off in a severe side part. His eyes are ice blue and have a well-practiced, piercing look that enables a pedagogue to strike fear into youths without yelling.

"Hello, Andrew," he says in a rough-textured voice, and extends a gnarled hand for me to shake. He is short a pinky and ring finger on his right hand, having lost them to his captors when he was a prisoner of war in the South Pacific. The fingers lost have given him more mileage in reputation and color than possessing the digits ever could have. "Glad to see you're feeling better, Grubman. I heard what happened. Shall I call for the school physician? He's a fine man."

"No, no thank you, Winston," I say, "I'm feeling better now. I just got a little excited out there. Playing ball with my boy, you know how it is..." He narrows his burrowing gaze at me and nods as if he knows all which happens in the realm of Dexter.

"So, Winston, we have things to discuss?" I say, tucking my gym clothes into my bag.

"Yes, we certainly do. What say we walk the boy over

162

to the dining hall, and you and I can continue over to the site." The three of us leave the locker room, and cross through the corner of the gym, exiting outside through the fire door.

"No, let's have Andrew take the walk with us. He can have a look too. I get to see so little of him after all," I say firmly to the headmaster. How can he refuse?

"Fine, fine," Pratt snuffles, irked at my subtly overruling him. He is quite smug in his omnipotence here at The Academy, but I want both he and Andrew to know that his domain does not include my boy. We walk as a group up a grassy rise, past the dining hall, and on past the amphitheater as well. "We're putting on a series of classic dramas here this spring," Pratt points to the half-bowl. Some Sophocles and "The Clouds," by Aristophanes, "Oedipus Rex," of course, all in conjunction with a local girls school. We're urging all parents to attend. Shall I put you down for tickets?" Pratt smiles.

"Are you in any of the plays, Andrew?" I ask.

"No."

"I see. Well, put me down for a row for each show anyway. I'll have my office send a check," I smile back at Pratt. He knows how little interest I have in coming to a play my son is not in, but it is an inexpensive position to maintain, even if I have to pay people to attend.

Presently we come upon a construction site, our destination. There is a vast, squared cavern cut out of the umber earth. The bottom of it has been made level. A cinder block foundation has been framed around most of the hole, and an idle backhoe sleeps in there, the shovel up in the air like a person eating and interrupted mid-forkful. It is a large project underway, and I can't think of a reason why no one is working on a perfectly clement day. I sense it is the reason for this little field trip though.

"Let's talk about the fieldhouse," I begin, for I do not prefer the passive role.

"Yes," says Pratt forthrightly.

"I'm thinking, 'The Hyman Lipshitz Pavilion,'" I say with majesty, letting the name unfurl grandly from my tongue. The headmaster goes pale. "After my cousin, Hyman. Remember our cousin Hymie?" I ask Andrew, who says nothing, but looks vastly uncomfortable. I turn back to Pratt, "I'd like a little ribbon-cutting thing, with a band, in the fall when it's done. Does The Academy have a band? Maybe they can learn 'Smelke's Nagel.' It was cousin Hyman's favorite..." The headmaster grows positively ashen at my words. It's as if I asked him to remember the Bataan death march, such is the discomfiture on his face.

"Mr. Grubman," he begins, that stalwart voice of his actually wavering, "here at the Academy we take a dim view of family names too prominently displayed on buildings. We try to emulate the more esoteric environment of schools like those of the ancient philosophers," he says.

Now it is my turn to look disconcerted. I am acting though. I allow my mouth to form into a downward crescent of disappointment. When I sense that Pratt is flummoxed as to what he should say next, I let it linger for another moment. I can feel how convincing I am. I should get a part in one of those productions they're staging over in the amphitheater. Then I turn my grimace around.

"That's very whimsical, Winston, but the Grecian clime is much more conducive to sitting outside under a tree and practicing sophistry. Here in Connecticut schoolmasters need actual *buildings* don't they? That is to say, where are the matching funds you spoke of last fall when I made my initial donation for this building?" The silence that follows my question is so profound that no less than Socrates or Plato could help but be moved by it. I refer to a little boiler room deal that Pratt and I struck last year when it was decided Andrew should attend Dexter. There were no spots available in the class, but it seemed the school desperately needed an athletic facility. My pledge of $1.2 million seemed to miraculously free up a slot. Pratt plays hardball though, the prick actually sent a tuition bill. If our talk right now was of a personal matter, perhaps I would be overmatched with the war hero and his legendary fortitude, but he cares about the young men and the institution, and this opens him up considerably. He clears his throat and swallows. He swallows formidably.

"While the idea of naming the place after your *relative* is a noble one, how about something *simpler?*"

"My mind is a blank. Can you give me a for instance?" I wonder. He fixes me with a bayonet stare, but then he wavers. Once the waffling starts it's over.

"Grubman Fieldhouse?" Pratt offers, his words weak and resigned.

"Grubman Fieldhouse, hmm." I try it out, as if for the first time. "I like it better. Fabulous. Now, what kind of completion funds are we looking at?" The rest of our conversation flies by with an airy, nearly chummy quality. It will cost me another $750,000 to finish the gymnasium, and for my humble moniker to be chiseled into Dexter Academy's granite facade next to Vandever and the rest. As we finish our handshake, I catch a glimpse of Andrew's face. He seems disturbed by what he has seen—nearly choleric. I experience a moment's horror as I wonder if the boy can actually respect Pratt more than he does me, his own father? Pratt marches away starchily into the Connecticut afternoon, leaving Andrew and I to walk back toward the dining hall.

"You wanted your name on the building in the first place, didn't you?" Andrew accuses me.

"*Our* name, laddie, *our* name," I correct. "I wanted you to see that, to learn how to negotiate."

"Do you think its right to try and break people down because you can?" Andrew says hotly. "Why does everything have to be some, some kind of a battle with you?"

"Life's not a battle, my boy, it's a war," I say seriously. "A holy war."

I wonder where to start in terms of all Andrew needs to learn. I've tried to give and give with my son, so he had every advantage. I've given, it seems, until that has become the problem. Andrew doesn't know what it's really like in the world.

"It's that kind of thing that gives Jews a bad name," Andrew mutters nearly inaudibly.

"What?" I bark, "What-did-you-say?" I ask again, my shock at his words causing mine to come staccato.

"Nothing," Andrew says quietly.

"I asked what you said, young man."

"I guess you heard me or you wouldn't be freaking out," he answers. I take a deep breath in order to calm myself at this.

"Listen Andrew, two things: I want you and I to sit down with Rabbi Weiss next week when you're home for Spring Recess. You don't have to be bar-miztvahed exactly on your birthday. You can learn what you need to and we'll schedule it for the end of the summer before school starts next year. Second, I'm going to take a house out in the Hamptons starting this summer. I'll have horses there, and we'll be near the beach. It will be great, you'll love it. I want you out there with me. I think we need to spend a *significant* amount of time together."

.My words sound dramatic, authoritative. I do not believe I have left room for comment, but Andrew is full of surprises today.

"Will Yvonne be there?"

"I don't know, maybe, what does that have to do with it?" I ask.

"I don't want to hang around with her," he says, as if she is *his* friend, from whom he wants to separate himself.

"I see. What about Ricky? Do you hang around with him?" I try to keep the jealousy out of my voice, but I fear that I fail in doing so.

"Not much."

"He's not *Uncle Ricky?*" Now I've lost any inkling of measured control over my voice. The antagonism in me for this man, who probably has a better rapport than I with my son, bursts forth in a completely unsatisfactory way.

"No, dad, he's not *Uncle Ricky*...Would you please grow up," he huffs. The little bastard sounds exactly like his mother. "Really, you lack any emotional fluency." *Emotional fluency!* What the hell is he talking about? He goes around repeating things he's heard and barely has a grasp of. I tighten my neck and my jaw. I clench my teeth together and screw down my will tightly over my anger. I feel the skin of my face and temples pulsing with a grotesque sub-dermal rage. I am just inches from exploding in a torrent of profanities upon my son.

"I may not be *emotionally fluent*, but I want what's best for you. That's a bar-mitzvah." Why is my toughest negotiation, my unwinnable one, with my son?

"I want to convert, dad. I feel more like a Catholic, like mom. Jesus was a real guy who I can relate to. Being Jewish has nothing to do with me. I don't understand Hebrew anyway, and neither do you. During Spring

167

Break there's a conversion ceremony at mom's church and I want to take my first communion," he spews forth in a rush.

The heat of the day settles heavy, thick, and silent. I am overcome with dismay. I've lost him. How can I begin to explain what it means to be a Jew, the suffering, the bond in the ostracism, the covenant, if this is the way he feels? My shoulders sag. I have the disgusting urge to drop to my knees. I am beaten by his turning away, and I have never been beaten, excluding my divorce, in the entire course of my memory. Lawyers and the I.R.S., co-op boards and Coach Kuhn, none of them could beat me. Only my stunning and cunning ex-wife and our frail spawn can wing me and send me spiraling to the ground. I've lost him.

"So that's what you really want?" I ask. I try to make myself come around to the idea, to deal with this compromise.

"Yes."

"I see. You're sure?" I feel a great sense of calm descend over me. My reason swiftly returns to me. The boy is the important thing, and even if he *thinks* he's Catholic, he is my son. As long as I remain close to him, there will be hope of him coming around...

"Yes."

"You little fool! You don't know what the fuck you're talking about!" I scream. My voice booms across the fields of Dexter as I grab him by his scrawny arm and jerk him about like a paper Halloween skeleton. He breaks loose from my grip and rubs his arm where I've held it. Then he starts to cry, his tears inciting me to yell louder, as if my volume alone can staunch them.

"You think you can convert, because your mother has confused you, but you're a Jew and you always will be, get it? It's not optional. People, most gentiles, hate you

168

for it, understand? Just like they do me, and the rest of us. They want to keep you out and hope you fail and die because of it. Here." I reach into my pocket and tear out a handful of one hundred dollar bills. "Get yourself a new VCR and watch a movie about life. Learn how it is." I unzip my gym bag and present him with my polo video tape. "Watch this and see how your father has managed to break into the game, to play with those who didn't want him there in the first place." He takes the tape in hand, while the money flutters to the ground.

I have so much more to yell into his tiny ears of stone, so much I have learned that he needs to know, but my throat has turned to sand. Suddenly Andrew breaks into a run back toward his dormitory, the video falling from his grasp about ten yards away. A few years ago I had to try and dump our race, when I could have easily run him down, but today I have no chance of catching him. His feet fly over the grass and blink in the sunlight. I do not want to run anyway. I am sick inside and in no condition for running. I am sick at this state of affairs, of my choices, and sick at myself. I am tired of chasing. I walk over to my video tape, my loafers moving wearily through the soft grass. I bend and pick it up. I have nowhere to go but back toward my Bentley.

I have no idea what to do when I leave The Academy but to throw the car in frustration at the snaking rural roads. Small farms and hay fields blur by outside as I run her loose for an hour as fast as I can push. I lose myself in the secret verdant interiors of Connecticut. The engine churns perfectly in the spring heat without a single hitch or ping, as I drive out the exhausted remains of the emotional fireworks. I consider losing control in the curves and stare at the stolid trunks of ancient oak trees lining the road. I picture myself dying in the wracked up Bentley, and the sorrow on all their faces at my funeral. Only an indefinable impulse makes sure I keep the car straight on the road. Finally, as the day fades into dusk, the adrenaline, the pungent edge of my angst, begins to leave my system. I feel like a cored apple as I point myself sadly back towards New York City.

There is a saying, "the mother makes the girl, but it is the father who determines the woman." I close my eyes in a moment of relief, a silent prayer of thanks that I do not have any daughters. What the hell would I have done in that case? If the saying is true though, to hear my family tell it, my daughters would have turned into monsters. I wonder if there is a parallel with sons? Am I responsible for the kind of boy he is, but Lauren for his manhood? It does not seem so. If it is true, then I suppose he is a difficult and unpleasant boy, as I am accused of being. When he grows into a man, will it be his mother's imprint on him? Will he turn out "sensitive and caring," as Lauren would claim herself? It is perplexing, the scope of these difficulties that come between sons and fathers. Nowhere do love and hate, desire and disgust, need and repulsion, reside so closely than within the male wing of a family. Within the family they are intimate, close-breathing bedmates.

Back in Manhattan, I tuck the Bentley into the garage and take a short walk to Tre Fiori in the fine evening weather. The events of the day leave an emptiness inside me that I can only think to fill with food. Throughout the ages my people have combated *tsuris* with food. Mountains and fields and oceans of potato pancakes, brisket, chicken in the pot, stuffed derma, stuffed cabbage, chopped liver, sturgeon, herring, kasha, kreplach, and kugel have fallen to our suffering. It seems illogical that food will help problems of the spirit, until you start shoveling it in and feel it begin to work. Food is life, and perhaps the heavy, starchy ethnic food of the Jews is the most sustaining of all. Rather than appetizing or other Hebraic fare, however, tonight my upsets will be soothed by regional Italian cuisine. As I round the corner off Lexington, I can already see a few people at the restaurant's door. I wade through the waiting couples and come face to face with Rez. He seems less than happy to see me, and is perhaps surprised that I have arrived at such an unusually early hour. I see right away that my usual table is taken. Louis Veith, an aging queen wearing his cravat and plaid blazer, sits there with his steady boyfriend, a young muffin with whiter than white teeth and wavy hair. After what I have gone through today this insult does hardly register. At least he is a regular. "Oh, hello-a Mr. Grubman. So nice to see you, but we didn't expect you-a so early," Rez greets me.

"Rez, how are you?"

"I'm-a so sorry, but Mr. Veith is at your table. You want-a sit in the back, or wait?" He smiles broadly. I scan his face for hint of sarcasm or derision. I detect none of course, as Rez is quite professional.

"I'd prefer to sit now if you can swing it," I say. With a hail of gestures and karate-chop consonant Italian from Rez, a small table is arranged for me in the back corner. I feel conspicuous as I walk through the restaurant. Heads turn as I make my way through the narrow aisles of chairs and closely placed tables. I wonder just how many diners have perused page 7 today. With their eyes upon me, it feels that they all have. It is my second solo visit to Tre Fiori in two nights as well, and this runs counter to the image I have endeavored to create. It is

171

too late now though, and I can only look forward to a dish of *fussili crudiaola* as consolation.

Once seated, I wait a moment for Rez to come take my order. Instead of Rez's attention though, I receive Massimo's less polished brand. He begins to tell me of specials, which I interrupt to ask for *fussili longo crudiaola*.

"I gotta go and check if we got it," he tells me. This is the difference between Rez and a regular waiter. If it is Rez waiting on me I can order an elephant steak and he'll ask me how I want it cooked, while Massimo has to go check. He crosses Tre Fiori and speaks to Rez at the front podium, who instead of coming to my table to assure me I can have whatever I wish, merely acquiesces with his shoulders. Massimo, flying by my table for the kitchen says, "Yeah, we got it," and I am left alone again.

I look around the restaurant a bit, and toward the front by the window, I see the Flachs family eating in a celebratory manner. They are an established Jewish clan with their name on the wall of the Manhattan Public Library, and with several tall and handsome sons, sons-in-law, and grandsons to administrate their real estate holdings worth over $900 million. That must be the magic number—$1 billion, or close to it—and the family becomes established and respected. I watch several people passing in and out of Tre Fiori paying respects to the Flachs. I am a long way off at $100 mil. With my $100 mil I am still faced with lockjaw accents so tight I can hear the wood grain of the Mayflower in them, whispering to Rez that perhaps there is an available table somewhere else away from me where "the air conditioning isn't blowing so beastly hard," or a similar excuse. If *I* contend with this, it is nothing compared to what must be faced by a pair sitting across the room against the far wall.

172

There I see two lanky-framed black men, an unusual sight in Tre Fiori. The larger of the two, his head shaved bald, legs protruding uncomfortably from beneath the table, I recognize immediately. He is Ike Stanley, a power forward on the Knicks. The other one I do not know, but rather than that of another professional ball player, he has the aspect of a friend or hanger-on. Rez walks over to them and spends several minutes talking to them, straightening out the dishes on their table, pouring them more wine and water. He is giving them a basic Mediterranean ass-polishing. I, on the other hand, receive several stares and hostile glances from people all over the restaurant. Here I am, twirling my fat noodles around a spoon, the purveyor of erotica and a social outcast. I am Mr. Reprehensible, while the rest of the be-suited business community is so noble. The *garmentos*, who buy their cheap fabric and have it stitched up by children in Third World countries for pennies in order to sell it marked up several hundred percent—they are moral. The bust-out joint brokers and fund managers, who take other people's money, invest it in ventures whispered of by their friends, who then whisper other information back to the same friends, and take their cut no matter how much of their clients' money they lose— they are ethical. The LBO sharks, the real estate developers, the venture capitalists who make their vig every step of the way—they are all so clean in their silk ties and shoe shines. The attorneys, forget about it, the attorneys who write contracts, litigate, threaten, cajole, and sue until everyone, *everyone*, pays them—they are virtuous, they are Esquires. While I, who sells pictures of naked women—women paid for their time—and arranges sexual telephone contact between wanter and provider, I am the exile. How many of them all have called me to arrange for *entertainment*—what they

173

really mean is whores—for their sons' bachelor parties? I cannot keep track of how many, yet *I* am the pariah. The only ones I cannot take issue with are the doctors. Not dentists and chiropractors, no, they're a bit junior varsity, but Medical Doctors. I don't care how minor the treatment, nor how much they charge, the doctors ease suffering on some level, and no matter how much I may hate them on the golf course, I cannot consider them guilty of the same hypocrisy as the rest.

The line at the door grows, and I see Rez regretfully break off from the basketball player's table and re-take his podium in front. A moment later Ike Stanley's friend stands, unfolding himself from his small chair, and stretches. He is fairly thin, not the weight of a ballplayer, but perhaps 6'9" vertically. He strides through the restaurant, on his way to the men's room I surmise, when he veers and redirects his course toward me. I am uneasy for a moment, wondering what he might want with me, and cast a glance up front for Rez. I can always count on Rez to act as a buffer between me and people who like or dislike me too much. But Rez has stepped away.

"Excuse me, sir," the large man pulls to a halt before me, "I am so sorry to interrupt your dining experience, but allow me to introduce myself." He hands me a business card. "My name is Laront Stewart." I glance at the business card, which reads "T. Laront Stewart, Sports and Entertainment Representative and Facilitator" I take in his seemingly endless height. He looks like a willowy tree in an olive hued suit, and the back of my neck aches from looking up at him despite his leaning down considerably. "I understand you are Mr. Elliot Grubman, yes?"

"Yes, I am," I admit, "what can I do for you, T. Laront?"

"As you can see I am in Sports and Entertainment

Representation and Facilitation." He repeats the enigmatic phrase on the business card in a dulcet, overly precise manner. "I am proprietor of a catering and beverage concern, as well, but that is neither here nor there at the present time...Tonight, one of the key clients and friends within my ventures, is seated over there." He gestures toward Ike Stanley, once again enmeshed in conversation with Rez, who has miraculously reappeared on the scene. "My venture attends to a heretofore unresponded to need within the professional sports establishment—that is to say the area of post-competition entertainment of athlete-entities in a discreet manner. For a minor compensatory percentage, we do the difficult, at times unsung, work of arranging enjoyable recreation alternatives for players and celebrities of a certain strata, in a fashion that enables them to keep intact the precious integrity of their public relations images, per se." I am stunned at his ornate way of speaking. "Can you understand where I am coming from, my man?"

"No," I say, "I cannot discern what your reasons are for talking to me." It seems at any other moment in my life I would have responded simply 'no.' Perhaps, 'Fuck no,' if I were feeling flowery, but here I am, suddenly festooning my own speech with nonsense. Undaunted, Laront sucks at his teeth with a 'tsk' sound, and continues.

"We feel, that is to say, my principles and myself, as well as Mr. Ike Stanley, that a man such as yourself, who has inroads to certain desirable entertainment properties as a result of your business ventures within the publishing field, could be quite integral in what we endeavor to provide. That is to say, if you were willing to provide introduction to the lovely models featured in your magazine as evening hostesses of good will for certain professional athletes we are associated with, there could be a lucrative division of fees resulting from such

175

an arrangement." Despite the unusual way in which he presents himself, it is now fairly obvious what Laront actually does for a living. In the 70's he would have worn a large brimmed hat. The part that rankles me is that I am suddenly not safe from this kind of character, regardless of where I am.

"Go away, Laront," I say politely, "I can't help you. You've obviously mistaken my business for another— my man." His eyes flash angrily at my last words, and granted, it is a risk tacking them on, but he walks away from my table and toward the men's room. At his departure Rez and Stanley look over at me in time to see me crumple the business card and toss it into the bread basket. Massimo floats by and I manage to catch him by his apron string. "I'll take my check now, and make sure Rez is the one who brings it to me," I say forcefully. Moments later Rez stands in front of me.

"Was everything-a okay, Mr. Grubman?" Rez inquires solicitously.

"The food was fine, as always," I allow, "but I'm not too keen on some of the customers around here tonight."

"Well, we have in a Mr. Ike-a Stanley, from the Knicks. He's not-a bad, eh," Rez patters.

"I'm talking about some of the other *types,* Rez, do you know who I mean?"

"Perhaps-a Mr. Grubman, but you know in the restaurant-a business, you must-a take care of everyone." He supposes he will discourage me from buying Tre Fiori with this line. I wonder if *he* has had Laront approach me for this very reason. Rez smiles, his words are easy, his manner smooth and unconcerned. This disgruntles me further.

"No, no Rez, I think that we will have to be more careful about who we allow in when I become involved," I say, nodding at the decision within my words. "You remember where we left off don't you? By the way, I'll appreciate you holding my regular table for me in the future." Just then Massimo comes up on Rez's flank and speaks some muffled words into his ear about a certain couple wanting a table. They both look up to the front of the restaurant, where the line of customers has grown long, and swelled out the door. Rez glances back at me, and then turns to Massimo. His face grows red and his words bark out at the waiter in a way I have never heard him speak before.

"I don't care if it's-a Jesus Christ come down off-a the cross! No goddamn-a tables available before 9:30!" Several customers whip their heads around to locate the source of the outburst. Seeing the ever-silken Rez flustered and screaming like any other spaghetti peddler gives me an undeniable rush of pleasure. I cannot stop myself from discovering the joy in another's struggle. I put some cash in the check wallet and stand up.

"I can see you're busy, Rez," I say genially, patting him on the shoulder, "we'll take this up tomorrow." With that I smooth my suit and walk airily out of the restaurant, my mood having suddenly lifted.

There is hardly any traffic on the streets outside. It is the rarest of things—a quiet night in New York—and I decide to walk the few blocks to my apartment. Despite the way things turned around at the end, my recent meal at Tre Fiori has left me more concerned than ever about the newspaper story. I always considered those who looked down on me and what I do for a living as prudish or merely jealous of my money. Perhaps a restaurant full of successful people though, people who have some money, looking down on me is evidence that I traded too much respectability for my fortune.

I turn the corner and stop. I am across from the townhouse that was formerly my home. I stand looking for a moment at its crenellated white marble facade. The house is dark, no motion within. I do not know what I hope to find inside, even as I begin crossing the street toward it. The mention in the newspaper is as unacceptable as Andrew turning his back on Judaism, and I have a notion I will deal with the leaky staff. Lauren must know which of the help has slipped the information to Brancato, if not, I will talk to them myself and figure it out. It may be too late to change my business, but I can at least limit who learns about it in the paper. If I even sense a hint of a possibility that one or more of the staff have talked, I will fire them and pack them out of the house forthwith.

I reach the door, a large, black-painted, oaken thing, with a thick brass circle hanging from its center for knocking, and consider how to best interrogate the help. During our time together, in our heyday, Lauren rolled with six of them and an affected son of a bitch named Jerome who ran the show. I am gone now and he is still in charge. As much as I do not like dealing with him and his precious ways, I have to admit that his tart tongue kept the staff jumping and that the house was always filled with food, drink, and fresh flowers. We had countless staffers in and out the door before we settled on our semi-permanent line up. There were two cooks—Mason and Dana—a West Indian couple who went back to their home island, Tobago I believe, some time last year. We had two part-time nanny's who alternated taking care of the boy. They became unnecessary several years back when he started school. Then there are the maids. There were three as of my moving out, I'm not sure if Lauren has kept all of them on. One is a fat, blonde-haired Peruvian named Blanca. Lauren did the house in a style that is a direct imitation of the grand salon of Fontainebleau, Napoleon's old Chateau, and it takes quite a maid to keep it clean—this maid is Blanca. She is a cleaning machine. The others, her support staff, are a pair of small, dark sisters or cousins from the Philippines called Lady and Sweetie. They are neither. They stalk the house with their short, severe haircuts, doing little work and intimidating whomever they can. Even Jerome stays away from them. They are my lead suspects as the source of the story. They acted vindictively toward me right from the start, before they ever had reason to, and selling or giving a story about me to the papers seems like something they would love to do. The only reason we kept them around in the first place is apparently they didn't steal. Whenever I complained about the size of our staff, I was informed by Lauren, in no uncertain terms, that they were necessary due to *my* unceasing demands.

I fish in my pocket for my keys. I may have lost title to the place in the divorce, but I never did hand over my key. There is a good chance Lauren has changed the locks, or that once she sees me inside she will have them changed. Using my key is a one-time only deal, and I think about knocking. I swing the brass ring once, tentatively, and it makes a clacking sound. Nothing stirs inside. Knocking on the door to a house I once owned makes me fee wretched, so I quickly slip the key into the lock and let myself in.

I step into the foyer, which is separated from the main front hall by another door, and try to get a sense of the air of the house. The burglar alarm keypad on the wall in front of me blinks green inactive and the place is quiet. The polished Cippolino marble beneath my feet is without vibration, and I feel the staff in slumber in their wing. It doesn't seem as if Lauren is *entertaining* tonight.

179

It will be uncomfortable if I am wrong though. Half holding my breath, I put my hand on the cool brass handle and let myself into the house proper. I hear no sound.

The foyer is dimly lit by a crystal chandelier overhead and I see myself reflecting vaguely from a large antique mirror on the far wall. I take a few soft, automatic steps to my right, toward my study. I don't know what the hell I am so frightened of and begin walking briskly, letting my heels ring adamantly against the floor. I swing open the door to the room that was once my retreat. It is now empty of anything that would identify it as mine. The bookshelves have been cleared of my books, and now house only two sets of encyclopedia, an Oxford portable dictionary, which is gigantic despite its name, and a few other reference books that Andrew uses. An old crayon drawing of his is still taped to the edge of a high shelf. My desk and chair remain in the room as always, yet they have become ghostly to me as I have not used them for so long. I am beset by the temptation to plunk myself down into my green leather swiveller and to let it envelope me in sensations of the past, but I do not indulge myself. Instead I move to an old wooden wall unit and open up its doors. Inside is my mini-refrigerator, and a VCR. The television that once resided in there has been moved. There are several old and dust covered video cassettes pushed back into the depths of the cabinet. I fish around amongst them until I find one without a label. I forgot to bring it with me when I moved, such was my new state of freedom then, and I did not dare ask Lauren to send it to me for fear she watch it and then destroy it.

I put my briefcase on the desk, pop open the gold latches and place the video tape inside next to the epic of me playing polo. Shutting the crocodile skin lid, I do not bother spinning the combination lock as my case never leaves my hand. I turn around, my small-scale Watergate complete, and find my heart pounding lightly. The video is a lurid one of Lauren and I wedding our own sexuality, still alive nearly a decade and a half ago, with the then new technology of home video. I have vivid memories of that night but no memory is as vivid as a video tape.

I had just returned from Florida, having put my mother's affairs in order after her death, when that important night occurred. Is it possible that all of a lifetime's love can have truly existed only for one night? It seems so, as that night was more intense and captivating than any other year's worth of nights combined and multiplied by three. That night, I recall, our love was volcanic. Lauren worked my grieving cock, milked the damn thing dry, rocked it until it burst and I shuddered in *petit mal* seizures of pleasure. Afterwards—I believe we had turned off the video camera—we spoke to each other as tender lovers should, as we never had prior and never have since. We said we were each other's religion, the only thing in which each of us could have faith. We watched the tape only a few other times over the years, trying unsuccessfully to conjure the feeling of that lost night. We never did film ourselves again. I look to the spot where the television used to be, its absence being the only thing that keeps me from playing the tape and masturbating to it slavishly right where I stand.

I walk out of the study, and having taken everything with meaning for me from it, close the door behind. I look down the long corridor toward the kitchen, past which lies the servants' wing. I consider going there, charging in with my accusations and threats, but a greater purpose pulls me toward the staircase instead. I desperately need the infusion of sex-love feeling that exist only in Lauren's presence, perhaps I will catch her unguarded and be able to seduce her. Then, afterwards, once her emotions have come into play, I will ask her to help me talk to Andrew.

I start to climb, the plush royal blue carpet beneath my feet muffling my steps. At the first landing I stop and prepare to push in the brass rod that keeps the carpet runner down. The rod has been loose for years and it has become my habit to put it back into place each time I walk up. Tonight, though, I see that it is no longer loose, that it sits properly fastened against the base of the stair. This causes me to realize that the usually squeaking door to my study now swings quietly as well. Either Lauren has become more thorough than ever with the house upkeep, or someone *handy* has been hanging around. The idea curdles the *fussili* in my ballooning gut. I continue up to the second floor, toward the bedrooms, just one step ahead of dread at discovering Lauren upstairs with someone. I no longer belong here, yet I plunge in deeper. It was so miserable at the end, my living here, I have no idea what drives me.

At the top of the stairs I see the door to Andrew's room is shut. No light peeks from beneath it. I would like to once again look upon his sleeping form, as I did as a young father, but I am not that, and he is at school. There, on a hallway table, is a covey of family photos in sterling frames, mine no longer among them. I see a recent photo of Lauren and realize her lips have been taken back down to nearly their original size. She had them plumped up with collagen on two separate occasions, and now, as fashion has dictated the bee-stung look is no longer quite as sought after, she has had some removed. She seems to have progressed to a near spiritual level of plastic surgery. As the Buddhists believe in millions of incarnations of a single soul, she has gone through at least a dozen with her face.

182

I turn to walk the hall toward her bedroom, when I literally bump into Lauren coming down the stairs from the third floor. She carries a giant brown Luis Vuitton hat box embossed with gold LVs in front of her, and she accidentally knocks me in the chest with it.

"Elliot, you look terrible, what's wrong with you?" Lauren asks mildly. If she is surprised to see me in the house it is hardly apparent.

"You look great as always," I say. She is beautiful in a cream-colored satin dressing gown over champagne silk pajamas and black velvet slippers that have her initials embroidered on them in gold spaghetti lettering. I must be the only one in the world who ages.

"Are you sick? You look greenish—"

"I came to find out the origin of that newspaper item," I say, scrutinizing her face.

"Oh, that...," she smiles vaguely.

"Yes, that. Can you believe it?" I feel my blood start to agitate and my face grow hot.

"I know, it was hysterical..." She actually chuckles lightly.

"Hysterical?" I try to process her reaction. "You mean you found it funny?"

"Yes, very. Oh, come on now, Elliot, don't be so insecure. Nobody cares about what they read in the papers, and I'm sure your little friend isn't that little. How old is she anyway?"

"Who, Yvonne?" I ask foolishly.

"*Yvonne?* Is that it?" Lauren says with glee. I am angry at myself for giving away details unnecessarily. "How *foreign*. Andrew's told me so much about her."

Of course, I remember, she must know all about Yvonne after my ill-advisedly bringing her and my son together. It was a short trip to the Bahamas before this school year started. Yvonne had no compunction about going

183

topless on the beach in front of him. Rather than enjoy this, as I thought he might, he was intimidated by her, repulsed. Who would have picked my boy to be so demure, to have such class and standards? I thought they would get along well since both are young, but I suppose Andrew hasn't yet reached the age when women will hold interest for him.

"She'll be twenty this fall," I volunteer weakly.

"There, you see? C.B. had it all wrong."

"C.B.? What, do you know him?"

"We've met. We're friendly. You can't miss him out on the party circuit," Lauren says offhandedly. It's as if she is trying to be casual, but her effort betrays her. It makes me wonder just exactly how much she has to hide.

"I don't fucking believe this..." I gape, suddenly aware that it was not Jerome at all who leaked the story.

"He's a horrible writer, but an interesting sort nonetheless." Do I smell a whiff of gorgonzola in the air of the house? I peek behind her toward the bedroom door, half expecting to see his greasy face and beady eyes peering out from the darkness there. Perhaps I am experiencing a psychosomatic episode. After my mother's death there were times I was visited by her smell. The night she died I smelled her around me after leaving the hospital, though when I checked my skin and clothes directly they had no particular odor. At the time, I concluded I was being visited by her spirit. I shake off the impression of Brancato's gamy stink as imaginary.

"Why are you here, Elliot?" Lauren finally grows suspicious. "How did you get in?"

"I knocked, the door was unlocked," I say unconvincingly and then turn it back on her, "What were you doing upstairs?" Only guest rooms and closets are up there. I look up the stairs behind her to see if anyone follows.

"Clearing out the storage. I'm packing to move."

"Selling out, huh? After all the money we spent making this place like fucking Versailles." I know it was Fontainebleau she copied, but my intentional little inaccuracies drive her batty.

"Please, Elliot, the language. I can't carry the maintenance and taxes on a place this size with the money I have left now," she says. My heart is blue for her and her mere $15 million plus child support. "And it wasn't Versailles, Elliot. It was Chantilly," she says sweetly. She is always the one with the last word, always able to one-up me.

"Still the clever one, Lauren" I say, dismayed.

"I don't know what you mean, now if you'll excuse me..." My time is apparently up. Her tone is maddeningly distant. It is so easy for her to fob me off, I am in wonder at her capacity for feeling. At least I am in wonder at her feeling for me. I look at her and think of that night, the one I hold video record of in my briefcase. It makes me choky in the throat.

She stands at the top of the stairs and watches me descend. I look back and see her there, arms crossed. She calls out to me, "Elliot?"

"Yes?" I ask, leaning back the way I came. I see her face poking over the landing. I hope she will say something conciliatory. Even light and friendly from her would be music to me now. "Do you want to have a drink?" I nearly ask. It is on the tip of my tongue. I do want to stay here tonight, with her. If we start with a drink maybe I can arrange it...

"What was that fiasco up at Dexter all about?" She can bring a closing feeling of darkness upon me like no one else. I can try to be my best, or do my best for myself and others, but when she speaks, a realization of all my failures arrives fully formed. She has this power and it is past time I just admit to myself that it crushes me. A sense of one's futility can provoke either sorrow or anger—for me there is only one choice.

"Like I told Andrew, we *will* meet with Rabbi Weiss when he's home," I say. "I *will* see him bar-mitzvahed." The words crawling out from between my clenched teeth, lest I ruin my plan

"Shh," she says, putting a finger to her lips. She moves down the stairs past me and leads me into the living room. The room is illuminated by only a green-shaded banker's lamp resting on an antique secretary. I have a moment's irrational hope that her desire for privacy is a good sign for my plan of seduction. She closes the large French doors behind us.

"Elliot, I'm talking about our son's well being, not his religion."

"They're one and the same. At least they will be one day." My jaw aches from the high-tension crush of my mandibles, but I believe I sound intelligent, nearly philosophical about the matter.

"Well, I hate to tell you in this way, but Sunday he's undergoing his conversion." My knees turn rubber at this and I sit down before I fall. I sink into the cushions of the sofa and allow my head to loll back and gaze up at the gilded coffered ceiling twenty feet above.

"The service will be held at St. Paul the Apostle's on 59th and Columbus..." she continues, unsure as to the nature of my silence. I wonder why she will lower herself to going to the West Side, but then recall her stories of this great man, Father Harris, who was the priest there. Back when I first knew her she could only afford to live on that side of town. "I suppose you won't want to see it, but it's only *appropriate* to invite you," she says resignedly. Poor Lauren, so beleaguered from dealing with the world of motherhood and all the martyrdom it entails that even being *appropriate*, the highest of her priorities, is taxing when I am involved.

My eyes roam around the room and see nothing out of place, except a man's suit jacket hanging over one of the regency chairs. It has been carelessly tossed and I see the label inside the lapel. It is from Banana Republic. *Please*.

"He's here I assume." I say of the jacket's wearer.

"Upstairs, on the phone with Andrew," she motions above. I am disgusted by the intrusion, beaten utterly by it.

"Can I speak to him?" I ask, meaning Andrew.

"You'll talk to him this weekend, if you come to church."

"Fine," I concede for the moment, searching for calm. "They get along well then, Andrew and him?" I cannot bring myself to say his name.

"Yes. It might surprise you, but he always counsels Andrew to be open, to get along with you."

"*He* counsels..." I shake my head. "I suppose I should go up and thank him." Lauren ignores this.

"Don't be juvenile. He respects Andrew, and Andrew respects him as a *friend*," Lauren intones.

"Oh, what new age bullshit," I spit. My calm never seems to last long when my ex-wife is involved. Lauren is ruffled and it appears she's considering giving me the old heave ho'. My knees are near the coffee table, the same one that I once poured a shopping bag full of money on. With all the decoration and renovation, this one piece managed to remain from the beginning. It is the only thing that survived from those days. The proverbial days of wine and roses, and cash. The thing about Lauren and I is even our best days had costs. High costs. Now, though, all I have are the costs but not the days. I pat the couch next to me, and, a concession, Lauren

187

seats herself there. I stare at her golden hair for a moment, until it is too painful and then force myself to look at the Rothko hanging above the oversized fireplace across the room. His modern style and the mauves and rusts and purples do not go with the room technically, but a six figure painting really goes with anything.

I signal toward the cheap suit jacket again. "So are you taking this seriously?"

She looks at me for a moment and sighs. "I don't know. I don't even know what 'serious' means anymore. I don't know how much I'm ready for. It's just a good-company thing, and he has an amount of self-possession—not based on wealth or anything like that—which is so *un-New York*. It's refreshing. It allows him to just be *with* me..."

As much as I feel her words are affected nonsense, I see, for the first time and too late, that I have been wrong all along about Lauren. She is neither easy nor difficult to impress, as I have long thought. Rather, she does not want to be impressed at all. She simply does not want to be poor or alone. She never did.

"Oh, Lauren...Don't you know I love you," I wail suddenly and dramatically. Her eyes bulge in aversion.

"It's not love, Elliot, it's panic." Her words hit me like a body blow. I feel my senses reeling from too much understanding all at once when there has long been none. I discern clearly for the first time that she despises me, and it is *this* about her that appeals to me so much. It is a staggering realization about her, about us, about myself. It always comes as a surprise to me when an avalanche of real emotion rains down inside me. When feeling breaks through the many walls that have gone up within me brick by brick. Tonight is no exception. I am caught unawares as the urge for tears comes strong as a shore breaker. I know it is wrong to bring my sorrows to Lauren, for she is only a part of them, but I am a selfish animal in matters of my own release.

I come apart into a good, hearty, disastrous, epic, heaving, purging, blood-cleansing, lung-wrenching, wheezing, mournful, bowel-clutching fit of sobs. I surrender to it completely, blubbering and slobbering. The misery and pain floods out of me in a torrential, cleansing stream. I cry and drool and wait for Lauren to comfort me, to please comfort me. When she does not, when I see her pose of cool reserve through the watery sheet of my tears, I shudder anew in a fresh spate of agony and sorrow. I would hand over fifty percent of my assets on the spot for an embrace, for her fingers to run through my hair, for a mere pat on the wrist. I cry until I am wrung out, until I am as porous as a squeezed out sea sponge. It goes on until I have not a drop of spare moisture left in me for tear nor saliva. Then I begin to feel silly. I pull out my monogrammed Sulka handkerchief and mop myself off. I run the cool cloth all over the slippery surfaces of my face and brow. I work to regulate my breathing and straighten my clothes. I press down on my hair and put away my handkerchief. I allow myself one of these fits every twelve years or so when there is no avoiding it—and then I get on with things. Tonight I do the same. Wordlessly, I leave Lauren sitting on the couch, and creep out of the townhouse on my way home to a night of sleep or no sleep.

When I arrive at my building some time later, and I am not sure how long, for my walk home is circuitous and stumbling, Tommy, the doorman, greets me. Tommy is a lean and cadaverous American-Irish who fights the battle with the bottle. It is a sad thing to see his often clever wit slide into slurred speech when he has temporarily fallen from the wagon with a thud. Tonight he is okay though. He is well pressed and his face is only a rosy hue of pink and not beet red. "Hello, Tommy," I say as I move wearily by him.

"'Lo Mr. Grubman," he gurgles. He has a way of speaking from far back in his throat, as if he is afraid to let his words out. "Ms. Yvonne has been by."

"Really?" I stop. "How did she seem?"

"She looked beautiful, sir, but she looked like she'd been crying." I feel uneasy at his words, as if he says them for my benefit, to let me know he is aware that I too have been crying. Then I begin to doubt this is his intention. I stared into several reflecting glass storefronts on my way home and my face looked no different than it does at other times. Tears leave no real stain on me. Tommy naturally refers to Yvonne's running eye make up.

"Is that so? Did she say anything about coming back, any message?"

"No, sir," Tommy shrugs.

"If she stops back, buzz me and send her up." I give Tommy a hearty thwack on his uniformed shoulder and a healthy $50 for his trouble.

I move around my apartment for an hour or so, unable to sit still, to watch television, to make any calls. I pause and flip through a list of *Swagbelly* girls I have on hand, but calling any seems pointless, an activity from another life. I change into pajamas and a robe and sit down on my bed. I watch the videotape of me and Lauren twice through, and not only does it fail to inflate me, but the naked figures groping and writhing on the screen are so foreign and unrecognizable to me that they may as well be of another species. I don't even bother rewinding the tape before ejecting it from the machine and replacing it in my briefcase.

I am standing in the kitchen, staring at the refrigerator and drinking cold bottled water in great gulps, when the intercom sounds. It is Tommy downstairs telling me Yvonne is on her way up. I experience a moment's anticipation over her arrival. Will she be conciliatory, angry, erratic, morose? I have no idea what to expect.

I have not moved, my finger still on the intercom's 'talk' button, when I hear the doorbell ring. I breathe deeply and smooth my robe, then answer the door. Enter Yvonne, dressed in a Chanel suit, carrying an Hérmes bag, with strappy sandals by Prada on her feet. She is all fine fabrics in modest cuts, and well-made shoes that finish off the outfit and flatter her. Gone are the platform sneakers and tiny backpack. Gone are the ripped-knee jeans. Gone are the lime green mini-dresses. She is classed up. She can certainly take a cue. "Where have you been?" I ask, stepping aside and letting her in.

"I've been in church. I've been praying all of every day." Church. Fabulous. Suddenly it seems I have a religious order of Christian women and boys springing up around me. I should get a commission on all the business I'm sending over the Church's way.

"What have you been praying over?" I wonder. She can't have been praying over our fight. I don't flatter myself with having that kind of impact on a young beauty like her. Especially one who suddenly knows how to dress and carry herself. I am in no way prepared for her answer.

"Ellie, I'm late. I think I am with a baby." She begins to cry now, and that churning feeling—which has become near constant lately—starts to reverberate in the pit of my flabby dirigible of a stomach.

"But you—"

191

"Yes. And then the lesbians were out in front—"

"They were—"

"And I have no one—"

"Can't you—"

"Being so young—"

"There are things you can—" It seems neither of us can get a full sentence out.

"I would never kill my child by abortion. To do so is sin." This last bit brings us to a halt. I think for a moment, and try to gather myself. My life has just become messy. If there is one thing I endeavor to avoid it is mess. A man such as myself—not especially facile in matters of emotion, set in my ways, past fifty—I cringe involuntarily at a mess, and eventually come to resent those involved in creating it. Fear, cold and dark, unlike I have known it since I was young and poor, clouds the air in front of my face like breath on a winter day. "Who have you told?" I ask.

"No one. Just my sister in Karlstejn. And my doctor who give me the pregnant test."

"Your doctor? Forget your doctor. You're done with him. Tomorrow you see my doctor. He'll re-test you, then we'll see what happens."

"Tomorrow I go to Dr. Jameson?" Yvonne asks, her tone bright and nearly hopeful.

"No, a different guy, Dr. Bobby Gold. You see him first." She seems oddly disappointed at this. I wonder how she even knows Dr. Jameson's name. He's the obstetrician who delivered my son. A gentle and sure-handed man. I must have mentioned him to Yvonne. Dr. Bobby Gold, though, he's the man I can trust. "Now, Yvonne, I hate to say it," I continue, "but I have to at least ask. You're sure that it's—"

"Ellie, of course. Do you think—"

"I mean, yes, but. There were times—"

"We didn't use the protection, Ellie—"

"True, but I'm not. That is to say my—"

"I was not with any others." Her definitive words finally cut off the fresh round of stuttered half-statements. She begins a slow, forlorn bit of crying. I put my arm around her and pat her head. I don't really know what to do when someone cries to me. I was never much for the scraped knee or bumped head routine, or worse. That was Lauren's province. I never know whether I should I tell the crier everything will be alright, when maybe it won't. Will my insulting their intelligence really help matters? Should I try to *feel their pain?* Or will that just end up in my going under with them? This results in my just patting Yvonne's head and wondering.

Fuck, I curse myself. Why was I so sloppy about birth control? I figured my sluggish semen would keep me safe. It has for a long time. At the moment I have no choice but to trust her word about being with anyone else. I suppose I can trust her. But thinking about trust makes me remember another area where I now have my doubts. "Yvonne?"

"Yes, Ellie?" Her sobbing has abated, though she still speaks into my chest.

"Remember when you told me you were turning twenty this fall?" I ask hesitantly.

"Yes, when you told me you were forty-nine, what is it?"

"Never mind." Suddenly there are several lost years to account for between us. If she has possibly added to her age the years I have shaved off of mine, then we are both, but particularly myself, facing a good deal of trouble. I make a mental note to call Leonard Loeb first thing in the morning. I might have to forget about the Hamptons and look into a house next door to Roman Polanski's over in France where this kind of thing isn't so reviled.

Though I have to consider she might be telling me the truth, about everything, in which case I have nothing to worry about. Perhaps, the fact is, that I am the only liar among us.

I steer Yvonne into the kitchen, where my first instinct is to sedate her with a vodka and perhaps a valium. Just before I offer it, I realize this might seem particularly heartless since she might be "expecting." Instead I pour her some mineral water, and we stand there drinking together. I lead her into the bathroom and hold her hair while she brushes her teeth and washes her face. I watch as she slips into a set of my pajamas. Her naked body, which I now appraise with a cold clinician's eye due to the recent veritable detachment of my penis, shows no signs of heaviness or other change indicating pregnancy. What do I know about it though? I have watched my ex-wife go through pregnancy, true, yet I still have the strange sensation of actually knowing nothing about anything in life except how to profit in business.

Yvonne slips beneath the sheets and takes a curled up position on her side like a sad, floating shrimp. I sit down next to her and go back to my head patting. "Oh, Ellie, what will I do?" Yvonne moans.

"Shh, come on now. Don't cry, it isn't good for the baby." This seems to comfort her somehow, and finally she slips into sleep. I quietly leave the room and go off into my den where I call Dr. Bobby Gold at home.

"Dr. Bobby?"

"Yes. Elliot?"

"Right. I may have a problem." I briskly inform him of the situation.

I am greeted with silence. The silence lasts too long, but finally Gold speaks. His tone is devoid of human inflection. "Listen. Don't worry about it. Send her over.

Soon. I'll administer a pregnancy test. It only takes a few minutes. She's probably just late." His words, at least, seem fairly optimistic.

"And if she isn't?"

"Well. I can recommend some excellent clinics. Inside the city or outside. Cash. You don't even need to use a real name."

"She's religious, Dr. Bobby. She won't." More silence ensues.

"Hmm. Well, are you in love?" I am not expecting this question from Dr. Bobby. His question implies maybe I should marry her, or at least move her in and set up one of those "stable relationship with love child" situations that are becoming so popular for rich, older guys these days. I consider where this all leaves me. For quite some time I have held that for men in business their thirties are a time for finding the path one will take and setting out. One's forties are for rising in one's field. One's fifties are for consolidation of gains, for reaching the top, and making the big score if one is going to. I have made mine, back in my early forties no less. I could think about trying to take things to another level. To take a calculated risk, put up a good deal of my own equity and purchase my way into a mainstream publication or like investment. The idea of it seems daunting and exhausting, yet until recently I could have asked myself "what else have I got to do?" Except now I face teenage problems like unwanted pregnancy. I cannot seem to truly *progress*. The idea that being in love with Yvonne and having a family with her will lead me to salvation seems farcical, or far-fetched at best.

"Well, Dr. Bobby, she's a wonderful girl and I do care about her, but she's twenty. I'm fifty. You know?"

I can hear Gold rubbing his chin on the other end of the line. "Let's say the prego test comes up positive. I can put her up on the table and give her an exam. A little too far with the speculum and pop, whoops. A few days bleeding, I give her some methagene. You make sure there's no med-mal talk and—"

"Don't say anymore, Gold. 9:30?"

"Conference all day tomorrow."

"Shit."

"Day after, 9:30."

"Yes."

As I lay in bed next to Yvonne, awake all night, I hear her stir from time to time. Her sleep is troubled and her dreams obviously turbulent. At one point I look over and see her sobbing in her sleep. For a long time I am unable to move, to reach out for her. Finally, I force myself to extend my hand through the darkness. My palm contacts the flat of her back, between her shoulder blades. I rest it there, and try to breathe.

Such is my preoccupation the next morning that I walk right by Taylor, who jumps to her feet as I stride into my office. I put my case down on the desk and slump down into my Arbus open-arm desk chair. Taylor is two strides behind me, her arms full of papers and mail.

"Hi, Mr. Grubman," she pipes, sensing my heavy mood, nervous I may lash out at her.

"Taylor. What do you have for me?" I sigh. I pay her and I direct her. I order her about, and punish her. But I am fair and just with her as well. I have no reason to exact my frustrations and concerns on her. She smiles back at me in relief. She hands me a list.

"Your calls. Leonard Loeb called, so did a Mr. Hyde from the District Attorney's office. Ken Feinstein is looking for a check. Mercedes Benz of Manhattan needs a lease payment on Yvonne's convertible. Rabbi Weiss's secretary is requesting details on the bar mitzvah. A Colonel Darby called and says he needs 'fifty thousands dollars more for a top notch mare he has found.' The Dean's Office at Dexter also wants a check." Everybody with their hand out or bad news, like usual.

"Another day at the office, huh Taylor," I sigh stoically.

"Uh, yes, Mr. Grubman," she agrees reluctantly. I pop open my case and distractedly pass her a videocassette.

"Have a dozen copies of this made, I'll give you a list where we'll send them. It's me playing polo."

"Okay," she says, unimpressed.

I pick up the Post and the Wall Street Journal from my desk. I want to read the Journal first. I try hard to fancy myself one much more concerned with the stock market and the state of business than other foolishness, but I cannot help myself today. I flip to Brancato's column. The bastard has taken another shot at me. The piece is a blind item, thank goodness, but on the heels of the last one I don't think many people are going to be wondering about whom he is writing.

Guess Who?

Which prominent big-bucks smut peddler, in the news of late, is rumored to have a young girlfriend—a mere child herself—with child, while his ex-wife is busy putting the old family house on the market and abseiling away in her free time?

As I sit and read it, I am no longer angry. I am way past angry. I am also through fucking around with this oily,

197

old shoe-smelling *gavon.* "Taylor!" I bellow. She rushes to my door and seeing me holding the paper, her face goes ashen. "Get me Abraham Katz on the phone." Without a word she hurries to do my bidding.

I, surprisingly, am not the most successful graduate of Tilden High, class of 1963, but second behind Abraham Katz. Katz is a giant in publishing—so called legitimate publishing. There are no more than ten people in the City, not counting the mayor, who can get right through to Abraham Katz on the phone. The fact that when we were young Katz was the intellectual type, and no kind of athlete, and that I did my best to look out for him back when that stuff mattered is the reason I can reach out to him. For certain outer-borough guys these bonds last long.

"Katzie? It's Elliot." Though he takes my call, we do not have tons to say to each other.

"Grubbie, how are you?"

"Getting too much tough ink in that fish wrapper of yours."

"I seen it." Katzie can speak three languages, but when it is me on the horn, Brooklyn is our *mama loshen*. I picture him over there at his office. The presses of one of the city's beloved organs rolling beneath him. His life is like a movie, the way he is mentioned favorably in all the society pages. He was appointed special envoy to Israel a few administrations ago. He is the rarest of things—the respected Jew. And rich, whoa-boy. He is as rich as God, while I am mere Pharaoh next to him. The fact I can get him on the phone swells me up.

"Do me a favor Katzie, can the greaseball."

"Why Grubbie? He'll just end up working across the street—"

"He's that popular?"

198

"He's getting there. And then I wouldn't be able to control him."

"You call this control?"

"You shoulda seen what he wanted to write."

"I'd hate to have Lenny Locb get involved."

"Christ, Grubbie, don't do *that* to me."

"Well..."

"Whatta ya want me to do, retraction and apology?"

"Can him."

"Come on Grubbie, have some *rachmones*."

"He don't have none."

"And his lawsuit?"

"Send me the bill."

"Suspension?"

"Do what you think is right."

"'Bye, Grubbie."

"'Bye, Katzie."

I sit in my office until late in the evening, trying and failing to develop answers for my situation with Yvonne while working, signing the check authorizations and checks themselves going out to the many people who want them from me. I do not take lunch, and as the day ends I turn off my office lights, put on my telephone headset, and return calls like a blind air-traffic controller. I am soul sick over my spate of worries. I need to make something right, but I do not even know where to start.

"What about Ken Feinstein?" Taylor asks over the intercom.

"Call him up. Remind him I quit smoking cigars, that should drop the premium," I instruct her. A few moments go by and Taylor appears in the doorway. "He wants to talk to you." I press the blinking light on my telephone panel.

"Kenny," I am cold.

"Elliot, how are you?"

"Fine."

"Listen, if you want the binder to go into effect, we need that check."

"I think you can do better on the premium, can't you, Kenny? Someone can."

"Sure, if you want to undergo an exam, they'll run all the tests. Do some blood work. They're very accurate."

"Is this about cigars? I haven't just cut down, I don't smoke them at all."

"I see. Good for you. One less vice, one more step on the road to heaven. Also enzymes, there's a test for that. I heard about an incident up on a basketball court..."

"But we're bindered as soon as you receive the check?" I inquire. "Is that what you're saying?" I can change gears fast when I need to.

"Right." What you want in an insurance man is an ethical guy, but not too ethical.

"I'm sending you a check for $135,000."

"Thanks, Elliot. The balance to be paid out?"

"Thank *you*, Kenny." I disconnect him. Fuck you, Kenny. "Taylor, have Grabow send a check for $135,000 to Kenny. Have him mark it paid in full." Miss a few tennis lessons, Kenny. Go to Europe on the American Plan.

I return Colonel Darby's call. I reach him at a phone in the barn down in Palm Beach. "Darby, what's the good word?" I say. I picture him there in his oversized pants, his reddened bald pate shining enthusiastically.

"Mr. Grubman, sir, I've been finding suhm t'rrific ponies for us. They're on th' way to South'ampton."

"Very good. There was a matter of some more money?"

I ask him. Already I am feeling a little less interested in polo than I had been two days ago.

"I tried one little Argie mare. She won runner up fer best playin' pony during the Gold Cup. She's fast, she turns smooth as can be, and she stups on a darm and gives ya narn pennies change."

"This is clearly some horse, Cuh-luh-nel, but another 50K already?" Even I have limits.

"You'll be playing three goals on her by the end of one season," he says crisply.

"I see. When *do* we play?" I wonder.

"Soondays air game days, while Saturdays air fer practicin'. Startin' next month. We can scrimmage Tuesdays and Thursdays as well, if ya can make it out from work. It's a bit of a drarve from the city on a weekday."

"Yeah, no problem," I say, and then scream out to my underling. "Taylor, get me a Realtor out on Long Island. I need a five bedroom house in Southampton with enough lawn to land a helicopter."

"Very good, sir. *Very good.*" Darby is excited at catching me as a customer. I don't fuck around.

"What kind of vehicle will you require for the summer?" I ask.

"I'm comfortable in a Rangey Rover, Mr. Grubman..." Darby says hesitantly. Hell, I'm not *that* easy.

"You want four-wheel drive? I'm comfortable with you in a Cherokee, now hold on for my girl, she'll get the check out to you. Taylor, pick up line one!" I shout.

My next call is to Leonard Loeb.

"Len, what's the good word?" I say again. It seems to be my 'opener' for the day.

"Elliot."

"Yes, Len?"

"Elliot."

"What already?"

"I've spoken to Hyde from the D.A.'s."

"What about? I have him on my call sheet—"

"*Don't call him,*" Leonard blurts frantically, then calms down. "They've been poking around regarding the news story."

"Yes, Lenny?"

"They're considering an investigation for possible statutory—"

"*An investigation.* Are you serious? Based on unattributable gossip?" I feel my pulse racing staccato in my chest.

"I know, I know. I threatened them for even thinking about it."

"What else can *we* do?" I really want to know.

"How old is she, Elliot? If I can assure them she's of age, they won't proceed. Do you know? *I* can't give my word unless *you* assure me." When Leonard Loeb retreats from his stance as my lawyer and begins to protect himself, I become distinctly uneasy.

"She's nearly twenty," I say.

"Good. You have proof?"

What proof? She told me, what else should I do? "Sure, sure, Len. You've had dinner with her, you think they make 'em like that at age 13 for godsake?"

"I don't know how they make them, Elliot."

"Just take care of it. What else is there?" I wonder.

"I don't know, you tell me," he says pointedly. All of a sudden I am subject to scrutiny from all sides and all professions.

"That's it, for Chrissakes, that's enough for today," I breathe.

"Let me go then," Len says, ready to square things up for me.

"Buh-bye."

202

All the pressure has me looking for refuge. I look inward for escape, to the place that has always been haven for me. I try to conjure fantasy.

The Kneeler

That's the term I use when thinking about my second infidelity to Lauren. Five years back, I was sitting at my desk, much like this. Unlike the first time, when I was dying for some contact due to Lauren's pregnancy, the second time was pure weakness. Alicia St. Francis, maybe you've heard of her. She is now heralded as the 'porn queen of the millenium.' Back then she was unknown.

–Late afternoon. The executive sits at his desk. She, tall, lean, and blonde, appears at the door, lit in silhouette. A gap of light from outside peeks between her thighs where her tight skirt rides up high.

–She walks into the office, closes the door behind her, and crosses the room towards him. She drops to her knees, crawls the rest of the distance, slithers beneath the desk and takes him in her mouth.

–He has a wife and young son at home, but does not say a word, nor make a move in protest, although he has turned down this very scenario perhaps fifty times prior with fifty other women. His docility is a fact that much sickens him later, but does not stop him from reaching out and fondling her pendulous love globes.

–Hair flies wildly as she goes down smooth and easy. As he spasms to his conclusion, she bangs the back of her head against the unforgiving edge of the mahogany desk.

–The office, then done in a sparse, far-eastern style, has a fairly abrasive jute rug. The rug has eaten right through her stockings and she has large holes torn out of each of her knees. She is a pitiable mess when she stands up afterwards—make up destroyed, ripped hose, shredded knees, and bleeding head.

Many things are not right with the scene. Even my pictorial fantasies contain morals now, as well as the sordid earmarks of reality. She *had* showed admirable skill, yet not so much as her reputation these days would warrant. I ended up putting her in the magazine afterward, it was all she wanted. It was no problem. I basically want everyone around me to be happy in life, starting with me. I was fairly surprised when her pictorial in *Swagbelly* launched a distinguished career. Fortunately for me, floor work, and not tell-all books are her forté.

I touch my crotch wondering if anything is stirred from the memory. I come up with only a handful of expensive wool blend slacks. Panicking, I stab at the phone, dialing up Rabbi Weiss. His secretary answers smoothly. "Rabbi's study."

"Naomi?" I ask. I always write down the name of someone's secretary and address them personally, it makes them feel human, and they put my call through with more alacrity. "Elliot Grubman here, is the Reb in?"

"Just a moment please." I listen to the strains of "Sholom Aleichem" on muzak for a little while before I hear the booming voice of the Rabbi.

"Yes, Elliot, how are you?" Rabbi Weiss speaks with the authority of Moses. Not the sometimes unsure Moses from the Book of Exodus, but the imperious tone of Charlton Heston himself in "The Ten Commandments."

"Things have been better Rabbi, and yourself?"

"Do you have that information on Andrew's upcoming bar-mitzvah?"

"That's the problem, Rabbi, it's Tisha Bov come early. The kid wants to become a Catholic, but I would rather speak about it in person. Can you meet for dinner?"

"Calm down, Elliot, of course I'll meet you," he agrees and we set Tre Fiori as the place. It is a night like this when I really miss my old indulgence with Havanas. When I once might have enjoyed a soothing cigar, I now wait edgily until it is time to leave.

Tre Fiori

It is after 7:00 when I depart my office, and I hesitantly peek out through the lobby's glass doors to the street, should any protesters have decided to give it another shot today. There are none, just passing pedestrians, and I have my limousine waiting for me at the curb. Mamoo lets me into the car and I feel quite secure with my bodyguard and my suit.

"Take me to the restaurant, Mamoo," I direct.

"Yes, sear," my man smiles into the rear view mirror.

Soon we arrive on the narrow side street out front of Tre Fiori. The door to the restaurant is bustling with the Upper East side power crowd and I grow unaccountably nervous. I pick up one of the telephones and place the receiver by my ear, although I have no one to call at the moment. I wait in silence for several seconds, hoping to catch a glimpse of the Rabbi, until I am startled by the blast of a large truck's air horn. The horn sounds its impatience again, and I hear the diesel engine's rattling accompaniment. My limo is blocking traffic. I take a deep breath and open the door. "I'll beep you when I've finished, Mamoo."

"Vedy good, sear," he responds and puts the car in gear. I straighten my tie and enter the restaurant.

As I step inside Tre Fiori, my senses of sight, sound, and smell seem overly sensitive and ordinary stimuli exaggerated in effect. The place is darker than usual, and what light there is in the room is deep red. The music, Italian opera, is quite loud. For some reason there is much more 'atmosphere' at Tre Fiori tonight than most other nights. There seems to be much more odor in the air as well. While the fragrant aromas of rosemary, tomatoes, olive oil, and garlic usually stimulate my appetite and fill my mouth with anticipatory moisture, things are a bit too pungent now. I get a queasy feeling as I am overcome by the hot stink of cooked food. Perhaps I am overly hungry from skipping lunch, my stomach acidified, but as I look around at the half-filled plates in front of the other diners, a strange bubbling sensation takes place in my belly. My glance darts around the room, and the usually well-dressed clientele are shabby looking to me tonight. Instead of successful people dining leisurely, I am overcome by the impression that they are all a bunch of baleful, dead-eyed cows, heads bent over their plates, methodically feeding.

"Good evening, a-Mr. Grubman," Rez smiles, striding up to me and breaking my reverie. "We have-a your table."

"That's swell Rez," I say. "Listen, a holy man will be joining me this evening. Rabbi Weiss. You'll recognize him."

"Of course." Rez shows me to my regular table by the window. At last, a little respect. This is more like it. I take my seat and arrange myself at the table. The usual restaurant bang and clatter goes on around me for a moment before I see Rabbi Weiss appear at the door. He walks in and says his name to Rez, who makes a brief mark in his reservation book and takes the Rabbi's hand with a deferential bow. Rez's Canali-clad arm then sweeps out, showing the Rabbi the way to my table. I take in the figure Rabbi Weiss cuts. He is a reformed Rabbi and wears no yarmulke outside of temple. He wears a shiny suit, well-tailored, a gold watch, and a delicate, twinkling pinky ring. His gray hair is swept back smoothly. The buffed black cap-toe lace-ups on his feet march purposefully toward me. He looks much more like a successful *schmata* man than a humble Hassid. I stand and we shake hands. The Rabbi leans in and gives me a warm embrace and light kiss on the cheek. "How are you, *bubby?*" Weiss says, his powerful voice tuned low. I can smell an expensive lilac cologne on him. His hand is manicure soft.

"Such *tsuris* I have," I say, as we sit down.

As is often the case depending with whom I speak, my dialect is pulled inexorably in their direction and I affect their style. In this instance the Semitic side of my speech evidences itself.

"So, how are Lauren and Andrew?"

"Lauren's been dating this *shmendrick* climbing instructor and letting Andrew run wild."

The Rabbi shrugs philosophically. "So Andy doesn't want to be bar-mitzvahed," Weiss says, sniffing in skepticism, indifference, sympathy, and question all at once. "*Oy, nebech,* it's worse for him, you know." Words come so easily for Rabbi Weiss, he makes me immediately comfortable. In another lifetime he could have held a nightclub or Las Vegas showroom at his mercy. He could probably still pull it off in this life if he chose to. When he gives a sermon he thunders and lilts in concert with his particular theme, taking his audience, his congregation, along every step of the way. I remember back when I married Lauren. The ceremony was held outside in a lovely garden on Long Island. Since my father had long passed on, Rabbi Weiss walked me down the aisle. As we proceeded, he whispered, "It's not too late. We can make a hard left and be out of here. I have the fastest car, no one will catch us." I looked over and there was his Corvette, the license plate read 'REBBIE-1'. His words can almost be made out on the wedding video, and they removed any jitters I might have had.

"He's running from his heritage, but mostly from me," I lament.

"You know Elliot, his circumcision was when he was entered into the covenant and joined our people. He can choose not to observe, but he cannot choose to be other than he is." I snap the breadstick I have been playing with and dip an end of it into sundried tomato paste. I chew on it with pleasure-less vigor. "I think it best for you to remain a father to him now, and hope he comes around." Awfully moderate talk for a Rabbi. Weiss surprises me.

"I have no authority over him. It's maddening. And Lauren is no help. I want to just shake the kid and tell him to get these cockamamie ideas out of his head. I forbade him to become Catholic." Rabbi Weiss nods his head at my frustration.

"Elliot, obedience isn't what it once was. The days of Abraham and Isaac are long past. Would you have listened to your own father if his wishes were so against yours?"

"My father? Forget it, Rabbi. You didn't know him. There were some things I just had to do though. Duties and responsibilities as a son. My bar mitzvah was one of them. Why can't I demand a little respect from my son? I have to come to a lousy restaurant to get that? When one gets older, they're supposed to know better, get wiser about these things, right? So when is my wisdom going to come?" I'm not used to speaking with such self-pity and desolation, but with Rabbi Weiss it is possible. Talking with him is completely different than with Dr. Gerry.

"There is a saying Elliot, 'There is no wisdom without

210

kindness.' Just try to be kind to the boy. And Lauren. And yourself." I can only wonder at what he would advise in the Yvonne situation, but cringe at the idea of mentioning it. "As difficult as divorce is," he continues, "it is hardest on the children." He is no Talmudic scholar, but Rabbi Weiss's depth in these matters goes far beyond mine. I find myself unable to mount any real argument.

"So you're saying I just do nothing?" I shake my head at the idea as unacceptable.

"No, no. Vah, it has to be so black and white? Just don't do the *wrong* thing. No ripping of the lapels, eh?" He smiles broadly and pats my shoulder, then samples the fabric of my jacket. "Such a nice suit." His silver hair rises up and frames his tanned face as if a strong wind blew it there. "Just be a *mensch*." The waiter comes to the table then, a new guy I do not know.

"Shall we order, Rabbi?" I ask.

"You go ahead and enjoy, Elliot, I have to go back to the community center for a pot luck." We shake hands, and Rabbi Weiss motions me to stay seated, then he and his *chachma* disappear. I order a simple plate of spaghetti pomodoro. I am nauseated at the blanched and pathetic looks on the faces of those who blandly shovel in food all around me, and also painfully aware that I am dining in solitude yet again.

I choke down my dinner. The noodles are too *al dente* and clumped together, and the sauce tangy and sour, though I have no motivation to send it back or complain. When my meal progresses on to coffee, I notice that the lights have continued to dim incrementally and the music has grown correspondingly louder. As my steamy little cup of espresso is delivered, the wailing sounds of Placido Domingo boom throughout the normally intimate restaurant. Another voice, a loud and non-melodious one, begins to moan in live accompaniment to Placido. Several diners turn heads toward the source before jerking their stares back to their own business. I take a peek and see, tucked away in the corner, one of Tre Fiori's owners, Julius, a large forty-five year old man with a head full of his original black hair—the lucky bastard. My hand goes self-consciously up to my own artificially colored wiry mess. Sitting next to Julius is the singer, another hulking Sicilian type dressed in an excellent suit. I cannot be quite sure from this distance and darkness, but I could swear it is a Fulvanti. Whoever made it, it is several thousand dollar's worth of sartorial splendor. It is the color of a mako shark, not shiny though, with a steel blue and silver striped tie complimenting it. The tie matches the man's hair, which is styled in a fluffy pompadour and sprayed into place like a helmet. His skin is tan and glove-leather-soft looking. On his outstretched arm hangs the distinctive chunkiness of a gold Rolex Presidential, and several of his thick fingers are pinched behind the knuckles by large rings. This tenor singing along with Domingo is clearly a made man.

Rez descends on my table to give me my moment of customer's conversation. "How's-a everything here tonight?"

"Fine, fine, Rez. Isn't that Julius, the other owner there?" I gesture over to the table.

Without looking Rez answers. "Sure, Mr. Grubman."

"Who's that other guy he's with, the opera singer?" I wonder.

"That's Mr. Leonini. He's a partner too. We have-a lotsa partners. You want to meet with them now?" Rez asks casually. I look over at the pair. Five hundred pounds of hot-tempered Italian bulk between the two of them, with thick Mediterranean skin, raised on plum tomatoes and extra virgin olive oil, that does not cut easily in a fight. They are heavy of jowl and lip, their noses smashed down on their faces. Julius lights up a big black cigar that fills the room with a stench. Mr. Leonini belts out the final tragic words to some work by Verdi, virtually drowning out Domingo. Nobody in the restaurant says a fucking word, they all act like nothing is happening.

"Maybe later Rez, maybe in a little while." I turn my attention to my espresso.

"Very good, sir, whatever you-a like," Rez smiles and drifts off. My pursuit of an ownership position in Tre Fiori is over. I must be crazy, to do some of the things I do. Next time I see my waiter float by I ask him for the check. I pay it when it comes, and leave only a 20% tip. Any more than that does not seem called for. The restaurant clears out to half-capacity, and I am about to leave myself, when Rez comes over again. He picks up the check and my money, and nods with understanding.

"Rez, please sit down with me," I ask, and he does so. "Listen, I know some things about the restaurant business, more than you might think," I raise my eyebrows knowingly. "If you feel you don't want another partner, then I suppose I'm not interested in being involved either right now." Rez smiles broadly at me, and I feel that old current we used to share come back to life. I am beyond grateful for it too, such is my need for a friend right now.

"Sure, Mr. Grubman, let us just-a serve you for now. It is better this way. We're all be happy then."

"I'll just shoot for being #1 customer, try to knock old Judge Frusciante off his post," I joke.

"Ma, no, Mr. Grubman, *you* are-a the best. He is one of the worst."

"Really? He eats here every day though."

"Sure, but someone like-a you spends in a day what he spends in a week. He tips low and expects a free cognac everyday."

213

"You give it to him?"

"We have a bottle of Delamain filled with kitchen brandy. That is for him," Rez tells me conspiratorially.

"Get out of here. He doesn't notice?"

"He doesn't notice shit." Rez and I share a laugh. I am happy to be back on the inside. I do not even wonder what he says about me to other customers. After a few more minutes of banter I dial Mamoo's beeper with my cellular phone, his signal to come pick me up. As I leave the restaurant, Rez cheerfully calls after me, "All the best..."

Back inside the limousine, my mood has nearly begun to stabilize when I remember that Yvonne, and the state she's in, awaits me at home. As does her appointment first thing tomorrow morning. I feel my musculature, such as there is of it, my tendons and cartilage as well, contract. My skeletal system, unsupported, collapses in on itself too. Sliding across the large bench seat of the limo as we take a turn, I feel I am shrinking away to nothing in a literal sense.

I step into the apartment, leaving the lights off. I drop my briefcase and walk quietly into living room. There, resting on the sofa, is Yvonne's purse. I look at it for a moment, hearing Leonard Loeb's questioning tone in my head, then pick it up. I root around inside looking for her passport or driver's license, anything that lists her age. Something I suppose I should have checked many months ago. All I find is close to three hundred dollars in cash, a platinum credit card I gave her, and a video store membership card. I zip open an interior pouch and discover her license. My breath comes quick and shallow as I bring it up and read it. Her birthday is just as she said it was. She is nineteen, will be twenty soon.

Relief and a righteous sense of indignation flow through me for a moment. Then, in the dim light of the city that flows through the large window, I see that the print on the license is just a bit grainy, the resolution of her photograph a touch low-grade, and there is something asymmetrical about the state seal in the background. My stomach clutches in apprehension as I wonder if the license could be fake. I replace it and walk to the bedroom.

Yvonne is in bed, her face pure and relaxed in sleep. A sheer robe from La Perla, rests at the foot of the bed. The muted television flickers, tuned to the Lifetime channel. Face down in the middle of the bed, not far from Yvonne's hand, is a book, *The Day to Day Journal of Pregnancy*. I pick it up and turn it, and see it is open to week five. I read from it facts about the embryo. "Rapid brain and head growth continues. A primitive mouth appears. The arms and legs are tiny buds." I glance down to the bottom of the page, past more developmental information, where there is a quote from Elie Weisel. "*Once you bring life into this world, you must protect it. We must protect it by changing the world.*" I close the book and sit on the edge of the bed. I reach for the clock and set the alarm for 7:30, although I am quite sure I won't be needing an alarm to awaken.

The Morning

The morning comes upon me sleepless, but not tired. Gray light filters in the window shades, the tranquil unpeeling of another day. It is so quiet and unspoiled for a short while, until car alarms, engines running, bags and bottles being thrown, the hydraulic whine of garbage trucks, and honking horns rip the silence and smear it with activity. This activity will last for another eighteen hours straight, until it all rests again in anticipation of another chance, another early morning chance at peace. That is what each day is for a person— a chance at peace. Today I will have my own. If everyone in the world saw each new day this way, would peace emerge? Or would a sense of failure envelop us all by nightfall?

Soon Yvonne wakes, which prompts me to take an unsentimental and business-like approach to matters. "Come, come. Time to get up." Soon she is out of bed and the room is full of the ripping sound of nylon hairbrush on tangled hair and the hyper-fruit smell of cosmetic body products. I make inky black coffee and rustle myself into a suit of pure brushed wool armor. I bring in the papers from the hall and we sit at the dining room table dirtying our fingers with them.

Yvonne looks up at one point, both hopeful and lost at once, and tries to speak. "What if—"

"Yes, dear. I know. It will be fine," I say. After a few more minutes Mamoo rings from downstairs. We ride down in the elevator to meet him. Mamoo drives us the

216

few blocks uptown and east to the building that houses Gold's office. We pull up to the curb and Yvonne readies herself to go. I, however, suddenly feel that I cannot go along with her.

"Are you ready, Ellie?" she asks.

"Listen, Yvonne, I do have an appointment this morning. You're just going for an examination, so why don't we meet afterwards?" I hate the sound of my own voice. Yvonne goes white with fear, and looks at me pleadingly.

"You can't come with me?" she nearly begs. I steel myself and lean across her. I reach and open the car door.

"You go ahead, I'll meet you after. I'll be here by the time you are finished." I give her a perfunctory kiss on the cheek and nod her out of the car. I sit there and watch as she goes to Gold's office like a lamb. For several minutes I ride around the block in the limousine. I try not to think of what goes on up in the antiseptic doctor's office. I am driven past the building for the second time when suddenly I break out in a sweat of full panic. I feel sick at what I've done and lunge for the car phone. I call Gold's office and reach a receptionist I do not recognize. "Who's this?" I demand. It is not Kathy, Gold's usual secretary.

"This is Olga, who's this?" I hear back.

"I need Dr. Gold, right now," I say urgently.

"I'm sorry, he's in with a patient—"

"She's my patient!" I scream into the phone, as fear of the irrevocable washes over me. I throw down the receiver. "Stop the car, Mamoo," I command. I leap from the limousine and run back up the block towards Gold's building.

Inside the staid office building lobby, uncomprehending worker drones stagger around me. Waiting for the elevator is agony. I feel minutes tick painfully away, never to be seen again. Finally an elevator arrives, but two people step in with me. I jab the button for floor number eleven. They reach to press their floors. "Don't," I say. "I'll give you fifty bucks to let this be an express."

One of them, a skinny black kid, a messenger with wraparound shades and bicycle shorts says, "Serious?"

The other, a woman in a business suit frowns and presses floor number seven. "Get real," she says. She is hard core New York, and must be a mogul or have a rich husband. She takes her time exiting the car at her floor and I want to throttle her. At last the doors smoothly close and we resume our trip up. I get off on eleven, handing the kid a $50 bill.

He laughs at me and says, "I was going all up to six-teen anyway, but thanks, G." I hardly hear him as I tear down the hall towards Gold's suite.

My shoes slide to a halt on the slick marble floor in front of the doctor's walnut door. I nearly dislocate my wrist twisting the slippery brass knob, which is locked. I press the doorbell madly. Shortly, an aggressive buzzing sound frees the knob and I step inside. "Hello, Mr. Grubman," Kathy, the regular receptionist, now back at her desk, greets me. Behind her in a stack of file cab-inets I see a petite Hispanic woman, she must be Olga, collating an armful of color-coded folders.

"Hello, Kathy," I smile, and dart quickly past her desk toward the examination rooms. "Hey, you..." she shouts after me. I make the hallway and see the doors to Gold's four examination rooms. Small, clear plastic carriers hold files outside of three of the doors, and I take these rooms to be occupied. I stare at the doors and try to decide which room they are in. I hear Olga and Kathy getting together and coming after me. I look at the fourth door, it has an empty file holder. I know Gold's style—no charts, no records. I hit the door. I am right. Gold's back obscures the space between Yvonne's legs. The doctor turns toward me and Yvonne throws down the gown she wears to cover herself. She was already a bundle of nerves and my intrusion upsets her delicate equilibrium. She bursts into tears. Gold gives me an anxious and quizzical look.

"How is everything?" I question him as casually as I can. "I'm, ah, just so excited you know? I couldn't wait."

"We were just getting started..." Gold offers.

"Yes?" I ask.

"Yes," he nods.

"Then, you haven't—"

"No." I think we are both relieved. I know I am. Yvonne has now stood up and commenced shaking. I feel slightly sick as my adrenaline catches up to me, leaving a sugary taste in my mouth. I signal the door to Gold, throwing him out of his own examining room, and then try to calm Yvonne. I manage to stroke her hair this time instead of just pat it.

"Shh, shh. Take it easy. Listen, we'll make an appointment with Dr. Jameson next week. He's the right doctor for you. Don't worry, I'll take care of everything." I mean it too. I am craven and pathetic, but I have just learned I am not as small as I thought. "Come on, let's get you dressed and out of here," I say soothingly.

Back in the limousine I try to keep up a placid front, but inside I am jittery like I just swallowed a pot of espresso for what almost came to pass, and what will come. It is too early for a drink now, even a glass of wine to calm me down, so I do what I would not have even considered days ago. I direct Mamoo to 28th Street near Sixth Avenue, to Fabulous Smokes. I used to shop there sometimes, when my Punches were slow in coming from London. I speak to Albert, the owner. He is a paunchy guy with curly hair, who has a cigar sticking out of his mouth at all times. He takes me back into the humidor and shows me a small locked cabinet that holds his selection from Cuba. He has no Punch Double Coronas on hand, so I take a box of Montecristo Number 2's. They are solid cigars, torpedo shaped, with oily dark brown wrappers. The box costs me $500. We drive around and I smoke the first one, polluting the limousine with the sweet smoke of the Vuelta Abajo. Yvonne seems like she wants to talk, she has questions, but with the help of my big brown cigar, I am able to discourage most of the conversation. She leans far away from me, her head stuck out her open window for fresh air.

I finish my first smoke, throw the acrid nub out the sunroof, and light up my second. I see it is past 11:00, late enough to tell Mamoo to drive us to Tre Fiori. They have recently set up for lunch when we arrive.

"Good morning-a Mr. Grubman. So nice to see you Signora Yvonne," Rez greets us and then seats us outside on the terrace so I need not abate my chugging on the cigar. I slide two of the torpedoes into Rez's jacket pocket.

"We're twins now," I smile, signaling the pair tucked behind my handkerchief.

As for ordering, I skip the menus. Yvonne takes an asparagus salad.

"Do you have soy beans?" she wonders. Rez frowns no. She has read that soy beans contain all the amino acids, which she pronounces ak-cids, needed to synthesize protein.

"Bring me a *bisteca Fiorentina*, rare, lots of garlic lots of lemon," I say, "and a Macallan on the rocks. It is a glorious day with the sun sparkling down on our table. What an odd feeling, sitting here with my new family.

"Ellie, I don't want to talk too much, but have you ever thought of marrying again?" Yvonne is hesitant, but radiant.

"Yes, dear, you certainly don't want to talk too much," I agree.

"Would you at least think about it though?"

"Sure, I'll think about it." I'll consider anything.

"I would never make you go through a big wedding. You don't have to worry."

"I see."

"Nothing grahnd. Nothing bleck tie, you know? Maybe, perhaps something during the day. We could wear matching dahk suits with chocolate accents. Tasteful and appropriate," she continues. "I weel sign a pre-nuptial, of course. I want the child to learn about both our religions too, Ellie. He should know about being a Jew. This is important."

My steak arrives and I slice into it, magenta juice running across the plate. It is tough but tasty. My cigar was into the red zone and I'd finished my first scotch before I began eating, so I have quite a head on. I try to imagine myself actually marrying Yvonne. It is difficult to visualize. Maybe I'll grow into the idea. The inquiring glances and clumsy questions about 'daughter or date?' may now include 'child or grandchild?' Eventually I will become immune to the questions anyway. I do some calculations that leave me picturing myself attending the young one's graduation ceremony in a wheelchair, with Yvonne nearly the age Lauren is at now. I shake my head at this new world order.

My plate contains only fat and gristle by the time Rez comes to collect it and I re-light my cigar. The Montecristo is not half bad, perhaps an even better blend than the Punch.

"Ahre you going to staht smoking again, Ellie? I don't

221

think it is such a very good idea. I have to take care of you a little beet now," Yvonne informs me.

"That's right, dear. I may indulge in the occasional cigar. Don't you worry about it though, you just worry about taking care of yourself." I allow myself a glimpse in the rearview mirror of my mind, and recall the joyous day that Lauren was sure she was pregnant with Andrew. I was ebullient with thoughts of all I would do for her and the kid on the way. I was absolutely sure I would not commit the litany of poor fathering offenses my father did on me. I never hit my son, and never cheated on his mother in a blatant or extended way. I paid him as much attention as I could. I endeavored to understand him and his problems. So I succeeded in not doing as my father had done, but instead came up with an original list of mistakes with which to drive him from me. I have joined the great pantheon of fathers in this way.

I begin sipping on my second scotch when I discover that one problem with reflection is that it leads to more reflection. I can continue on with the single malts and the retrospection and end up like one of those war vets with a thousand-yard stare, or I can force myself to look ahead, to the future and the yet-to-be mistakes I will make with the new woman and child. I light my third Montecristo of the day, my blood roiling with nicotine, when I see a pudgy figure in black bounce down Tre Fiori's three stairs and come towards our table. It is Brancato, in a sweat, the brilliantine from his hair running down over his brow in a sheen it would take a squeegee to remove. He is not just fat with success around the middle like, for instance, myself. He is shambling and sloppy and all heavy nasal breathing with lack of discipline. I smile at his arrival.

"You son of a bitch...You son of a bitch," he sputters.

222

He wants to make things physical between us. He figures he is younger and stronger and he'll thrash me and then things will be evened up. He probably has visions of himself overturning my table and pummeling me, making me beg and cry, and him kicking me hard in my ass. There is no way in hell any of this will come to pass. I will not stand up and enter into this arena. I don't fight at a disadvantage. This is one of the key differences between Jews and Italians.

"Me?" I ask innocently, all sweetness and light.

"You think you can go around interfering in people's—"

"Hey, *goombah*," I interrupt, "*I'm* not the one interfering in people's lives. You walked into my office, remember?" Out of the corner of my eye I see Rez and two busboys waiting at the door just past Brancato. I'm covered here. I rest my hands across my own paunch. Yvonne looks at me and doesn't even seem nervous. She may be a teenager, but she is sharp and she knows who is in control.

"I've got a job to do. You have no right to—"

"Do you? Have a job, that is?" He says nothing and all of us hear his breath puffing in and out of his drooping nose. His close-set eyes sparkle in search of inspiration. I decide to help him out a little. "It's a shame about what happened, just when you finally got something right. Listen, I want you to take this," I remove a torpedo from behind my handkerchief and extend it toward him. Reluctantly, he takes it. "Understand what I'm giving you. Don't write about it, even when your *vacation* is over. And call my office, we'll see if we have something for you," I say graciously. He hates me. He hates himself for needing me. He hates everything about everything at this moment, beaten as he is. This moment, he'll come to learn, is what life is all about.

Brancato stares at Yvonne, then tries to laugh sardonically, but it comes out a gurgle and then he gathers his squidgy flesh around him like a greatcoat and turns with as much dignity as he can muster. "We'll fucking see about that," he says dramatically, and stomps off.

I sit at my outdoor table until the lunch crowd has come and gone, until the waiters have given up their huddled conversations about me, have had their own afternoon meal, have laid up, rested for awhile, and have even set up for the dinner service. Yvonne grows tired of waiting for me after four scotches and the beginning of my fourth Havana, and goes home for a nap. After the next whiskey has been delivered, Rez leaves me the bottle, and a large bowl of ice. This is the manner in which I while away my afternoon, until it is past six and old Judge Frusciante leads in the early dinner crowd. Today he is yellow. He wears canary slacks, meringue shirt, and a pilly lemon-colored sweater vest.

"Yer at my table, Grubman," he growls.

"And you look like Tweety Bird," I cough and toast him with scotch and cigar. He glares at me then goes inside to read Rez the riot act. I smile. Then the liquor and tobacco conspire against me. I go green and feel queasy and thick- headed. I stub out the smoke and push myself back from the table. I want nothing more than a couch to lie down on after a day like this. My head aches in a way that makes it difficult to remember it not doing so. I leave money on the table and stagger into my waiting limousine.

I stagger back out of the car in front of my old townhouse. I make my way to the door and fish around in my pocket for my keys. I put the key in the lock and turn. Nothing. I turn the key with force, but still the tumblers do not budge. Any harder and I risk breaking off the key. Lauren has had the locks changed. That was quick. I set to banging the brass knocker with an inebriate's gusto and sense of rhythm. Within moments, Blanca's moon face peeks out from behind the lace curtains hanging in the small window next to the door. She looks startled, as if she doesn't know how to handle my arrival.

"Is the Mrs. in?" I shout at her.

She nods her large head.

"Well go get her, please." I yell.

Blanca disappears and I stand alone for several long moments. My excruciating wait ends with the jingle of chains and the clack of bolts. Lauren pulls open the heavy door, a stern look on her face.

"I need to ask you something," I fairly lunge toward her.

"What is it?" Lauren asks, then leans back, waving a hand in front of her face. "You smell like a pool hall."

It is then that I catch a glimpse, over her shoulder, in the shadowed foyer, of Andrew.

"Andrew," I call out, stepping toward the inside of the house. Lauren braces in the doorway and it is clear my only way in is to physically push past her. I cannot rough my ex-wife in the slightest, especially in front of my child. "Can I speak to our son? Please." She glance back over her shoulder and he edges a step forward toward me.

"I'm sorry for what happened up at school," I begin, urging my thickened tongue to dance as it never has before. "I know you didn't understand what I was trying to tell you, and because of it you think I'm cruel..." At this, his brow uncreases, and years seem to fall from his face. He appears more like a five year-old than a near

225

thirteen year-old at this moment. "I do know that what I said is true—you're a Jew, whether you want to be or not..." He gives the slightest of glances toward the staircase and freedom from me. I pause as long as I dare. "Maybe one day you will. But this is now." He looks back toward me. "I know you blame me for a lot of things, and you're probably right..." I begin to lose clear focus on what I should argue, how I should convince. I feel the scotch and tobacco heavy in my bloodstream. "I love you, son. I love you. I'll come to Church." Emotion plays across my boy's face, and he begins to cry. I hoped for my words to be a balm, but I do not know the exact nature of their effect. I want to go to him, to comfort him, but Lauren begins to close the door on me.

"Go sleep it off, Elliot."

I scream at the evaporating sliver of space between the closing door and its frame. "When you see me in that church, that's when you'll know how much I love you, son..."

I turn back to my waiting car. I go home and take Lauren's advice.

Sunday, Critical Mass

The next few days pass painfully slowly. The headache I left Tre Fiori with hangs on with persistence for the rest of the week and throbs even now. I am unable to reach Andrew, and give up trying after leaving several messages on his blasted answering machine. I have wrestled and struggled with many problems in my day, ranging from financial to legal, but none have caused me such grief as the fact that my son will turn his back on being a Jew today and join the Catholic faith. It leaves me feeling empty and poor, like a pocket full of dirty change. Despite my money, I feel two steps away from the scrappy twelve year old I was back in the neighborhood, coming home from Hebrew school to hear my father was dead. I am yet another Grubman in the short line of Grubmans who will not live to see his first son bar-mitzvahed. I know now that there are many forms of poverty, but emotional poverty seems, after all, to be the most difficult one from which to escape.

Yvonne and I arrive early this Sunday morning at The Paulus Fathers Church of St. Paul the Apostle on 59th Street and Columbus Avenue, near Lincoln Center. It is a massive stone building dominated by two towering transepts which flank a large blue and white limestone frieze. This frieze is something to see. One of those grandiose and holy-seeming Christian jobs that give me such a strange feeling. It is a decorative scene of God reaching out with one hand, the good book tucked under his other. He is held aloft by a flock of angels and

227

has beams of light radiating from Him. The light extends out toward a flying lion, a griffin, I suppose, which a live pigeon rests on ignobly, and past the lion is a man on horseback straining backward to touch God's outstretched hand. Far below the frieze are the church's massive blonde wooden double doors, perhaps six inches thick, sufficient to seal a tomb.

I could vomit or cry as I trudge up the stairs and enter the place of worship. Through the doors, the first thing I see is a large font of holy water, with a great pool full of the stuff just beyond it in the background. As we step inside, Yvonne kneels on the three-colored marble and inlaid wood floor, as glossy as any basketball court, and makes the sign of the cross upon herself. I witness this with something close to horror. I look around trying to gauge my unfamiliar surroundings. To our right is a reading room, to our left, oddly, a small gift shop and book store that takes both Visa and American Express. The church features vaulted ceilings, which span upwards a breathtaking several hundred feet. Row after row of oiled wooden pews stretch into the distance before me. Hanging lamps that look like giant censers combine with the natural light coming through dozens of ornate stained glass windows, yet the place remains shadow-filled and murky. A set of steel organ pipes is suspended on the left of the nave, just past the confessional booths, which a small sign designates as the 'Reconciliation Chapel.' Dead center a hundred yards away, past all the pews, is the altar, which is vacant at the moment. We walk down the center aisle, our footsteps echoing in the cavernous hall, and draw near the fifty or so people sitting in the first few rows of benches.

I focus my eyes straight ahead, beyond the altar, to an elaborate chancel that houses a large golden dome resting on marble pillars. Beneath the dome, a bewildering

228

display of crucifixes glow under pin spotlights. I experience a prickling sensation along my arms and the back of my neck at the foreign-ness of this place. The sight of a crucifix has always made me feel strange, as if I did not belong, and superstitious of harm that could come to me at the hand of those who worship the cross. These feeling are heightened on this black morning. We move down the aisle toward our seats, and I can see several small chapels lining the walls. They are decorated by excellent, somber oil paintings done in dark hues, and granite statues with votive candles at their bases, as well as much gold leaf and gilding. I have to hand it to the Catholics, their art is impressive. I've been to the Vatican during a trip to Rome, and that place is a palace filled with treasures of art that dwarf any king's. So many gallons of paint, tons of gold, sweat and tears have been spilled by artists in tribute to their Savior and their Church, it is fairly awesome.

At last we arrive near the front of the church, where there are some seats reserved for us as family of those involved in the ceremony. We sit down and Yvonne drops her knee to a padded bar along the bottom of the pew and makes the sign of the cross on herself again. I really wish she would stop that, but I say nothing. I turn my head to the right and there he is, the big J. himself, in bronze, pegged to a large cross. The spikes go right through his hands. It looks painful, but He can take it. His head is lolled in peaceful anguish down and to his right. It seems he can hang there forever.

I grow hot and uncomfortable as the vast church becomes oppressive. Several large fans attempt to circulate the stagnant air, but it does not help. I pull at my collar which feels chokingly tight. There seems to be no oxygen in the stale, incense laden atmosphere. Things are too quiet. I am miserable. This mass is sparsely attended, I suppose since the main mass has already taken place according to the schedule out front. I surmise this one is more of a conversion ceremony only. I can barely imagine the suffocating heat that would be pressing down on me if the church was full.

Sitting a couple of rows back and off to the left are a few of Lauren's friends, including Jennifer and Sandy Kleiner. Sandy is of course my friend, but today he is in attendance solely for Lauren. I cannot return their smiles—Jennifer's gloating, Sandy's sympathetic—with one of my own. Also to the left, but proudly in the front row, sit Lauren and her beau, Ricky. He is in a deacon's black suit that has my money written all over it, and she, painfully appropriate in a mint green Donna Karan two-piece with white gloves to her wrists and a silk scarf knotted at her throat. Yvonne, too, has presented herself well today in a charcoal Dolce and Gabana number that downplays her surgically large breasts, but Lauren looks like the head flight attendant on the social register airlines. She is the blonde Jackie O. herself.

From where I sit I can see a large painting of an old, white haired man on his knees in the road. His tunic is a dirty ivory, and he has a halo of gold around his head. Nearby, a Roman soldier in sandals stands haughtily, his weight leaning on his sword, ready to finish off the old-timer. Although a Jew like me would have been fed to the lions even before this old guy, the captioning, in gold lettering above and below the painting make me understand his plight. It reads: "I Have Fought A Good Fight, I Have Finished My Course. I Have Kept The Faith." This is what happens. You fight a good fight. You lose. You end up kneeling, and waiting for the sword's slash.

The organ starts up with a low hum and the priest enters. He is a dandruffy, gray haired man with thick glasses and a dirty, wax-stained chasuble. I suppose this is the vaunted Father Harris I once heard so much about. He leads in those to be converted. There are about fifteen of them. Three quarters are kids Andrew's age and younger, as well as a few adults. Andrew is third in line, smiling shyly, standing in his white gown. He wears a neat side part, his hair pasted into place. Seeing him there, in this tableau before me, looses a howling wind of abject emptiness in my chest. My head swirls at the sight of him, just out of my reach. He is right there, but so far away. I don't know his reasons for all this, but I suspect that he resents me for some things, he blames me for the divorce, and he is only a kid and doesn't know any better. What would possess a grown man or woman, though, to convert to some other religion so late in life? Do they have a religious epiphany, replete with a visit from God or a saint? Or is it a more intellectual procedure? "Well, I've read the book and I like what this Jesus fella' has to say..." I try to open myself to the mystical for a moment. I'm *in God's house* after all, maybe He will reveal Himself to me and I will understand. If he sent *me* a signal I could stand up there and join Andrew. I could become Catholic and make my families, both old and new, intact. I wait for my sign.

The organ breaks off and the priest begins speaking in the most haunting of languages—Latin. It does not sound harsh and throaty like Hebrew, which is so vital and full of life. Latin sounds ethereal and beyond, from a wispy realm of clouds and mystery. I do not know what the priest says. I catch an occasional familiar word, but I am lost. I suppose Yvonne or Lauren could explain things to me, but there is no time for asking. The priest swings a small censer around with a clinking of metal chains, and incense smoke puffs out from it, making the air of the church stink like rotten talc. He holds up a large, round wafer and breaks it, says some more prayers, and puts the pieces in a cup of wine. Signaling off to his left, the priest summons a tiny altar boy, who struggles over to him with a marble bowl. The priest smiles on his little Christian soldier and takes the bowl from his hands. He sets it down on the table in front of him and dips his fingers in. They come away wet and he touches his own forehead and breast with them. We are all directed to stand and sit several times during the course of the ceremony, and at one point everyone kneels on the padded kneeling bar. I remain seated during this, and look over at Sandy Kleiner who also refrains from kneeling. He shrugs his shoulders and gives me a blinding, apologetic smile with his big, super-white choppers. I look away from him.

We have reached the crucial point in the ceremony. The priest calls forth the first candidate, a Latino woman about thirty-five years old. He has her lean back over the bowl, says some prayers, dips a gold ladle into the holy water, and pours it over her head. She kneels and accepts a piece of wafer on her tongue, and moves off to the side. She is beaming. She is all smiles. She is Catholic now. There is a little stir in the row in front of me as her family or friends writhe in excitement over her salvation. Next in line is the young man standing beside Andrew. He is perhaps ten years old. He gets the same treatment. The holy water mats down his hair and drips onto the shoulders of his gown. This entire proceeding has grown surreal.

Yitgadal v'yitkadash shmay rabba, be-olma di-vera chiru-tay ve-yamlich malchutay...I swear I hear the lamenting cadence of the Mourner's Kaddish sounding in my head. It is Andrew's turn, and he is called forth, his feet treading silently across the red carpeted altar...*Yitbarach ve-yishtaback, ve-yit pa'ar ve-yit romam*...I imagine his life from now on, his learning catechisms,

232

saying 'Our Father's,' feeling guilty over masturbating, feeling guilty over sex, making confession, flirting with joining the priesthood, not doing so, going to bingo and raffles, Midnight Mass, caroling, pig roasts, beer drinking...

As this smelly old priest goes to dip my boy's head with his filthy water, I don't believe I can endure it any longer. Andrew moves into place and begins to lean down over the bowl, when his eyes miraculously find mine across the entire church and audience, and what I read in them is not beatific resolution, but doubt. I need to act. I don't know what to do. I stand bolt upright and shout out at the clergyman, "Take him!" Startled faces turn toward me. It is unanimous, the entire lot of them are aghast. Suddenly, all my suit wearing and decorous ways are gone, and I'm the storming through doors, the standing up and shouting public outburst type of guy, constantly covered with the greasy-rancid sweat of my own panic. I shout too loud, even for a church this size. I shout above and beyond that priest, into the organ's main set of pipes far behind him. I shout loud because I want him to hear me, and I want everyone else around to hear me too. I shout because I want the Archbishop Edward *Cardinal* Egan—what a stupid fucking name—to hear me in the great beyond. I want all the bloody Cardinals, Bishops, and Monsignors all the world over to hear me as well, that is why I scream. I want the Pope back in Rome to hear, and I want God himself in his heaven to fucking hear me. "Take him then," I bellow again. "Go ahead and fucking take him!"

Things seem to go into slow motion for me at this moment, and I am somehow able to absorb the congregation's horror and disbelief at what I have done. It is incredible, but I even manage to see some individual faces standing out from the overall sea of faces around

233

me. I see Jennifer and Lauren and Ricky in freeze frame, so slowly are things moving. I see the bewilderment on Yvonne's face as she sits next to me, and amusement and awe on Sandy's face. Then I make out the terrible shame on Andrew's, as he flies from under the priest's fumbling hands and runs from the church.

Everyone gasps collectively as Andrew charges out the side door and runs down ten steps through an iron gate onto 60th Street. I am right after him, running full speed. There were the days when I had to let him win a foot race, and there have been some when I couldn't beat him, but today I am committed to catching him. I see him run up Columbus Avenue to 62nd Street, past Fordham Law School's Ned Doyle building, just shy of Lincoln Center, where he cuts right. "Andrew, stop!" I shout after him. He does not heed me. This is the only time I call out, as I need all my wind to try and keep up. The boy continues past a few luxury high rises and on toward Broadway, where he foolishly tears right across the flow of two-way traffic. I wince as I see the hem of his initiate's habit actually touched by a speeding panel van. He glances back and sees me puffing after him. This causes him to pick up his pace. He catches the 'Walk' signal, fortunately, near the edge of the Mayflower Hotel as he crosses Central Park West. When I get there a moment later there is miraculously not a single taxi in front of the hotel to aid me in my pursuit.

Andrew has now turned uptown, and runs beneath the heavy green trees that line the park. I have no choice but to put my head down and dig, trying to close the distance between us. Perhaps I gain a step, perhaps I lose one. Andrew runs like a deer. He bounds by the Ethical Culture School across the street on his left as if it is the quarter mile post at Belmont. Beneath the inscription on the school's wall, an infant in his mother's arms howls

234

for some unknown reason. The motto reads: "Dedicated to the ever increasing knowledge and practice of Love and the Right."

Whatever the hell that is, I consider, my breath coming in painful stabs. I make a gasping notation to myself to come back some day with block and chisel and take off the lettering. Then I am beyond it. On the next block, at 65th Street, there is a Lutheran Church with red doors, and I can only wonder if their Sunday Eucharist is this action packed. Andrew shows no signs of slowing, to say nothing of stopping. It seems he will run this way indefinitely.

The soles of my Ferragamos are smoking as we pass 66th Street, when suddenly Andrew dips his shoulder and cuts right, up the stairs toward Tavern on the Green. He runs through the parking lot, past the awning and the fake gaslights, past a gold-braided doorman, past a valet parking a Volvo, and past two vacant hansom cabs. He steers himself toward the main park drive, which is choked by bicyclists, roller skaters, joggers, and strollers on this warm spring day. At times I have wondered how far I could run if I absolutely had to. With something important spurring me on, I always fancied that I could simply run as long as I needed to, with sheer will driving me onward. That was merely my will spouting off though, for today my body's firm answer to the question is: from St. Paul the Apostle's to Tavern on the Green. As the Sheep's Meadow comes into view, things finally start to come apart for me. My stride goes ungainly and my arms begin to tingle and flail. My heart seizes, and my body goes tight, as if I have all the phylacteries in the world wrapped around my chest. I think I may spit up on myself, and I begin to see the scene from above. I stagger and croak, "Andrew," then I go down like a pinwheel. I go down like Foreman in Zaire.

235

In my mind I read of myself in my last headline:"*Reviled Pornographer Found Dead In Pool Of Piss.*" I flash on my first heart attack twenty-five years ago. I fell over like a chopped tree in a crowded restaurant during lunch and woke up having wet myself. It was humiliation on a baroque scale. I see Andrew look back at me. He slows as I flatten upon the ground. The pavement comes close in my vision and I am wracked by searing pain. Hot light bulbs burst inside my torso and behind my eyes. Every part of my body is visited by sizzling demons who lay into my millions of nerve endings with their flaming pokers. The asphalt smells like tar as I writhe on it and hear Andrew's footsteps slow down further, and then stop somewhere off in the distance. I cling to the frayed ends of consciousness listening for his steps to grow louder, hoping for him to return. I close my eyes and my face contorts.

I cannot stand up for all the riches in the world. I cannot speak a sentence to save myself or my son. Only my mind ticks slowly, like a damaged but unstoppable clock. My memory begins to run. I leaf back, the past in front of my eyes like magazine pages. On one page is Barbara, young and innocent, cowering in her nakedness. I can only stay with her for a moment as the next page falls and she is gone. On the next is Lauren, sleek and sure in her dominance of me. I want to stop and stare at her image, but again the page is turned. There is Yvonne, perfect and young, just the way she is, smiling and pointing to her abdomen. Then the images begin to come more quickly. Their clarity is blurred as the pages are briskly feathered. Faces, body parts and places travel by too rapidly for me to register. I see wonderful breasts hanging down as a shoe strap is buckled. A back hunched over a make-up table. There is a neck bent and cradling a telephone. A mole on a stomach. A foot with a slight callus on the ball of it, extended for me to kiss. My mind's eye is deluged by a delicate, fleshy montage of all the women I've tasted and known and tried to drown myself in. Hands, hands reach for me, painted fingernails, and fingernails bitten, lean fingers, and stubby ones, touch me, rest on my shoulder, play with my hair, grasp for my wallet, accept a jeweled ring, punch me playfully, slap me hard, alight on my chest, guide my penis. The hands pick up car keys, and count money, pincer around credit cards, take up pens and sign checks, receive gift wrapped packages, pluck at ribbons and tear at paper. The hands take and take. They take everything. They begin to claw at my chest. Strong hands, stronger than my mother's and cooler even than Lauren's, begin to claw at my chest. They tear into my flesh and peel it back easily, though I feel no pain. They move my ribs apart without effort, the bones gone soft. They poke through spongy lung tissue with a sucking sound. The hard hands become wet with my fluids as they keep reaching inward and inward toward my organs...

My head lolls flat on a pillow. I awaken in a room that is white, so white I feel it has been painted by clouds. Outside, in the hall, I hear the business-like sounds of carts rolling about, and soft, orthopedic shoes on linoleum. I have tubes sprouting from my left arm and leading to an intravenous pole. Several flattening plastic bags of fluid are suspended above me. The skin of my wrist is sallow beneath the surgical tape holding down the line. I feel a two-pronged oxygen source blowing into my nose. On my right middle finger is a clip with a wire trailing away from it. I roll my head to the right and see a black and white television screen with a broken and jagged line blinking across it. It is my heart monitor. My every fiber is involved in flaming pain.

Suddenly a shadow crosses over me. I squint to focus and make out the perimeter of a woman's blonde hair. I cannot tell who she is. Something is wrong. I do not recognize her. It seems a hairstyle that Yvonne has never worn before. Then I gather who she is. She is Lauren. It is her cool, slender hands which reach down and do not claw at me, but smooth the wires, cables, and cords running all over my body. It is Lauren! After everything, it is her. I see a defibrillator resting menacingly in the corner. "That...," I say weakly, gesturing at it with my chin.

"Yes. They used it. You finally cycled," Lauren says. "You shouldn't talk. You need a bypass when you stabilize." Lauren. She's here. I want to smile but my face is frozen and suddenly everything hurts still more than before. Every nerve, muscle, tendon, and fiber of my being feels raw and mishandled, and the most interior chamber of my self, where my newborn feelings are hatched and housed, feels ripped apart and violated.

"Yvonne's outside. She's in a dither she's so worried. She seems to care quite a lot for you."

"Andrew?" I breathe. Now Lauren smiles, her beautiful face glowing in kindness. Finally.

"He's fine. You scared the hell out of him...out of all of us, really, Elliot...but he was the one called the ambulance. He doesn't want to lose you." I close my eyes. My boy came back to me. Thank you, God. My boy came back to me.

"Oh, Elliot," Lauren says, sitting down on the bed next to me. Far off, deep inside me, is the realization that it took my near death to gain this moment's tenderness from her. I want the realization to remain far off. I don't want to face what I know: that this tenderness won't last once I've recovered.

"Lauren..." My throat is dry, and cracking, but she has mercy for me. She runs a cloth across my brow. I lift a hand weakly, and she takes it between hers, her cool palms pressing against mine. She places it in her lap. I feel her warmth there. Instantly I feel a stirring and my blood begins to rush forcefully through my system like hot lava, as it once did so long ago. The light hospital sheet covering me starts to rise. A tingling, throbbing, welling up of fluid and emotion collects in my groin. The long rusted wheels of desire's chariot start to roll. With a metal on metal screeching, a sound surely only I can hear, my penis defies the realm and laws of gravity and points aloft. I am hard as a lance. I turn my face toward Lauren. A tear rolls from the corner of my eye. She wipes the salty deposit away from my cheek with the side of her finger and rubs it with her thumb. Perhaps she is not aware, but it is a tear of joy.